Amethyst Dreams

by
Phyllis A. Whitney

Published by Random House Large Print
in association with Crown Publishers, Inc.
New York 1997

Library of Congress Cataloging-in-Publication Data

Whitney, Phyllis A., 1903–
Amethyst dreams / Phyllis A. Whitney.
ISBN 0-679-77436-X
I. Title.
PS3545.H8363A8   1997
813'.54—DC21   96-48170
CIP

Random House Web Address:
http://www.randomhouse.com/
Printed in the United States of America
FIRST LARGE PRINT EDITION

This Large Print Book carries the
Seal of Approval of N.A.V.H.

For Sharon Summers
Dear Friend
and
Wise Counselor

Foreword

I have sometimes thought that if I spread out a map of the United States, blindfolded myself, and took a pin to pick out any spot on the map, I would find a wonderful place to write about. Every location has its special history and treasures that belong nowhere else. Topsail Island was just such a pinprick on a map, discovered because I was led there by chance.

When I was collecting the background material for *Daughter of the Stars*, the last person I met in Harpers Ferry (and almost didn't meet at all) was Kate Richie. She and her husband were about to move to Hampstead, North Carolina, and I said in parting, "Tell me if you find an interesting locality I might write about." Later, when they'd settled in, she suggested nearby Topsail Island as a possibility. My daughter and son-in-law drove me down from Virginia, and I could hardly have found a richer speck of earth to use as a story background.

Something that often surprises me is how little people know about the history of the place in which they live. The first thing on the island to catch my interest on arrival was a square cement tower. There were seven of these marching down the narrow strip of land that was Topsail. Inquiring about them, I was told by one resident that they had something to do with the Coast Guard. You'll find out how wrong that was!

Fortunately, I found more knowledgeable people to help me. Kate and David Richie had purchased a home on the mainland and bought a boat in which they traveled the Topsail Sound. The sound is part of the intracoastal waterway that offers boats clear passage all the way to Florida. They had become fascinated by the beauties of these waters, so rich with wildlife. I thank them both for becoming my eyes and ears for places I could visit only in my imagination.

Jeanne Nociti, executive director of the Greater Topsail Chamber of Commerce and Tourism, met my request for help with enthusiasm. She phoned Betty Polzer and we were able to visit Betty in her charming pink house on the oceanside. Betty became my friend-by-mail. Her lively mind and vital spirit were helpful to me through her many letters. Her extensive research into the history of the island, her published writings, and the many clippings she sent me enriched my knowledge. Dear Betty, I miss you and I am sad because I couldn't show you this finished book, into which you put so much before you went on to another dimension.

Jeanne also introduced me to Evelyn Bradshaw, president of the Topsail Island Historical Society, who has been a great supporter and source of information. Evelyn took us to visit the Assembly Building, which had been used to store and assemble rockets before launching. The Historical Society had saved the building from commercial uses and was planning to house a museum there that would preserve island history. The museum, Missiles and More, is now a reality and there are exhibits and displays that show early Indian life, the history of Operation Bumblebee, the Gold Hole, and much more.

Evelyn Bradshaw also gave a great boost to my story by introducing me to the island's famous Gold Hole. Here I have tampered with fact. The Gold Hole exists on private property, so I have changed its name to the Pirate's Pit and moved its location to where it serves my story. The booster rocket did wash ashore on Topsail, but my characters were not present at the time. There really was a Cabbage Island, but

I borrowed the name for the imaginary speck of land that my characters visit. Don't look for Susan's "secret room" under the Assembly Building—though that hollow sound in the floor near the door is real. Thank you, Bill Morrison, for thumping it and inviting my imagination to take off.

Ken and Evelyn Ottoway were warmly hospitable when we visited Spyglass, their tower house home. Thank you for loaning it to me for my story. Ken gave me a shark's tooth he found on the beach, and that, too, took its place in a scene.

Sloop Point Plantation, across on the mainland, was a delight to visit. James and Mae Graves had restored it with love and meticulous respect for the original house. It has been designated as the oldest plantation house in the state. In my novel it has become Gulls Cove, and the people who live there bear no resemblance to the far more gracious hosts at Sloop Point. When I am doing research for a book, I always take a great many pictures, both still and video, so I was able to re-create bits of Sloop Point for several scenes.

I want to thank Ralph and Bettie Shipton, whose beautiful modern house, across the sound from Topsail, we were able to visit. I am especially grateful for the use of the Shiptons' elevator. I don't know what Captain Nick would have done without it!

The manager and staff of the handsome Soundside restaurant were especially helpful, inviting us in during off-hours to take pictures. Thus my characters could dine in accurate surroundings.

Strangely, I feel closer to Topsail now than I did when we were there. After all, I have spent many months on the island watching my characters work out their various destinies. It will remain forever real in my memory and as it existed in this story.

Amethyst Dreams

Hampstead, North Carolina

"She must be stopped from coming here. We must stop her. We don't want her here, Ryce." Louise Trench, a woman obviously accustomed to getting what she wanted, spoke across the room to her husband.

Ryce Trench wished that his father's money didn't matter so much to Louise, but he had always known that it would. In her mid-fifties she was still beautiful and all too well aware of the fact. Her hair had been kept carefully blond, and her face was still smooth—as though all strong emotion had been suppressed. She had never grown fat and her figure was perfect in her expensive, well-cut clothes. Ryce, too clever for self-deception, had known why she'd married him, but her beauty had captured him from the first. And he'd been lonely since Ellen's death.

The three people in the long living room at

Gulls Cove stood apart, but they were all looking out a window toward the beautiful rippling water of the sound. Richard Merrick, the Trench attorney and friend, turned to pick up Louise's words.

"It's too late to stop her. Mrs. Knight received my letter and her plane from California is due to land in Wilmington in a few hours."

"At least she can be discouraged from staying," Louise insisted. "We need a plan."

"My father is dying," Ryce said, "and he's the one she's coming to see. She won't be here long. He just wants to talk to her about Susan."

Ryce still looked devastated whenever he spoke his daughter's name. He knew she was dead. He had felt the loss of her from the first, though it was something his father, Nicholas, had never accepted. The tie between Nick and his granddaughter had been unusually close, and throughout Nick's recent long illness he had spent thousands of dollars to find out why she had disappeared. Sending for Hallie Knight, his granddaughter's oldest friend, was nothing more than a foolish last attempt, but perhaps the most threatening in Louise's eyes.

"Nick will live forever," she said tartly.

"I hope that's true," Richard said, picking up his raincoat and briefcase. "In any case, I'd better get started for the airport. I'll phone you after I've delivered Mrs. Knight to the island."

Ryce was aware of the look in his wife's eyes, the way she smiled at Richard. He'd seen that look before, whenever a handsome man was in her vicinity, and as always he held his anger deep inside. Louise couldn't help the way she was. She needed to be admired, but he knew she would never leave him as long as she had the lure of his father's inheritance, his father's money.

Richard paused on his way to the door. "There may be nothing to worry about. She may not accept Nick's terms."

"How did she sound on the phone when she called in answer to your letter?" Louise asked.

"Curious. Puzzled. Nothing more. I had the feeling that she was distracted by some difficult private matter. She's only coming because of her friendship with Susan."

"If you play your cards right, Richard, you can scare her off. Why, that awful house Nick lives in should be enough to do the trick." Louise shuddered at the thought.

Ryce managed to speak mildly. "Of course, we don't really know what my father intends. I'll tell you one thing—I feel sorry for this woman. Who will protect her?"

"Protect her from what?" Richard asked. "She's not in any danger."

"How can we be sure?" Ryce asked, taking a

deep breath. "After all, no one knows what happened to Susan."

"We'll know when she chooses to let us know," Louise said. "Your daughter was always unpredictable. This Hallie Knight may stir things up. If Susan is the bait, anything can surface."

"Susan has been gone for two years," Ryce pointed out sadly, "and I don't think my father will ever give up trying to find an answer to what became of her."

Impatient, Richard glanced at his watch. "We're getting nowhere. The reference to his will in the letter he sent to Mrs. Knight means nothing. It was only intended to coax her to come, I'm sure."

Louise sniffed.

"Anyway, I must start for the airport. Once she's here, once Mrs. Knight has seen Nick, we can play it by ear. There may be nothing to worry about. We'll talk again after we've sized her up." He hardly looked at Louise as he went off.

After he was gone she made a slight grimace in her husband's direction and walked out of the room.

A pall of helplessness settled over Ryce Trench as he stared out across the sound toward Topsail Island. He'd been born there fifty-five years ago—in the very house where his father still lived. When his first wife, Ellen, was alive, she and Ryce and their daughter, Susan, had lived on the island with his mother and father. Ellen died before his parents separated and his mother had gone her own way. But in those early days they'd all lived together happily enough. Or so he'd thought.

Ellen had loved Anne and she'd loved Nicholas Trench's house and the island—loved the beaches, the maritime forest, the island's unique history. Susan had felt just as passionate about the place even though she had hardly known her mother, who had died when she was three. It was her grandmother, Anne, who'd looked after her. Ryce had been so devastated by his wife's death that he had created a busy life of hard work for himself. Though he knew he hadn't been much of a father to Susan, he had loved her deeply. Now he was secretly looking forward to meeting the woman who had be-friended his daughter when she was away at col-lege. Perhaps getting to know Hallie Knight would return something of Susan to him.

He'd often wondered if his dear Ellen would ever have understood this marriage to Louise. Sometimes he hardly understood it himself. She had been impossible to resist, though he had never fully understood what drove her besides her desire for money. She had told him about her well-connected family in the North. They were all dead by the time she came south, so Louise was lonely, too. He had never asked probing questions about her past because it obviously hurt her so much to talk about her family.

He didn't expect to ever find another woman like Ellen. If there is one person in the world meant for each of us, he thought he had found his and lost her all too soon. At least Louise was an attractive companion and, at this stage of his life, he considered that enough.

Lately, however, the spark of anger that had come alive in him earlier had shown signs of being all too ready to ignite. For the sake of his own sanity and whatever life he might have with Louise, he knew he must never allow that to happen. He must keep his emotions under control.

Across the sound the island stretched long and narrow, its shadows deeply slanting in the setting sun. It was an island that knew how to keep its secrets, no matter what probing this woman who was coming to Topsail might attempt. Secrets were meant to be kept—to be buried too deep to ever be found.

1

It was over. I would never forgive Paul, and I would never live with him again. Our eight years of marriage had seemed wonderfully happy, even though we'd had no children. I had trusted my husband in every way, and I'd never worried about the Hollywood crowd he mixed with as a West Coast literary agent . . . or had I?

It was Paul's special talent to find the movie buried in hundreds of pages of a novel, and he had an instinct for knowing the right director or producer for a project. His enthusiasm and charm did the rest. *Everyone* knew, or wanted to know, Paul Knight; his successes were notable.

There had been the attraction of opposites to bind our love. Paul was gregarious, always ready to go to parties and meet new people, while I preferred a quieter life and the company of a few friends. Nevertheless, the tie between us had been *real* and I'd expected our love to last. Love and trust and dependability were my touchstones. I'd been that naive.

Paul had always seemed blithely, even mockingly, aware of the make-believe aspects of the world in which he worked. He recognized tinsel when he saw it. I suppose that's why I would never have believed that he'd become involved with a sexy blond actress who wasn't really very bright. I confronted him, once I knew what was going on, and he'd given me no excuses. I, who had always been so controlled, so understanding, had exploded in rage—outrage. He listened to me with some astonishment, admitted his affair, and then simply moved out, leaving me to decide what I wanted to do. He'd loved me as little as that.

The letter from Susan Trench's grandfather had come the next day, while I was still reeling. I didn't understand what it meant, and I didn't much care. I only knew that it offered me an opportunity to *do* something concrete—to get away from my life until I could work things out. This letter, like the one I had received two years before, telling me of Susan's disappearance, addressed me as "Dear Hallie," not as "Mrs. Knight," so I supposed that Susan had talked about me affectionately.

I thought of Susan often, troubled as I was by her sudden disappearance. At first, after I'd left Berkeley, we had kept in touch, calling and writing and occasionally rendezvousing in some beautiful but not too expensive spot for a week of relaxation and fun and catching up on our lives. We were really good friends for a while, but I was living in Palm Springs and Susan was on an island called Topsail off the coast of North Carolina. When we'd roomed together—and during those first years after college—Susan had been the wild and unpredictable one; my nature, as I liked to think, was more stable. I'd listened to Susan's troubles—trouble always seemed to be part of her life—rescued her from a foolish scrape or two, and loved her like a sister. Of course, we'd always promised each other undying friendship, but after a while we each became busy with our own lives and drifted apart. Eventually even our letter writing lapsed. We still managed Christmas cards with return addresses, but nothing more.

Then, two years ago, Susan's grandfather, Nicholas Trench, sent me a newspaper clipping about Susan's disappearance. I had been shocked and grieved. I'd asked questions in my return letter, but Captain Trench chose not to answer, and I'd never heard from him again until now.

Apparently he'd remembered my friendship with his granddaughter. He wrote that he hadn't much longer to live and would like me to visit him soon. He wanted to remember me in his will because of my "many kindnesses to Susan." But most of all he wanted to talk with someone whose memories of his granddaughter might comfort him. Enclosed was a check to cover the cost of a first-class round-trip plane ticket from California.

Accompanying his sealed letter was a more formal note from an attorney, Richard Merrick, whose letterhead indicated he was connected with a law firm in Wilmington, North Carolina. The note asked me to contact him as soon as possible. He hadn't sounded particularly friendly when I called, but arrangements were confirmed for my trip to North Carolina. So here I was flying over the eastern edge of the continent on a trip I'd never expected to make.

I'd hated the long hours on the plane, with nothing to do and too much time to think. All the pain Paul had caused me flared up more intensely than ever, pain that was laced with an anger that made me feel a little ill. In the airport in Los Angeles, and again in Chicago, where I'd changed planes, the world seemed filled with couples traveling together, as Paul and I had always done. The worst moment had come at the start when I was boarding my very early flight in Los Angeles, and there'd been a man in the line ahead—not very tall, with brown hair cut a little long at the back. He'd had a quick way of moving his head, and my heart had almost stopped beating. It wasn't Paul, of course, but by the time I reached my seat, I was shaking. I'd always thought Paul distinctive—far more interesting than other men. Yet now men who reminded me of him seemed to appear all too often.

On this last stretch of the flight I hadn't even had a seatmate to talk with, so I was stretched a bit taut, and all the more relieved when we were nearly there.

A soft grinding sound shivered through the plane, ending in a thump that meant the landing gear was down. As we emerged from cloud cover, I could see miles of North Carolina forest, with the Cape Fear River winding through the trees. During the flight I had distracted myself for a while by studying the maps in a guidebook I'd hastily bought the day before, so I knew a little about the country below. I'd made good connections and it was still light down there. Topsail was a tiny barrier island off the coast north of Wilmington, but I couldn't make it out from the air.

When the plane landed and I filed off with the other passengers, Richard Merrick was waiting for me. The briefcase under his arm was the identifying clue he'd given me—that and the fact that he was quite tall. He looked the way he had sounded on the phone—competent and a little cool. His voice was deep-timbred as he greeted me—a strong voice, though not entirely reassuring—and it seemed to suit his large frame. He settled me in his comfortable Buick and we headed north up the coast. While he didn't study me directly, I was aware that he was sizing me up, and I tried to give him very little to read.

"Tell me about Captain Trench," I said when we were well on our way. "I believe Susan told me he was a captain in the navy. Is he very ill?"

"The doctors give him another month or two. Sometimes he's in considerable pain. I'm glad you've come in time. He remembers Susan talking about you, and that's important to him."

Even though Merrick said the right things, I doubted his sincerity. "Glad to see" me, he obviously wasn't.

"Did you ever find out what happened to Susan?" I asked.

He didn't answer for a moment. Then he spoke sadly. "We just don't know. That's an unhappy story, so let the captain lead the way when it comes to talking about it."

"I remember Susan's fondness for Topsail Island. Is that where we're going?"

Merrick nodded. "Nick—Nicholas Trench— still lives there in the house he built for Susan's grandmother. She left him many years ago." Merrick paused and I had the feeling that he'd meant to say something more, but when he went on he changed the subject. "Before we arrive, you'd better get used to calling the island Top'sle. Merchant ships used to make stops where inlets cut in from the sound side of the island. In those days pirates roamed the coasts looking for ships to raid. The merchant captains could see the topsails of pirate ships over the dunes and get away in time. So the island began to be called Top'sle, using the seafarer's pronunciation. Now it's an ideal spot for vacationers who enjoy fine beaches, and for a good many retired people who live there the year round. Young professional people are finding it as well—writers and artists and others who are self-employed. We'll cross over soon at the swing bridge out of Hampstead."

His discourse, I suspected, was to distract me from the real subject of Susan and her grandfather.

"Does Susan's father live on the island?" I asked when he came to a pause.

Merrick glanced at me and then looked back at the road. "No, he doesn't."

"There's a stepmother, I believe?"

This time he merely nodded, and I realized then there were topics he was reluctant to discuss. This, of course, made me all the more curious. I was glad to have something to focus my attention on.

He put an end to my questions by pulling into a gas station. When he'd filled the tank, he turned the car into a parking place and switched off the engine.

"I don't know exactly how to say this," he began, "but you need to know that there may be some people who won't welcome your coming here. Don't plan to stay very long, Mrs. Knight. There's nothing you can do for Captain Trench anyway."

I looked at him in surprise. "What do you mean? What could anyone have against me?"

"It has nothing to do with you, really. It's just that you might get in someone's way. Nicholas Trench will leave a considerable fortune when he dies, you know."

I didn't know and I could only protest. "What have I to do with that?"

He spoke quietly, probably in his best soothing lawyer's fashion. "I saw a copy of the letter Captain Trench sent you. He mentioned a legacy."

"I'm sure he meant no more than a token gift. Though I don't know why he would do that."

"There are those who won't want to share," Merrick said.

"Then I'll ask him not to leave me anything. When we've talked about Susan—which he seems to want and need—I'll just fly back to California. So there's nothing for you to worry about."

He gave me another long look, then smiled more warmly. "I'm sure everything will be fine. He's an old man who has suffered a great many losses, so we must humor him and listen."

Something about the way he said this irritated me, and I nodded vaguely as he pulled the Buick back onto the road. I was probably much too edgy. The bridge was in place, and we crossed to the island without further delay. The car cut through the small business area of Surf City, where there were restaurants, gift shops, an artist's studio, a small Chamber of Commerce building, and other commercial enterprises. Then we drove out along a main road that led south along the narrow island.

Houses of every size and variety lined the road on either side. All were set on columns that raised the living floor above flood level. Sometimes these supports were neatly enclosed behind walls, while other owners had left the ground level open and exposed. On our left I glimpsed sand dunes that rose along the ocean, which I couldn't see. At intervals wooden steps and walkways led over the dunes and down to what I supposed was the beach.

"The dunes are fragile," Merrick told me, "so protection is necessary. No one walks on the dunes. The island's a little over twenty-four miles long, in the shape of a shallow crescent. It's never very wide at any point. On the soundside, inlets can change the width. On the oceanside, there's the curved line of the beach along the Atlantic. You're lucky to be here ahead of the summer season. Many of the rental houses are still unoccupied, so the year-round residents have the island mostly to themselves." Again he seemed to be talking to distract me.

I watched the sandy roadside on my left, where houses faced an ocean I still couldn't see. They were built fairly close together, mostly painted white or brown, with a few bursts of color here and there. One pink house made a particularly dramatic statement. Most of the houses wore name signs—some poetic, some a bit cutesy. I saw WINDWARD, SECOND TIME AROUND, and BACK A BIT, among others.

"Is the island all one town?" I asked.

"It's divided into three towns—Topsail Beach, which is south, where we're going; Surf City, where the bridge came across; and North Topsail Beach, which is filled with condominiums, and like another world. The two ends can be critical of each other. There's another bridge serving the north end. The island breaks into two counties as well."

I noticed, running beside the road on the soundside, a narrow strip of low, wind-twisted trees growing densely, their tops so intertwined that they formed a tangled canopy.

Merrick noted my interest. "Those trees are part of the island's maritime forest. Once the forest covered everything. Mostly the trees are live oaks that have been stunted and twisted by ocean winds. A great deal of the forest has been destroyed by rapid building, but now there are laws that preserve what's left of the trees."

Ahead on the right an odd-looking structure came into view—a sturdy concrete tower three stories high, with square corners. There were centered windows and what appeared to be a door at the bottom.

"What's that?" I asked as we drove past.

"Those towers were built after World War II, when there wasn't much else on the island except fishing communities—mostly shacks. There were nine towers originally, but one of them is gone, so now there are eight. They were part of what was called Operation Bumblebee. Ask Captain Trench about all that. He was here as a young man in the navy at that time."

The maritime forest's thick green growth lined the way on our right, with occasional lanes cutting through here and there, leading down to the sound.

Merrick turned into one of these lanes, where thick, dark foliage grew abundantly all around, nearly meeting overhead to form a shadowy tunnel. At the far end of the lane a patch of light showed the water of the sound. Before we reached the water, Merrick turned the car into a clearing where two houses had been built among the trees. One, set back from the water, had been painted a creamy white—a sturdy foursquare house. The other, facing the sound, was a gray clapboard that rambled into wings on different levels. Both houses were raised on exposed supports, and a three-car garage occupied the space under the clapboard house. We pulled up in front of this.

Stairs inside the garage area led up to the main floor. At the top of the steep flight a thin, middle-aged woman waited for us.

"Hello, Mrs. O," Merrick said as we reached her level. "This is Mrs. Knight, Susan's friend. Hallie, Mrs. Orion is Captain Trench's housekeeper and right hand."

I noticed the way he had slipped easily into using my first name, but I still didn't feel comfortable with him. At least he sounded less like a tour guide now.

Mrs. Orion took my offered hand, but her smile seemed restrained, as though she was waiting to decide about me. She wore a garment of blue seersucker that suggested a uniform and enveloped her like a pillowcase.

"The captain is waiting for you, Mrs. Knight," she said, and looked at Merrick. "Will you stay for supper, Mr. Merrick? I'm sure Captain Trench would like that. We're having it a bit late tonight because I wasn't sure when you'd get here."

Merrick shook his head. "Thanks, but I need to get back to Wilmington. I'll come over tomorrow, Hallie, and see how things are going. Perhaps you'll need a ride back to the airport by then."

"Thank you, Mr. Merrick," I said, sounding formal and a little stiff. His assumption that I would be quickly ready to leave, as well as his eagerness to hurry away, left me with a deepening irritation. Nevertheless, when he had disappeared down the stairs and I heard his car leaving, I felt alone and altogether uncertain. Here at the back of the house near the stairs, the rooms were dark, with branches pressing against the windows. A gloom that was both physical and psychological settled over me. I wished that Paul could be with me now—and then remembered with a stab that I could not call on him anymore. A sense that I had not been brought here for some innocent purpose settled over me and made me feel increasingly alone.

Mrs. Orion was waiting and she led me into the relief of late daylight as we stepped into a wide living room that stretched across the front of the house. The furnishings seemed old and rather shabby, as though no one had bothered to refurbish for a long time.

"You might like to go out on the deck and see the view before the sun goes down," Mrs. Orion said. "I'll tell Captain Trench that you're here."

I crossed the room, moving toward the sunset light that had begun to gild the sky. The sliding glass doors were open, and I slid open the screen door and stepped out onto wide gray boards that cantilevered out across the front of the house. When I approached the railing, I saw that the ground below sloped toward the water of the sound, where a dock ran out from the shore. A small boat tied at the far end of the dock bobbed gently as ripples from a passing boat reached it.

The glowing sky had sent out wide streamers of gold. On the far shore of the sound lights were on in several houses. I rested my hands on the gray railing and tried to let my inner disquiet subside in the aura of peace around me. My breakup with Paul had made me all too ready to see ominous signals everywhere. I wasn't here without a choice. I could leave anytime I wished. To go where? A change of scene, a new perspective, was what I'd wanted. Captain Trench had given me this and I must use it to gain some sort of equilibrium.

As I stood on the wide deck, breathing wonderfully clear sea air, two brown pelicans flew by flapping their wings, and I felt a small surge of delight. No wonder Susan had loved this place. The dark house behind me began to seem less threatening.

When Mrs. Orion returned, I was ready to meet Susan's grandfather.

2

icholas Trench's room occupied the left front corner of the house and there were enough windows to let in plenty of light. To my dismay, however, Mrs. Orion immediately began to draw all the draperies, with quick, nervous gestures, leaving only a side window uncovered for air.

The old man looked lost in his wide bed, propped by pillows that seemed larger than he was. The four dark walnut posts of the bed were carved into corn shapes at the top, and they stood like guardians around him.

Mrs. Orion had turned on several lamps, so the gloom was not complete. "I'll get back to fixing supper," she said and hurried away without any formal introduction.

I wasn't sure whether or not to offer my hand as I approached the bed. In fact, I wasn't sure that the old man was even aware of my presence. Mrs. Orion had murmured, "She's here," but I didn't know if he'd heard her.

"Thank you for inviting me, Captain Trench," I said hesitantly.

He turned his head slightly and for a moment he stared at me from eyes sunken deep in their sockets. His nose must have grown even more aquiline with age, and his cheekbones rose above hollowed flesh. Perhaps as a young man his lips had been full—a mouth eager for life— but now they pressed into a straight, thin line that spoke only of pain held in check. Pain that might be emotional as well as physical.

He came at length to some conclusion about me, and when he spoke, a crackle of life came into his voice. He had not lost the habit of command. "For God's sake, open those drapes and let in the sunset!"

For an instant I was too surprised to move. Then I walked to the windows and flung back the draperies so that light flooded the room, bringing in outside patterns of yellow and lavender.

"That's better," he said more quietly. "The Owl—Mrs. Orion—is a nervous Nelly, and she's afraid of prying eyes, though there's nothing out there to look in but pelicans and gulls."

I returned to the bed, able to smile at him now.

"You remind me of Susan, Captain Trench. She must have gotten some of her spirit from you."

He waved a bony hand toward the straight-back chair beside his bed. "Sit down, Hallie. You won't be comfortable—that's part of the plan. To keep visitors from staying very long. They're supposed to wear me out if they stay. The Owl never understands that what I want is to have something demanded of me so I can be worn out!"

I sat in the stiff chair and found that he was right, but discomfort didn't matter. I would stay as long as he wanted me to. At the same time I was a little wary. Something more than his illness tugged at my sympathy. His body may have failed him, but a tough, unbeaten spirit looked out of his eyes, compelling me. To do what? He was a man accustomed to having his own way— which might not be my way.

"I remember Susan with a great deal of affection," I told him. "We were good friends, even though we weren't anything alike."

He nodded. "I can see that. Susan always jumped before she thought. You look as though you'd think first and figure things out."

"Not always," I admitted. Certainly I hadn't done much thinking before rushing out here. I'd wanted only to run, to escape, to postpone the decisions I needed to make.

"I suppose I was more cautious than Susan. She was like a hummingbird, only alighting here and there, always in motion. It's a wonder she ever stood still long enough to listen to me. Though sometimes she did."

"She wrote me about how much you helped her. You were the person she trusted. She could get mad and fling herself thoughtlessly into situations, the way I sometimes did when I was young. Too often she had regrets later. I never did. I never regretted anything . . ." His voice seemed to die out on his last words, as though he'd suddenly remembered something he did regret.

There were questions I wanted to ask, but I knew I had to move slowly. In spite of the flash of life he'd shown, he was clearly very ill. He had to have felt trapped and helpless in the hands of those who cared for him, even though they had his well-being at heart.

His hand reached out suddenly and caught mine, taking me by surprise. "Come closer, Hallie, so no one will hear. Do you know why I asked you to come here?"

"You wrote me that you wanted to talk about Susan."

"That, of course. But what I really want is for you to find out the truth about what happened to my granddaughter."

For a moment I could only stare. "How could *I* possibly do that? Surely you've tried—"

"Of course I've tried. I've had the best people I could hire searching for her. They found nothing."

"Then why do you think I—?"

He broke in, weary and impatient. "Perhaps you would search from the *inside*. You knew her and you would use your heart as well as your head."

This didn't reassure me. "What do *you* think happened to her?"

His grip on my hand tightened. "I think she was murdered. That's the only possible answer."

Shock held me silent. I was more sure than ever that I couldn't help him. I understood his love for his granddaughter, but I was no detective. I wouldn't know how or where to begin. Besides, I was starting to get the sense that there was horror here and it was nothing I wanted to face.

"What about her father? What does he think?" I asked.

He threw my hand aside, dismissing the idea. "Ryce has never had any real gumption. And ever since he married again—to a woman Susan detested—he's been of no use at all."

Neither would I be of any use. But I couldn't

crush him with a flat refusal. "Let me think about this."

He tilted his strong, bony chin in my direction. "Fine. Take your time. I hope you'll stay awhile. I've had the Owl prepare Anne's room for you. Anne was my wife—Susan's grandmother. Susan used to stay in her room when she came home. When she was a child, Susan's own room was downstairs, where she could run outside easily. But when she came back from college, she wanted to be near me, so she took her grandmother's room."

Strangely, I couldn't remember Susan ever mentioning her grandmother.

"She died long ago," the captain said grimly, as if reading my thoughts. "We don't talk about her. I'll call Mrs. O now and she can get you settled."

A brass bell that looked too heavy for him to lift rested on a low table beside the bed. Evidently, though, there was still enough strength in his arm when he needed it, for he raised the bell and sent a clamor ringing through the house.

At once Mrs. Orion appeared in the doorway. "All right now, Captain. I'm here. You needn't bring the fire engines."

He grinned at her, and I suspected that an affectionate war of wills must go on between them.

"Will you show Mrs. Knight to Anne's room so she can rest a bit before supper? Good night, Hallie. I'll see you in the morning whenever you're ready."

Mrs. Orion was busy closing the draperies again, and her movements suggested that they would now stay closed. Neither of us said a word.

Before I left, I dared to pat his hand. That much I could offer. "We'll talk tomorrow," I said and followed the housekeeper from the room.

Mrs. Orion, thin and wiry in her semi-uniform, moved lightly on soft soles as she crossed the wide living room. I had to hurry to keep at her heels. As we passed a stairway leading to the floor above, a young man came running down, shouting a greeting.

"Hello! Hello! Ma didn't tell me you'd arrived." He looked at me in open appraisal. "I'm Corey Orion. And of course you're Hallie."

Exuberant was the word for Corey, and I suspected he was a little older than he looked or acted—probably around Susan's and my age. I stiffened as he threw his arms around me and kissed me on the cheek. His uninhibited behavior took me by surprise, and I didn't know how to react. He saw this and I caught a spark of amusement in his eyes.

His mother shook her head, but her expression was one of fondness. "Behave yourself, Corey. It was a long time ago that Mrs. Knight knew Susan, so don't presume." Her son only grinned at her.

Corey Orion was as dark as Susan was fair— thick black hair, a little long, snapping black eyes—and much too good-looking. Often looks like that in a man mean self-interest and self-satisfaction. His full mouth, I suspected, had kissed far too many girls. Yet Susan had never mentioned either Corey or his mother, which seemed puzzling. In fact, Susan had never talked about anyone on Topsail Island but her grandfather. Even her father had been mentioned only in passing, and the fact that her mother had died when she was small. I had guessed that painful happenings on the island had kept her from wanting to talk. Still, the one person she seemed to have loved wholly was Nicholas Trench.

Corey regarded me with a look of curious anticipation as I turned to the door Mrs. Orion held open for me.

"You can rest for a half hour," she said. "Corey has brought in your bags. I'll set a table for us out on the deck, since it's warm this evening, and we can have supper out there." She paused as though an afterthought had come to her, but I sensed that her effort to be casual was false. "There are pictures hung in the room that were painted by Anne Trench, the captain's wife. I hope you won't mind."

I didn't know why I should mind, but she hurried off to tend to her duties, as though she wanted no questions. Her son still waited, as if for some reaction on my part.

"Thank you for bringing up my bags," I said. "I'll see you later." And I closed the door upon his waiting curiosity.

Mrs. Orion had turned on a lamp near the bed, and I looked around, receiving an immediate impression of clashing styles. If rooms long lived in held the imprint of former occupants, this room surely displayed confusion.

Basically, it was a quiet room of cool blues. Like the captain's, this was a corner room, with glass doors opening onto the deck. A side window looked into the twisted upper branches of live oaks, and I walked over to look out, turning my back on what I wasn't ready to see.

Dark foliage blended into the dusk of evening, as I stood, shielded here from sunset. A single light standard had come on in the clearing and I could see across to the neighboring house, where lamps shone in several rooms. I would need to talk with the captain's neighbors if I was to find out more about Susan. I smiled ruefully at the commitment I already seemed to be making.

As I looked down, a young girl in jeans and a pullover came out of the house next door. I could see her clearly in the light from the standard. She appeared to be around ten. Her long hair lifted on her shoulders as she ran across to look up at the window where I stood. For an instant our eyes met before she turned away, but I had the curious feeling that there had been hostility in her manner.

I shrugged off the encounter and faced the disquieting room. There were no curtains or draperies here, and none were needed. Shutters had been set into each deep window space, and these were folded back. I didn't close them, but stood looking about the room—at least at the lower part of it. I wasn't ready yet to raise my eyes, since I had already glimpsed what was there when I came in.

The bed was wide, and I winced at the sight of it—a bed in which I would sleep alone. The woven coverlet matched the blue-gray water of the sound as I'd seen it today when Richard Merrick and I had crossed the bridge to the island. The carpet was slightly deeper in tone. A small table for writing and a slender-legged chair that sat before it were made of pale birch. Near the glass doors that opened onto the deck stood a round table with a rippling skirt of blue cloth that hung to the floor. Haviland china in a tea set for two offered hospitality. Two more light-colored chairs were drawn up to the table.

The sense of loss flashed through me again. Everything came in pairs, except for the chaise lounge in one corner, its cushions displaying a tiny design of bluebells and primroses, offering an invitation to rest and dream. If it were not for the walls.

When I'd stepped into this room, I'd averted my eyes, but I could no longer avoid what was there. I could understand now why Mrs. Orion had been uneasy.

Against the off-white of the wall facing me, pictures had been hung almost frame to frame. All were paintings, and all clearly came from the hand of the same artist. Most were abstract, and the clash of colors and forms suggested extreme emotion. The artist must have been furiously angry as she painted. Some were oils, some acrylics, but there were no watercolors. Perhaps watercolor was too gentle a medium for the artist's moods. In one picture bright droplets fell clear to the frame, as though the painting bled.

If these had been painted by the captain's wife, her anger must have lasted a long while to result in all this work. Only here and there had the abstract style been abandoned, and then a totally different spirit had taken over. Set among the wilder paintings were lovely portraits of Susan as a child, and here no tormented brush had wreaked its fury. Clearly the artist had loved the child.

The whole effect of the main body of paintings left me feeling a little sick. I knew now why Corey Orion had waited when I stepped through the door into this room. He had wanted to see how I would react, and I was glad I hadn't given him that satisfaction. How could I possibly stay in this room with Anne Trench's anger and pain splashed across the wall? Had Nicholas Trench been the cause of all this emotion?

Weariness suddenly overtook me and I chastised myself for my dark imaginings. Once the lights were out, I wouldn't see these flaming colors. Besides, wasn't this the same sort of wild anger *I* had felt for the last few days? And yet as spirited and brash as Susan was, she was also highly empathetic, so it was hard to understand how she could have stayed in this room with her grandmother's pain.

For now I was simply here; I could solve nothing, and I didn't want to think about this room or why Nicholas Trench had brought me to this house. I flung myself on the inviting bed and closed my eyes.

3

I awoke a half hour later to a blissful gloom shrouding everything that had disturbed me. I got up and found the adjacent bathroom without turning on a light. Only when the door was closed did I touch a switch. Here the tiles were a clear blue and white, with nothing to disturb the senses. I bathed my face in cool water and smoothed back my hair with my fingers. Unpacking would have to wait. I didn't return to the darkened room until I heard Mrs. Orion tapping on the outer door and calling my name.

When I opened it, the housekeeper noted that no lamps had been turned on and nodded her understanding. "I told the captain that he shouldn't put you in Mrs. Trench's room. But then he hasn't set foot in here since Susan hung all those terrible paintings of her grandmother's on the wall."

"Susan hung these! But why?"

"I wouldn't know," Mrs. Orion said, squinting at the paintings with an unpleasant expression on her face.

"You've never told the captain they're in here?"

"Would *you* want to tell him? When I came here I heard a rumor that she had committed suicide."

The paintings might bear that out, I thought, for they seemed to be the work of a disturbed individual. I followed Mrs. Orion through the sliding glass doors onto the wide deck, where a table had been attractively set. Subdued lighting, supplied by several votive candles, offered a pleasant ambience and the light, fragrant breeze lifted my spirits.

Corey was waiting for us, and he seated me with a flourish. My chair faced the sound and I could look out over dark water to where scattered lights shone on the mainland.

"Did you rest well?" Corey asked. I caught a hint of mockery in his voice, so I ignored his question and spoke to his mother.

"I'm still trying to understand why Susan would hang those paintings in a room she meant to occupy. How could she live with them?"

It was Corey who spoke. "They're really bothering you, aren't they? But they're not that bad. Actually, they're rather beautiful."

I turned again to his mother. "Could you possibly put me somewhere else?"

Mrs. Orion looked doubtful. "The captain was definite about where you should stay. The other bedrooms are upstairs and he wanted you close by."

Corey suddenly seemed genuinely concerned. He dropped his mocking tone and spoke more quietly, surprising me. "I'll take the paintings down, Hallie."

I thanked him stiffly. I was still trying to get a sense of him. He seemed chameleonlike in his personality. But at least he was considerate toward his mother, and rose to help her bring food to the table.

My offer to assist was waved aside, and I sat down, suddenly realizing how hungry I was. Meals on planes left me indifferent, so I'd eaten little all day. My emotions would be better in hand after I had some food.

Corey brought in a big bowl of oyster stew, and his mother carried a tray to the table with fresh salads, small, crisp oyster crackers, and homemade hot rolls and butter. Mrs. Orion ladled the stew into smaller bowls and I took a first spoonful. In spite of burning my tongue, the stew was perfect—the oysters barely curled at their edges, and yellow pats of butter melting on the creamy surface. Even the amount of salt was exactly right. Clearly Mrs. Orion had a gift.

As I crumbled oyster crackers into my bowl, I asked, "Who are the people next door? I saw a young girl outside a little while ago."

Corey and his mother exchanged looks. "You tell her, Ma," Corey said.

Mrs. Orion looked thoughtful. "They're an odd family. I don't like to gossip—"

Her son was quick. "You love to gossip. Go ahead."

"Well . . . there's a lot of history to the story next door. They've a mix of Spanish and Scottish blood, to begin with."

"With a little gypsy stirred in for good measure," Corey added. "All of which make for volatility."

"Mrs. Cameron is hardly a gypsy," his mother said. "She's lived in this country all her life. And I must say Fergus Cameron dotes on her."

Corey picked up the story. "Fergus was here on Topsail after World War II and got to know Nicholas Trench when he and Nick were pretty young. They made an unlikely pair because the captain was Annapolis and Cameron was an enlisted man in the navy. I guess work on Operation Bumblebee threw them together. Later,

Cameron left the navy to work for a while at Cape Canaveral after the Bumblebee project was dropped."

"What is Operation Bumblebee?" I asked.

"You mean nobody's told you?" Corey's tilted eyebrows lent themselves to poking fun. "Usually that's the first story we tell outsiders."

"As you're doing now," I said. "So go on."

He grinned at me. "Right after World War II ended, the navy took over Topsail and kicked off the few fishermen who lived here. It was all hush-hush because the island was to be used for rocket launching. Camp Davis was already located across the sound and could serve as a base for the men who worked on the project. You saw the cement towers that run down the island, didn't you?"

"Yes. Mr. Merrick told me to ask the captain about them."

"He can tell you a lot more than I can, since he was here when it was happening, but I know the towers were used to track rocket launchings, and I guess there were a number of firings." Corey, in spite of his irritating manner, seemed genuinely caught up in the story.

"They called the project Bumblebee, and it was intended to give defense support for the navy in the event of another war. The missiles could shoot twenty miles out and supposedly knock off any incoming attack. Anyway, that was the idea—until they gave up on Topsail and moved out."

"Why was that?"

"Topsail's climate didn't cooperate. Too much dampness. So around 1948 the whole experiment moved south to Cape Canaveral, and the navy gave the island back to North Carolina."

"By then, at least electricity had been brought in," Mrs. Orion said, "and artesian wells had been dug and roads built."

Corey nodded. "That's what helped open everything on Topsail to the outside world. Nobody had been interested in the island for development purposes before. The captain and Fergus Cameron had become close friends and I guess they kept in touch. They both liked Topsail, so they bought land here and built the two houses they now live in. Fergus went on to become a noted rocket scientist until he retired."

Mrs. Orion elaborated again. "Fergus Cameron's second wife, Carlina, is a lot younger than he is, and Dulcinea—the girl you saw—is the daughter of that second marriage."

"Dulcinea?"

"After Don Quixote's beloved," Corey said. "That kid carries an interesting mix of legends in her head."

The look of hostility the child had given me

was still puzzling. "She didn't seem friendly," I said.

Again I caught the look exchanged between Corey and his mother, but neither commented. Suddenly I realized I was about to doze over the dish of fruit that had just been set before me, and Mrs. Orion patted my arm. "You're tired from your long trip. Let me see if you have everything you need for the night. Would you like Corey to take those pictures down before you retire?"

I shook my head. "Tomorrow will do. With my eyes closed I won't see a thing."

I told Corey good night and followed his mother to Susan's room. When she turned on a light, I averted my eyes from Anne Trench's paintings and waited until everything had been checked out to Mrs. Orion's satisfaction.

The moment I was alone, I flicked off the switch. Enough light came through the bathroom door for me to find my bags. For a few moments I stood at the side windows, looking down through treetops to the clearing where the child called Dulcinea had played. It was empty now.

Leaving the window open, I unpacked a few things I needed and got into bed as quickly as I could. Darkness shielded me from the strident wall and I fell deeply, soundly asleep.

It was nearly morning when a dream wakened me. Susan had been sitting on my bed whispering, "Help him, Hallie, help him." She murmured the words several times before I blinked myself awake. Suddenly the day loomed ahead depressingly.

I tried to go back to sleep, turning to stretch my arm over the other pillow, but my efforts were met with that still-unfamiliar emptiness, and at once I was wide awake with more than Anne's paintings to worry me. I stared at the soft light coming in through the open window and indulged myself in the satisfaction of despising Paul.

When he'd come into my life nearly ten years ago, I'd been new with the literary agency. Though I was born in Connecticut, I'd been living in San Francisco and working at various secretarial jobs. When a position with a literary agency in Los Angeles was offered, I'd jumped to take it. The climate appealed to me, and the proximity of all that movie glamour was fascinating.

Paul Knight was constantly in and out of the office, and I was assigned to work with him on a manuscript he was grooming for one of the studios. He had been an editor with a publishing house in New York, so he knew that end of the business. "The book comes before the movie script," he often said, and he would work with authors to give their stories the right touch to appeal to a producer.

Paul seemed to be everything I wasn't—dynamic, charming, successful in a spectacular way. The office lighted up when he came in. I'd been surprised when he asked me to have lunch with him one day. I'd expected him to want to talk about the manuscript we were working on, but to my surprise he wanted to talk about me.

I remembered. I remembered every detail much too clearly.

"You're a deep one," he told me, teasing a little. "You don't talk a lot, but when you do, what you have to say matters."

Most people regarded me as shy and not particularly interesting. It never occurred to most people to wonder what I might be thinking behind my protectively quiet facade. And there'd been no one since Susan Trench to make demands on me.

Paul poked holes in my smoke screen right away. He wanted to know about *me.*

By our third lunch I was telling him that my parents had died in a boating accident when I was five, and that I'd been raised by an unmarried aunt in Berkeley—a woman who had taken me in out of duty to a dead brother, but didn't really like children. As I grew up I discovered more and more that my aunt's strict precepts could never be mine. The "don'ts" that were dinned into my ears had seemed unfair and senseless. Of course, most teenagers go through a stage of rebellion, but at least the girls I knew had family love to see them through. I made a few good friends, but until college and Susan, there had never been anyone who looked to me for affection and guidance. Though we were only a year apart in age, Susan quickly became the younger sister I'd never had. We had both lost our mothers as young children and that understanding of pain and loss formed a solid bond between us.

Paul listened to all this. He understood and sympathized without being sorry for me. He believed that I had enough character of my own to succeed at whatever I wanted to do, and he told me so. As we worked together, he took me to meet some of his authors, and a confidence began to grow in me that was new and satisfying. Paul actually valued my opinion and he listened to what I had to say. Perhaps he was a born teacher, and I was a willing student.

Before I met Paul, it had always been hard for me to trust anyone in a close relationship. After all, I had been the victim of my aunt's repeated warnings. Her basic refrain was that men couldn't be trusted. She never revealed what had happened in her own life to sour her, but she inoculated me with whatever poison she had absorbed.

Paul was the least cynical person I'd ever known, and eventually he cleansed me of the poison, turned me in new directions. No matter what he'd done, I owed him that. He called me his "balance wheel," and he would listen when I thought something through in my own careful way. We became friends as well as lovers, and when we married I couldn't imagine ever wanting for anything more than I had.

Until now—when I didn't want the man I'd married or anyone else! My aunt had been right about men, after all.

I found that my pillow was wet with tears that I hadn't meant to shed. I rolled out of bed and headed for the shower. I couldn't spend my time weeping and bemoaning. I was worth more than that. I would turn my back on what I'd thought was my life and let the people here distract me. I already liked Susan's grandfather, and now in the clear morning light, I began to feel brave. Trying to help the captain might do a great deal toward helping me—even though the prospect for success in locating Susan was anything but encouraging. Besides, if he had some other motive for bringing me here, then I wanted to know what it was.

4

⌾⎯⎯⎯⎯⎯⎯⎯⎯⌾

*S*trangely, the paintings on the wall no longer bothered me as much as they had the night before when I was tired. I would let Corey take them away, but I wouldn't allow myself to be upset by them. I felt sympathy for Anne Trench. I didn't know what had tormented her, but I could understand her anger. It must have been a release for her to pour it out in this work. The captain was probably no better than most men, and Anne had undoubtedly suffered at his hands.

"Good for you for walking out!" I told the artist. I doubted that a woman who could vent her feelings like this would ever commit suicide. That she'd died when she was relatively young—like my own mother and Susan's mother—was sad.

When I'd dressed in jeans and a loose blue

shirt, I slipped sandals onto my bare feet and went out to the front deck. If no one was stirring yet, I would find my way across the main road to the beach and walk in the sand. Perhaps an ocean wind would blow the cobwebs away and I wouldn't think of Paul.

But Mrs. Orion, again in her semi-uniform of blue seersucker, with a white apron tied around her waist, was already up, setting a table outside for breakfast. "Good morning, Mrs. Knight," she said upon seeing me. "Would you like something to eat now, or do you want to see the captain first? He's up and expecting you, whenever you're ready."

"I'm ready now," I told her and hurried across the wide deck to the captain's corner room.

His door stood open, and when I tapped and walked through, I found him sitting in a wheelchair, wearing a blue silk dressing gown, with a jaunty yellow scarf at his throat. He didn't look as desperately ill as he had the night before; perhaps my arrival had given some new interest to his life.

"Good morning, Hallie," he said. "You look rested and more cheerful than you did last night."

In that case my look was deceptive, but I smiled at him. "So do you."

He flicked a hand at a tray nearby. "I've finished breakfast, and for once I had an appetite." He glanced past me to Mrs. Orion in the doorway. "Will you bring another tray in here for Hallie, Mrs. O?"

Mrs. Orion nodded at the captain in approval. "Of course. What would you like, Mrs. Knight?"

"Toast and coffee would be fine, please," I said, and sat down beside the captain's chair. He watched me intently and I sensed that some unspoken question hung in the air.

I gave him what little I could. "I'll stay for a few days, even a week, if you like. But I'm still not sure that there's anything I can do. Mostly I'd just like to get acquainted with Susan's grandfather. She talked about you a great deal, you know."

He dismissed sentimentality. "You can do more than you think. You can begin in that room where you slept last night. When Susan was last seen, she was writing a letter at the desk in that room. Where did she go when she left? Or was she taken away? What happened to her?"

This morning all the draperies were open in the captain's room, and light spilled in, rippling on the ceiling in a reflection of water from the sound.

"Perhaps I could wheel you out on the deck, since it's such a beautiful day," I suggested.

He shook his head. "Not now. I may go out there later. No one can hear us in here. Whatever I decide to tell you is for your ears only."

Mrs. Orion returned with a tray for me, a sprig of dogwood lending its white beauty to the simple breakfast. I drank orange juice, sipped strong coffee, and spread marmalade on toast. I was grateful for the sliced banana that had been added and ate with a better appetite than I'd expected. But the captain's fixed attention was disconcerting, and the long silence seemed heavy. Finally I had to break it.

"Last night at dinner Mrs. Orion's son told me a little of Topsail's history."

"Operation Bumblebee, I suppose? Do you know why it was called that?"

I said I didn't, and he pointed to a framed script on the wall nearby. I went over to read it.

The Bumblebee Cannot Fly

According to recognized aerotechnical tests,
the bumblebee cannot fly because of the
shape and weight of his body in
relation to the total wing area.
But the bumblebee doesn't know this, so
he goes ahead and flies anyway.

I went back to him smiling. "I hope you'll tell me more about that time yourself, Captain Trench."

"That was a long while ago. I was a green kid." He dismissed the subject. "I must tell you something—warn you. My son's wife, Louise, is coming over to take you to lunch today. It's her idea. I didn't suggest it."

I wondered about his use of the word *warn*.

"That's kind of her. Will I meet your son?"

"If he happens to surface. Sometimes I don't see them, even when they come to the island. His wife doesn't like this house."

While I could sense the captain's disapproval, I could understand that this place might have unhappy memories for Susan's father.

Perhaps it was time to tell him something about myself, and I spoke frankly. "You might as well know that I'm here because I'm running away."

His searching look intensified. "From what?"

"My husband is in love with another woman. I found out only days ago. Your letter came just in time to rescue me."

He asked a strange question. "Did your husband know you were leaving?"

"*He* walked out first. I suppose he'll only return to pick up his things."

"And he'll find you gone?"

"That's what I wanted. I hoped he might even be hurt a little."

"You'll let him know where you've gone?"

"Of course," I said stiffly.

"I never heard from Anne, my wife—after she went away."

He looked so weary that I knew he needed a break from a conversation that had grown unhappy. "Perhaps you can rest a little and then we'll talk again later."

"Go across to the beach," he said. "My property runs clear to the ocean—not very far at this point. When you cross the main road you'll see steps leading up to a gazebo built on this side of the dunes. The far steps will lead you down to the beach."

I thanked him for the directions and went downstairs through the garage. The little girl, Dulcinea, was outdoors again. She sat in a swing that had been hung from the sturdy branch of a live oak tree, and was reading a book. Now and then the child touched a toe to the ground to keep the swing moving gently. She didn't respond to my presence—in fact ignored me so completely that I knew how conscious of me she had to be. The frown she wore further suggested an awareness of me, rather than simple annoyance with her book. Hair curled about her face and hung long down her back—a gleaming red, with streaks of gold where sunshine touched it. I hadn't been able to see its full, rich color last night.

"Good morning," I said cheerfully. "I'm Hallie Knight. I'm visiting Captain Trench."

This time she looked up from her pages and I saw a freckled nose, and bright green eyes that surveyed me with scorn. "*My* family doesn't speak to *his* family," she announced, glancing toward the captain's house.

The hostility I'd sensed the night before was even more evident now, and I tried to offer reassurance. "That needn't matter to us. After all, I'm not family. I went to college with Susan Trench a long time ago. You knew Susan, didn't you?"

She left the swing so abruptly that the seat sprang away crookedly, striking the tree. In her haste, she dropped her book as she raced toward the Cameron house. In a moment she had disappeared around its south corner in the direction of the sound. An astonishing reaction.

As I watched in surprise, a woman came to the front door and stepped onto the porch. She was a colorful figure in a full skirt that suggested the green of the ocean. A rainbow pattern ran around the hem, shimmering as she moved. Several strands of bright beads cascaded over the front of her white blouse, and above its rounded top her neck held her head high like the stem of a flower.

Dulcinea's green eyes clearly came from her mother, and they seemed as watchful in mother as in daughter. Carlina Cameron's hair, however, was a glossy black mass that waved down her back. Gold hoop earrings caught the sunlight as she descended the steps. Altogether, the effect was striking, and I recalled Corey's term for her—"gypsy." She was probably in her forties, so Dulcinea must have been a late child.

I walked toward her, holding out my hand. Her fingers were cool, her touch quickly withdrawn, and the green eyes watched me, questioning.

Again I tried for reassurance, and began introducing myself, but she interrupted at once.

"Yes, I know who you are," she said. "I am Carlina Cameron. I understand Captain Trench has invited you to come visit because you were Susan's friend."

She was, I realized now, even more than striking: She was vividly beautiful, her smooth skin slightly olive in tone, and her features perfectly formed. When she smiled she would probably be stunning, but there was no smile for me now.

I tried to explain my presence. "Captain Trench wants me to share my memories of his granddaughter. She and I became friends when we went to school together."

"He probably wants more than that," the woman said sharply. "Susan didn't make friends, but she had a talent for making enemies."

"I was her friend," I said, and then added deliberately, "The captain wants me to find out what happened to her."

Carlina stood very still, staring at me. "Do you realize how many detectives he's had searching for her?"

"Yes, but they didn't know her. I'll stay for as long as I can and try to help."

"I don't think he's told you the real reason why you're here. Have you met Louise and Ryce yet?"

I shook my head, feeling lost in a mire of relationships that I didn't understand. "But I'm having lunch with Louise today."

She considered this for a moment and then said, "All of us are concerned for the captain."

"Your daughter said your families weren't speaking."

"Dulcinea dramatizes and exaggerates. All that was in the past. Just try not to upset Captain Trench any more than you can help. Listen to Mrs. Orion. She's the sensible one in that house."

And probably Mrs. Cameron's informant. Either she or her son, Corey.

Without waiting for a response from me, Carlina Cameron went back up the steps and into the house. The screen door closed behind her—and that was that.

As I crossed the yard, I saw the book the child had dropped and picked it up to look at the title. It was called *The Power of Gem Stones*. Colored pictures of semiprecious stones ran through it, and the pages fell open readily to a section on amethysts. I remembered that Susan had been fascinated by the lore connected with such stones. Perhaps she had introduced the subject to Dulcinea.

I placed the book on the seat of the swing and walked away from the two houses toward the road. Again I was aware of dark, tangled branches meeting overhead as the road climbed to the highway. Now and then a car went by on the higher road, but there seemed to be little traffic this morning. It felt good to move quickly, yet with a special consciousness of the scene around me. I listened to snatches of birdsong and heard children's voices as I passed another house half hidden by the low green trees of the maritime forest.

When I reached the main road, I saw the gazebo the captain had mentioned. It rose between low, intertwined trees that separated two small houses.

I crossed to follow a wooden walkway that led to steep steps, and climbed to the floor of the gazebo. There I stood looking out over a long crescent of white beach toward the Atlantic Ocean.

5

The roof of the gazebo was supported by six white columns. Open lattice-work came partway up on either side, and benches offered a place to rest out of the sun and watch the Atlantic roll in. I stood for a moment at the top of the far steps, looking out over the long stretch of sand. The beach ran the length of Topsail Island, white and clean, with surf forming a lacy trim. In the morning's sunny calm the ocean was green near the shore, deepening to gray-blue as it spread out in a vast rolling plain that reached to the horizon and other continents.

This was certainly a barrier island. Considering the assault of ocean storms over the centuries, it was a wonder it had survived long enough to become inhabited.

Steps at my feet descended to a landing and

then dropped to where the sand began. I left my sandals on the bottom step and rolled my jeans above my knees. Mrs. Orion had told me that later in the day the sand would become too hot for bare feet, so I should enjoy it now. I ran down to where the waves curled in and walked on the damp sand. Doing pleasant, physical things kept me from thinking too much.

Two children played beside a beach umbrella that sheltered their mother, and they waved as I walked past. Farther along a man knelt beside a collection of flotsam thrown up by the ocean. He was bareheaded and his dark hair caught glints from the sun. He had tied his shirtsleeves around his waist. Rolled-up jeans showed strong brown legs. When he moved, I could see it was Corey Orion, and I walked up the beach toward him.

On the land side, beyond the dunes, the roofs of houses showed in all their variety. At intervals more steps came down over the dunes, offering access to the beach. The darker waterline, marked by broken shells, seaweed, and other detritus from the sea, indicated the reach of the water.

Corey, his dark head bent, was so absorbed in picking through whatever treasure the waves had washed up that he didn't see me until I stood beside him.

"Any good finds this morning?" I asked.

He smiled at me—a nice smile, when he chose to use it. "Something for you," he said, and held up a small black object, perhaps an inch long, with three smooth, rounded points. The ocean had polished it to a glassy surface.

"That's a shark's tooth," Corey said. "Maybe a mako shark, since the edge isn't serrated the way the teeth of the big whites are. Those teeth are fossils, of course—maybe a million years old."

I examined the object with respect. "Thank you. Do sharks lose their teeth very often?"

"They're lost easily because they aren't rooted in the jaw. They grow in the gums, and when they fall out, the shark develops another set. Very convenient."

This morning Corey's dark eyes were friendlier, and there was no mockery in his manner as there'd been the day before. Clearly this treasure from the sea interested him and lifted his spirits.

"It's a funny thing," he went on. "Everything else that goes into the ocean is consumed in one way or another, but not the teeth of the shark. So they're always being washed up for us beachcombers to find."

"Are the teeth always black like this one?"

"That depends on the silt they were buried in. They aren't black in the shark's mouth, of course."

He held up a shell and again I accepted his gift. It was shaded from white to gray with corrugated ridges, perfectly shaped and unbroken.

"It's only a cockle, but pretty," he said. "I have a collection up at the house of things I've found down here. In the summer Susan and I used to come down to the beach early to find what had washed up overnight. When she went away to college she gave me her collection, and I still have it. I'll show you sometime, if you like."

"Thank you," I said. But there was more on my mind this morning than what had been left by the sea. I dropped down beside him and traced an absentminded pattern in the sand.

"Corey, I saw the little girl, Dulcinea, again when I came out of the house this morning. She told me that her family and Captain Trench's don't talk to each other. I met her mother, too, and she didn't seem all that friendly. Tell me what's going on."

One eyebrow lifted. "You aren't going to let anything alone, are you? You like to dig for treasure, too."

"People are more interesting to me than shells."

"Besides, you're supposed to play detective, aren't you?"

"Not really. I won't be around long enough

for that. But Dulcinea and her mother made me curious."

He shrugged. "Susan told me a little about what happened between the families. She didn't care much for Carlina Cameron. But with Susan I could never tell how much was exaggerated and how much was true."

I remembered that trait of Susan's—how she'd liked to embroider.

"Tell me what she said, Corey."

He gathered up a handful of sand and broken shells and tossed them toward the water. "I didn't always like the games Susan used to play. She could really bug people."

"Don't *you* play games?"

His smile was gone. "Sometimes I tease. But teasing comes at different levels. Don't you ever like to tease?"

Now and then Paul had told me to lighten up—that I lacked a sense of humor. I didn't think that was true. People didn't always find the same things funny.

When I didn't answer, Corey produced his ready grin. "I knew Susan pretty well. My mother and I moved in after her grandmother left, and we were thrown together. She was my girl for a while when we were in our teens, but when she went off to school in California, we eventually stopped writing. And when she came back on vacation, things had changed. She wasn't ready to settle down and be serious—and I wasn't either."

We were both quiet for a while and I studied the little cockleshell in my fingers. When I looked up he was staring at me openly and I again felt the challenge in him.

"I know why you're here," he said. "The captain talks to me sometimes. He'll never stop trying to find out what happened to Susan. I suppose you're the last straw he can reach for—being her friend."

A pretty weak straw, I thought. "This morning the captain told me that the last time Susan was seen she was in her grandmother's room. Did you see her the day she disappeared?"

"Sure. I could have been the last one to see her. I went to her room to ask about something, and she was sitting at her desk writing a letter. The letter disappeared with her."

"No one saw her walk out of the house?"

"Nobody who would talk."

"What did you want from her that day?"

He got up from the sand, dusted off his jeans, and then held out a hand to pull me up. "Let's start back. We can walk while you're playing detective."

Corey had a knack for rubbing me the wrong way. "Stop that! I'm no detective, but I am curious."

His grin was growing all too familiar. "So that calm, controlled exterior hides a temper? Interesting."

I wasn't always so edgy, and I managed to respond quietly. "Susan was my friend. *I* want to know what happened to her. Besides, I like the captain, and I'd be happy to help him in any way I can. You didn't answer my question about what you wanted when you went to see Susan that day."

"What I went to ask her about isn't important." He didn't look at me as we walked on across the loose white sand. When we neared the steps he added, "I can't remember what it was, anyway. Maybe something trivial, like 'Where did you put my—' whatever. I suppose she didn't know, because she went right on writing. I didn't see her again. What happened afterwards—all the commotion when she couldn't be found—knocked that little stuff out of my head."

"Do you think she's dead?"

He backed away from that. "I don't think she'd have willingly left the captain without a word. He meant more to her than her father ever did."

"The captain thinks she was murdered. Do

you suppose she could have been killed in her grandmother's room?"

"You're reaching," he said. "There was never any evidence."

"There's an answer somewhere. People don't just disappear. There has to be a lead."

He had no answer for that.

I brushed sand off my legs and rolled down my jeans. When I slipped on my sandals and climbed the steps, he came with me. I pulled him down on the bench in the gazebo.

"Tell me about the captain," I said. "What's wrong with him?"

All the fun went out of Corey. "It's cancer. He should have been dead months ago, according to the doctors, but he won't have that. He's like the bumblebee. He doesn't accept that he can't be alive, so he goes on living. I don't think he'll die until he's ready to."

"I like that. Good for Captain Trench!"

Corey smiled grimly, but he wanted no more questions. He left me sitting there and went off alone. I felt more unsettled and anxious than ever as I walked slowly down the lane that led to the house. For a little while Paul had been no more than a shadowy presence at the back of my mind, but of course, the moment I had time to remember, he was there—not the angry man I'd last seen, but the husband I had loved and counted on. That was the worst part of all, since, as I'd recently discovered, that man didn't really exist.

When I reached the captain's house I hurried upstairs to his room. The door stood partly open and I heard a woman's voice. I tapped and he called to me to come in. He was sitting up in bed, and a striking-looking woman sat in the chair beside him. She turned as I came in and rose to hold out her hand.

"Hello. I'm Louise Trench, and of course you must be Susan's friend. I do hope you can manage some good talks with Captain Trench about Susan before you go home."

Though her handclasp was strong, her clear blue eyes were cool. Susan's stepmother was still beautiful, with a good deal of charm at her command—something she now turned on me in a welcome I didn't altogether trust. Her carefully tended hair had been drawn into a shining twist that crossed the back of her head and was tucked into place with small amber combs. Her dress was made of amber silk, with a tiny pink figure in the print. She was probably in her fifties, though she wore her years well. I felt immediately conscious of my sandy jeans and windblown hair, and wished that Susan had told me something about her stepmother.

The captain was watching us from beneath

half-closed eyes, and I went around the bed to pull over a chair so I could sit beside him and look across at Louise Trench. Again I noticed his fine blue dressing gown and elegant scarf. I suspected that he still chose whatever he put on, and that he had once worn a uniform with pride.

"I'm early," Louise went on pleasantly. "I wanted a little visit with Father before we left. We'll have lunch in Wilmington, Mrs. Knight, if you don't mind a drive. That will give us some time to get acquainted. I was very fond of Susan, you know."

I didn't know, and when I caught a glint in the captain's eyes, I wondered. I hadn't warmed toward this woman and I disliked the idea of spending hours in her company, but, obviously, I had no choice.

"Richard is meeting us at the restaurant in Wilmington," she explained. "Richard Merrick, who met your plane yesterday."

That would help a little—not to be alone with Louise.

The captain spoke grumpily from the bed. "Well, you'd better get dressed and get going, Hallie. Tell Mrs. Orion to come in. I want to get up in my chair again and go out on the deck for a while."

"A good idea," Louise agreed. "It's a lovely day. I'll call her for you."

I stood up. "Can I help you into your chair, Captain? If you like, I can wheel you outside."

He scowled at me. "Can't you call me something besides 'captain'? I seem to be caught between people who boss me, like Mrs. Orion, and those who hold me off with a lot of false respect."

He seemed to be ignoring the "Father" title that Louise Trench had produced.

"I'll think about it," I said. Being impulsive wasn't my thing, but something prompted me to lean over and kiss the captain's cheek. "How is that? Fresh is something different, isn't it?"

"Fresh I like. Now get me into my chair. No, don't bother yourself, Louise. This one will manage."

As I wheeled his chair over to the bed, I caught the look on Louise's face and was startled. For just an instant a look of antipathy had rested on me. Then she was smiling blandly again.

"Of course we must humor him," she said archly. "Even when he's being naughty."

I could tell by the look on his face that, in a moment, Nicholas Trench was going to roar at his daughter-in-law in his best topside voice.

"I'm not sure how to manage getting you into the chair," I said quickly, and the distraction served.

"I can get up on my own," he said. "Just put

the brakes on the chair and give me a hand if I need it."

He didn't need it. He stood up on legs that were only a little shaky and sat down in the chair. At his direction I drew a light blanket over his knees, and he was ready by the time Mrs. Orion came bustling into the room. "I'll take him out on the deck," she told Louise. "I know you want to get started for Wilmington."

"I'll hurry and change," I said quickly. "When I get back from lunch I'll look in on you again, Nicholas."

His sudden warm smile expressed his approval of me, but Mrs. Orion spoke with authority. "Please see me first, Mrs. Knight. The captain likes to have a long nap in the afternoon."

The captain snorted and winked at me openly. "You see what I'm up against? You have orders to see me as soon as you get back to the house, young lady!"

Mrs. Orion wheeled him abruptly out onto the deck and Louise followed her. "Ryce and I are so glad you're here, Mrs. O. It's wonderful that you've stayed with him all these years."

Mrs. Orion gave her a stolid look and said nothing.

Louise tried again, though I sensed the artificiality of her manner. "How is your son? Is he working somewhere on the island?"

Mrs. Orion's shrug indicated resignation. "He's about to start a job working part time at the Soundside restaurant—waiting on tables at night. That leaves him time for all the things he feels are important during the day."

Louise's smile was sympathetic. "He's a good boy, I'm sure. And he'll grow up eventually."

Since Corey was close to my own age, this seemed terribly patronizing, but I imagined that he could take care of himself. I was beginning to suspect the "young" act he affected. However, his mother's reaction to Louise made me curious. I had the feeling that she didn't trust her, and was uneasy with her, but wanted to keep up a front of courtesy.

I left them on the deck and hurried off to my room and a quick shower. Then I put on a sheath the color of ripe wheat, and added antique coral beads and earrings. Never mind that Paul had given them to me. I wouldn't think about that now.

When I rejoined Louise, we went down to her blue Mercedes, parked in the driveway. As we got in I saw that Dulcinea was outside again. I waved a hand at the girl, but there was no response.

"An obnoxious child," Louise said as we drove back to the highway that would take us to the bridge.

I couldn't agree. "That's a pretty strong word. Dulcinea told me that her father's family and the captain's don't speak to each other. Though I understand they were once friends."

Louise turned onto the crossroad that led to the bridge. "I don't know the details, but undoubtedly it was Fergus's wife who caused the trouble. Nick had a thing for Carlina before she married Fergus. Anne, Nick's wife, was the one who suffered the most from what happened."

"At least *she* got away," I said.

"She'd never have been one to stick around and take second place. I can't say I was fond of her, but I never blamed her for leaving."

"What happened to her exactly?" I asked.

"You'd better ask Ryce about that. After all, she was his mother."

I determined to ask no more questions during our drive to Wilmington, since Louise obviously didn't welcome them. I would simply watch the great stands of pine trees that I'd seen from the air, and offer no more ideas of my own.

6

ouise drove competently, sure of her car, and very sure of herself. Now she kept up what was not exactly a conversation, since she did most of the talking. Perhaps she wanted to prevent my asking questions. Everyone I'd met since I'd come to North Carolina seemed to be harboring some secret, and Louise was no exception. My attention wandered until she mentioned her husband's name.

"It's been dreadful for all of us, of course," Louise ran on. "But poor Ryce has had more than his share of unhappiness."

That was certainly true. He had lost his mother and his first wife. Then his daughter had disappeared. I still found it strange that Susan had talked so little about any member of her family except her grandfather.

"Were Susan and her father close?" I asked.

"Not exactly close. Susan had her own interests, which weren't always ours."

I could imagine that was true.

"Ryce and his father tried in every way possible to find Susan, but of course nothing worked out."

"Why 'of course'?"

"If Susan chose to disappear, I think she could do it without leaving a trace. I know the captain believes she's dead, but I have never been convinced."

"When will I meet her father?" I asked.

It seemed a natural question, but Louise's hands tightened on the wheel. "He's very busy right now. We'll have to see if we can work something out."

"Was there anything Susan was running away from?"

"I wouldn't know. I never tried to figure out her motives. She always seemed to follow inner promptings of her own."

That was a good way to put it, I thought. Susan had had a taste for the mysterious and dramatic when we'd been close. I'd often thought that she enjoyed tantalizing people. And her temper could be explosive.

"I was very fond of Susan," I said. "She was

different from other girls I knew, and a lot more interesting. I could never guess what she would do next."

"She was always like that. I doubt if we'll ever find her—until she wants us to."

I spoke quietly, watching Louise's profile as she drove. Seen from the side, she had a sharper look than when one saw her full-face. "Both the captain and Corey Orion think she is dead."

"That's because they can't accept that she would go off without telling them. The captain is lost in his own fantasy about his granddaughter. And of course Corey was foolishly in love with her. I wouldn't pay much attention to anything he said."

"Foolishly?" I repeated.

She didn't turn her head. "Just figure it out."

"I can't see why anyone would want to harm Susan," I said. "It's true that some people disliked her, but I never heard of her having serious enemies."

"She was worth more alive with all that money behind her," Louise said. "Not even my husband knows how much Nick has put away. Richard Merrick takes care of his affairs, and he's not talking. But I'm sure there's a great deal."

Which would now come to Louise's husband when the captain died, if he was the only heir.

Would Nicholas have bypassed Ryce and left his fortune to his granddaughter? I wondered.

Louise went on. "Eventually Susan would have been a wealthy heiress—the captain would have seen to that. So there were always interested young men around."

"When I knew her, she wasn't attracted by the idea of marriage. But of course people change. She told me that her mother died when she was very young and she was raised by her grandparents. Though she only talked about her grandfather—never her grandmother. From what I've learned since coming here, Anne Trench must have been a strong character. Didn't she get along with Susan?"

"Who ever got along with Susan?"

"I got along with her fine," I said mildly, but firmly. "Can you tell me when her grandmother died?"

Louise looked at me in surprise. "Whatever made you think she was dead?"

It was my turn to be surprised. "The captain told me that."

"He would! I suppose he regarded her as dead the minute she went off and divorced him. She moved to Boston and she's been up there painting ever since. She's had a few notable shows and won some awards. Several museums collect her paintings. This began to happen soon after she left the captain, so Susan would have known about it."

"Does Ryce hear from his mother?"

Her answer was indirect. "Ryce was always on his father's side, which didn't please Anne. But I've looked her up once or twice when I've been in Boston—though not since Susan disappeared—and she was perfectly cordial."

"I'm puzzled that Susan never talked to me about such a talented grandmother."

"She probably never forgave Anne for leaving Nick."

I noticed that she'd stopped calling him "Father."

"It's a wonder the captain didn't throw out those angry paintings his wife did. Have you ever seen them—the abstracts?"

Louise spoke softly. "I think it was Susan who rescued her grandmother's work when her grandfather threw them out. But he couldn't very well throw out what was in his own mind, could he?"

"Does he know the paintings are still in the house?"

"I can't believe that he does. He wouldn't stand for it. She painted them to hurt him, and she succeeded."

"Perhaps it was a release for her to paint them. Perhaps he deserved what she did."

Louise threw me another look of surprise, but she didn't comment. "We're coming into Wilmington now, Hallie. It's a wonderful old city that lies between the Cape Fear River and the Atlantic Ocean."

The subject of Susan and her family had been dropped for the moment, and I was just as glad.

We were following the side of a hill that ran parallel to the river below, and after a block or two Louise turned down toward the waterfront.

"This is the old downtown area," she said. "The Cotton Exchange has been restored and turned into a collection of shops. If you were going to be here longer, I'd take you through it one day."

Whenever Louise mentioned my "visit," she seemed to imply that I would be here for only a few days at most. I let her think what she liked, since I didn't know myself how long I would stay. A lot would depend on the captain and what he expected of me.

On the riverfront street she turned left. "We're going to the other end—to Chandler's Wharf. Richard thought you might enjoy a table beside the river."

Elijah's, where we were to have lunch, was only a few blocks from where we left the car. We walked the rest of the way on old cobblestones.

Inside the restaurant we were led to a table in a porch area. Richard Merrick had already arrived. I was seated where I could look across the wharf below us to the river. The bridge was close, built with a high section between two towers that could be raised for the passing of ships.

Richard had risen to greet us, with a special smile for Louise and a questioning look for me. He was almost as fair as she was, and they looked very handsome together. But these relationships were none of my business, and I knew better than to judge anyone.

"I'm sorry Ryce couldn't make it," Louise told Richard, and then explained further to me. "He manages our small farm, you know, and it keeps him very busy. It's not really a plantation, though the house is historic and is called a plantation house. If you're still planning to be here, perhaps you would come to dinner tomorrow night? Ryce is anxious to meet you. And of course we'd like you to come, too, Richard. Perhaps you could drive Hallie over?"

"A pleasure," Richard said, though I wondered if it was. Something about Richard Merrick's manner left me feeling uncertain. Now he put his question into words. "So what do you think of the captain, Hallie?"

Above our row of window tables, ceiling fans alternated with hanging light fixtures, and I studied a soup spoon in the bowl of which a miniature fan reflection turned lazily. I wasn't sure what to say about the captain.

"I like him—though I hardly know him yet. Mrs. Orion treats him as if he were a helpless invalid, which I'm sure he resents. Anyway, I can't do what he asks."

"What is that?" Louise asked quickly.

There seemed no reason not to talk about the captain's impossible request. "He has a notion that I can find out what happened to Susan."

Louise and Richard exchanged looks. "What could *you* possibly do?" Louise asked.

I tried to explain how I felt. "I told him there was no way I could think of to help him, but he didn't listen. I'll try to make him understand that there's nothing I can do. Then perhaps I can go home. Unless he has some particular task for me."

Richard seemed concerned when it came to the captain's well-being. "There's a deep pain in that man that has never stopped gnawing at him. And I don't mean his very real physical pain. It was eating him alive even before Susan disappeared. He won't rest—he can't rest—until he finds some sort of answer to what happened to her."

"What if there is no answer that can ever be discovered?" I asked.

Louise agreed. "Exactly. But he's never been a man you could argue with."

I tried to give my attention to the menu, and when our waitress came, I ordered simply— Maryland crab cakes, a baked potato, and salad. While the other two decided, I looked out the window to the river flowing beyond the wide wharf. The water had a dark, almost reddish tone.

"What a strange color," I said.

Richard explained. "The color comes from tannic acid leached by cypress trees upriver."

"If you don't do anything else during your brief visit, you mustn't miss exploring the Cape Fear area," Louise said when the waitress had gone. "There's a stern-wheeler that takes passengers downriver, so if there's time you could make that trip."

I smiled and nodded, but I wasn't here for sightseeing. As I looked out at the water, a freighter came downstream. The bridge span was high enough for it to pass under without the center span needing to be raised. The sight held my attention, until Louise made a soft sound of dismay. She was looking down the porch area toward the end of our row of tables, and I saw that a man was coming toward us.

He was a rather small individual whose basic

coloring seemed to be gray—gray suit, gray hair, gray eyes. Perhaps a sad, gray nature.

Louise was clearly not pleased to see him. She watched coolly as he approached our table.

He nodded at the other two and held out his hand to me. "I'm Ryce Trench. I'm happy to meet my daughter's friend." His handclasp was firm, even warm. When he glanced at his wife, however, his expression seemed carefully blank, and he went on speaking directly to me. "I decided that I wouldn't wait until you came to see us as my wife had planned, but would join you for lunch. May I sit down?" Without waiting for an invitation, he took the chair next to me. "How is my father since you've arrived?"

Louise broke in before I could speak. "I had a visit with him this morning, Ryce. He seems weaker every time I go to Topsail."

Ryce kept his eyes on me, and it was as though she hadn't spoken. I had been wrong about him. He wasn't entirely gray. A spark of barely hidden fire burned in his eyes. Not even his Southern good manners held it entirely in check, and I knew that he was a deeply angry man.

I answered quietly. "I like your father very much, but I haven't any comparisons that I'm able to make about his health. I hope I can be of some use to him. He wants me to tell him some of my memories of Susan, and I'll certainly be able to do that."

The spark I'd seen so briefly had gone, and the grayness again predominated. "Susan is dead," he said flatly. "That's not why you're here, Hallie. Father is trying you out, testing you while he makes up his mind."

"To what purpose?" I asked.

The waitress arrived to take Ryce's order, and he waved her away with a request for coffee and key lime pie. When she'd gone he looked at Richard for the first time. "You haven't told her?"

"There's hardly been time," Richard said. "Mrs. Knight needs to orient herself a little. Besides, I feel that it's up to the captain to tell her when and whatever he chooses."

Ryce ignored this. "My father wants to write you into his will because he is grateful for all you did for Susan. But I'm sure he wants to get to know you a little better before explaining his plan."

"He mentioned his will in the letter he sent me. I've told Mr. Merrick that if it is more than a token gift, I won't accept it."

Ryce shook his head. "You don't know it all, Mrs. Knight. My father is setting certain conditions that you may not want to accept. You can resist by refusing the conditions."

"Then that's probably what I will do."

Louise made a sound with her pursed lips—perhaps meant for a laugh.

"We all know your opinion on this, Louise." Ryce spoke mildly, but I sensed that smoldering spark in him again. "It's up to my father to tell you, when he's ready, Mrs. Knight. I hope you will remain until then."

I knew I would remain a while longer, in any case. Not because of the captain's will, but because I wasn't ready to return to the reality of an empty apartment.

"I'll wait," I said, looking at each of them for a moment. "If it's not too long."

Ryce's smile was kind and he seemed to approve of me. I couldn't read what either Richard or Louise thought.

Another freighter was going past on the river, and this time the suspension section rose between the towers to allow for its passage. I watched until the freighter had gone through, and relaxed into silence while our meal was served.

As we ate, Louise engaged Richard in conversation while I spoke quietly to the man beside me.

"When Susan told me about Topsail Island, she only mentioned her grandfather. So I know nothing about the rest of the family."

"Susan carried a load of unforgivingness," Ryce said sadly. "Perhaps she was too much like her grandmother in that. My mother was not a forgiving woman and her anger could be a match for my father's."

"Was she angry with you?"

"She was mad at the universe. I hear she's mellowed, but I wouldn't know."

He glanced at Louise, but she wasn't listening, and he went on. "Susan could be filled with more than anger. When it came to her family, *venom* might be a better word. But tell me about you, Hallie Knight."

That wasn't a subject I wanted to talk about. "There's nothing much to tell."

He saw my reluctance. "Did Susan ever discuss what she wanted to do with her life?"

I shook my head. "She had so many talents. She could have been a writer, or a dancer, or an artist like her grandmother. But there never seemed to be one thing that held her interest for long."

"Was she happy then? During college and before she returned to Topsail?"

"I don't think she was unhappy. Perhaps she was still searching, as most of us were in those days. Being young isn't always a happy time."

"Come to think of it," Ryce said, "I don't know very many happy people of any age."

But *I* had been happy. I'd been happy in my marriage, in my work. I'd felt that I was making up for the unhappiness of my younger years. Now—in a flash—that good life I'd made for myself was gone.

"Other than their mutual capacity for anger, was Susan anything like her grandmother?" I asked.

"In some ways she was. There was the same excitement in her that my mother always had. An eagerness for life. Perhaps a dangerous eagerness. But in the last years here she seemed to lose that spark."

The word *dangerous* caught my ear. "I think you're right. Sometimes Susan would take risks. I'm afraid I was the sensible one who often spoiled her fun."

"She used to talk about you, even after you stopped exchanging letters. She envied your happy marriage. Men were attracted to her, but she was always too restless to settle down. I used to think that she and Corey Orion hit it off well. Both Corey's mother and I would have been pleased, I think, to see something solid develop between them."

We'd been talking about her in the past tense, and I put my question bluntly. "Do *you* think she was murdered? It's what the captain believes."

He seemed to freeze, as though the word cut through some web of protection against inner pain, and at once I was sorry I'd spoken out.

Louise must have been listening, after all. She turned from her talk with Richard. "Murder? Who has been murdered?"

"The captain believes Susan was," I said.

"Nicholas Trench is not in possession of his right senses," Louise said sharply. "I've often thought that it would be better for everyone if he could be put—"

Richard rested a hand on her arm, stopping her. "Easy, Louise."

"Well, it's true that Ryce should be able to make important decisions for himself."

Her husband merely looked at her. Perhaps he looked *into* her, for she flushed angrily.

The word *murder* had touched some level of response in each of them. Even in Richard, who was watching me warily. Certainly it had ended our meal. Suddenly it was as if a silent signal had been given and we were ready to leave. No one had answered the challenge of the question I had flung down.

Richard signaled for the check, and while we

waited, Ryce spoke in his quiet way to Louise. "I'm planning to visit my father this afternoon, so I'll drive Hallie back to the island."

I suspected that Louise was pleased with this arrangement. When we walked out to our cars, she smiled at me. "We will count on you for dinner tomorrow night, Hallie."

I agreed and we parted quickly. I had the feeling that Richard would have liked some words alone with me, but he followed Louise's lead. Since he had walked to the restaurant from his office, she would give him a lift back.

Once in Ryce's car, I tried to settle down. Our time in the restaurant had been disquieting, and it was a relief to be with Susan's father and away from the other two.

Ryce wasn't given to idle chatter, so we drove in silence toward Hampstead and the island. This left me alone with my own thoughts, something I didn't much care for, because the moment my thoughts weren't otherwise occupied, they turned too readily to Paul. Now I wondered if it was ever possible for the male of our species to be true to one woman for a lifetime. I'd never questioned this before—I'd believed completely in Paul's integrity and his love for me. Now I could see how gullible I'd been.

Ryce startled me by interrupting this unhappy

reverie, and I realized that time and miles had slipped away. "The swing bridge is open, so we'll have to wait to go across. It shouldn't be long."

We were several cars back in the line, so I couldn't watch the operation of the bridge. For the first time since we'd left Wilmington, Ryce seemed ready to talk.

"You asked a question when we were at Elijah's," he said. "My father is obsessed with this belief in Susan's murder, but I don't think you should listen to him. What you have for him are your memories of Susan, and I think you should give him whatever you can that will comfort him and avoid anything he proposes that feels like sleuthing."

This didn't satisfy me. "What I asked was whether *you* believed that Susan was murdered."

The gray look seemed to descend like a fog that wiped out all expression. "That is a dangerous question to ask."

"What do you mean?"

"What if it's true? What if a killer walks among us? What if someone is waiting to see how close to the truth *you* get?"

I had no answer for that. Before he could go on, a man in a car behind us recognized him and got out to come over to the driver's side of Ryce's car.

"Hi, Ryce. Have you heard about the find on the beach?" he asked. "It sounds important, so my paper's sending me over. No one's sure what it is, but the thing came ashore in Surf City on the oceanside."

The car ahead of us started to move, and the man—obviously a reporter—dashed back to his own car, leaving us to wonder what he was talking about.

"I'd better find out what's happening," Ryce said as we drove across the bridge. "Shall I take you back to the captain's first, or do you want to come with me?"

I went with him, and when he'd parked the car on the oceanside, we climbed steps that led over the dunes. There was no gazebo here. The far steps dropped directly to the beach, and we could look down on the small group of people who had gathered there. Their attention seemed to be held by a long metal object that lay on the sand.

Ryce made a stifled exclamation as we started down the steps.

7

"*I* can see Fergus Cameron down there," Ryce said as we headed down. "Have you met him yet, Hallie?"

"I've met his wife and daughter, but not Mr. Cameron." I decided to repeat Dulcinea's remark and watch for Ryce's reaction. "Dulcinea told me that the families don't speak to each other anymore."

"Dulcie playacts. It's true that the relationship between my father and Fergus has cooled over the years, but that doesn't affect the rest of us. Though I can't say that Susan and Carlina liked each other much."

We started across the sand, and I could see the long, very large metal object more clearly. A tall, thin man was examining it, and as we approached he straightened, recognizing Ryce. His long face matched his body, and both showed prominent bones. He held himself in a stiff, nervous way that barely concealed his excitement.

"You'd better let Nick know about this, Ryce," he said as soon as we were close.

Ryce touched my arm. "Hallie, this is Fergus Cameron. He was here with the captain when the rockets were being launched. Fergus, Hallie Knight, a friend of my daughter when they went to college together."

Cameron nodded absently in my direction, his attention held by the object in the sand.

"It could be a booster for a rocket launched from Operation Bumblebee," he told Ryce. "Whatever it is, it's the first piece from a rocket launching that's ever washed up on Topsail." He looked around at the small gathering of curious islanders. "Has anybody notified the sheriff? This is a valuable artifact and it needs to be preserved in water."

The reporter who had spoken to Ryce earlier said that the sheriff was on his way.

"Then I'd better get the news to my father," Ryce said. "Fergus, will you let us know when it's been identified for sure?"

"I'll do that," Fergus Cameron said, waving a hand as Ryce and I started up the beach.

As we climbed the steps over the dunes, I asked Ryce, "What was the falling-out between the captain and Mr. Cameron about?" It had already been hinted at, but I wanted to know what Ryce would say.

He shrugged. "Who really knows? Though I expect that Carlina was the focus, or so gossip has it. It all happened years before Dulcie was born. Carlina's settled down by this time. When Fergus and my father first knew her, she was a trapeze artist in a traveling circus. From all accounts she must have been pretty stunning. Everybody thought her an unlikely wife for Fergus, but I guess he fell pretty hard."

We had reached the platform at the top of the steps, and Ryce was silent, stopping for a moment to look out again over the beach.

"There's more to the story, isn't there?" I said.

Ryce shrugged. "It's all ancient history. I guess my father was chasing her, too, even though he had a wife of his own."

"Your father was married to your mother at the time?"

"That's probably why Carlina turned to Fergus, who was unencumbered. She wanted to get out of the circus, and this was a way. Dulcie came along late in their marriage."

"Is Carlina why your mother left the captain?"

He didn't seem to mind telling me. "Not really. There was always some woman Dad had an eye for. Carlina wasn't anything new. Though maybe she was the last straw." He looked at me and seemed to see something in my face he didn't like. "Stay out of it, Hallie. I'm warning you. Don't go stirring up sleeping dogs. Come along and we'll go tell my father about this find. He's going to be pretty excited."

I made no promises, and when we reached the house I went with Ryce to the room where Nicholas Trench sat in his wheelchair. There was no warm greeting between father and son, and neither man seemed to expect one. But when he reported what had washed up on the beach, the captain brightened with the same excitement that had touched Fergus Cameron.

"Fergus *would* get there first," he grumbled. "You've got to take me down to the beach, Ryce. Right now!"

Ryce regarded him calmly. "You know that's not possible. We couldn't get you over the steps across the dunes, and a wheelchair won't move on sand."

The captain looked at me. "Get Corey for me, Hallie. I'll send him down to the beach to talk to Fergus."

I walked out of the room, to find Mrs. Orion waiting in the hallway, and she nodded to me. "I'll take care of it."

I went back to the room they'd given me—Anne Trench's room. Her paintings were still there, but someone, probably Corey, had taken them down and placed them against the wall, along one baseboard, facing inward. At least I didn't have to look at them anymore; I could live with their backs.

When I'd changed from my dress into jeans and a shirt, I took out the small treasures from the sea that Corey had given me that morning and put the shark's tooth and cockleshell on top of a bookcase near the windows. They shared the space with three books about gemstones that were set upright between the jutting wall and a large black rock that had been used as a book-end. The rock seemed an ugly thing, but when I turned it around I saw with delight that it was a geode. I had always been fascinated by this phe-nomenon of nature. A black chunk of rock, dug out of the earth in certain places, might hold a hollow filled with glistening gemstones. This piece had been sliced open on two sides. The strata of colors, ranging from yellowish white to pale lavender, burst at its heart into an amethyst cluster that caught a purple light in its many facets.

Dulcie's young voice suddenly spoke close by, startling me. Apparently she had the run of the captain's house—with or without anyone's per-mission.

"That strong color only comes when stones

are dug out from deep in the earth. When they lie near the surface, the color isn't nearly as strong."

She stood in the doorway watching me, her red hair windblown, her green eyes bright.

"It makes a good bookend," I said.

She came into the room. "It's okay, I guess. But you better not keep it too close to your bed at night."

"Why is that?"

"Amethyst makes you dream. Susan told me that. And it's written in those books besides." She pointed to the volumes on the bookshelf.

"Have you ever slept with an amethyst geode by your bed?"

Her wide eyes seemed to catch a gem fire of their own before she turned away. "*I* wouldn't take it out of Susan's room," she said so primly that I wondered if she had.

"Did Susan say what kind of dreams amethyst causes?" I asked.

She answered without turning. "She said they could be deep dreams and very clear. But they might be dreams she didn't want. Sometimes they scared her." Dulcie turned around. "She said if you looked into a true amethyst for too long, you could be hypnotized."

Of course, this might be true if one stared long enough at any bright object. "Have you tried that?" I asked.

Dulcie brushed a strand of hair out of her eyes and nodded. "I did once, but it was too scary. Everything went dark and swirly, and I could hear Susan's voice."

She threw me a frightened look and then started for the door. Just as she reached it, she turned and looked at me again. "You could ask that person her father married. *She* knows. Susan goes to see her sometimes because she lives in an old house where spirits like to go." Dulcie smiled slightly as though pleased with her own fantasy. "I think she scares Louise."

She whirled about and ran off, leaving me with the feeling that in spite of her tendency to exaggerate and fantasize, Dulcie knew more than she was telling.

I turned back to the bookcase. Perhaps the books on the shelf below the geode would tell me more about Susan's interests than she ever had. I pulled over the desk chair and sat down to study the titles. They revealed nothing that I didn't already know. We'd always shared a liking for mystery novels, and I saw that Susan had continued to read them. I recognized old favorites—Dorothy Sayers, Agatha Christie, Dashiell Hammett.

I turned my attention to the geode, with its heart of glittering purple treasure. Without realizing what I was doing, I stared into points of dark violet that lit the heart of the stone. Suddenly, opening ahead of me, awash in that glowing amethyst light, a tunnel without end seemed to stretch far into the infinite. As I continued to stare, literally spellbound, a human figure appeared at the distant end, bathed in violet light—whether it was a man or woman, I couldn't tell. The figure, in a long gown, stood very still as though it watched me from a great distance.

I spoke a name aloud softly: "Susan?"

In an instant the vision was gone and I seemed to hear a faint whisper of faraway thunder. There was no storm outside, and the violet facets of stone continued to sparkle in their own eerie light. From somewhere a memory came to me. Geodes were often called thunder eggs.

I felt dizzy, and I shook myself hard. I didn't like what had just happened to me. Mystic amethyst visions were not a part of my existence. And they were certainly not what Nicholas Trench wanted of me.

Dulcie had left my door open, and when Mrs. Orion looked in, I turned from the geode in relief.

"The captain would like to see you," she said. Her clipped words told me that she still didn't approve of my presence. During the worst of his illness she had undoubtedly been able to protect him from outsiders whom she considered disturbing. But since I had arrived, he'd grown stronger and found enough energy to ignore her. I wished I could find a way to placate her.

She strode off and I followed, glad, for the moment, to be away from a room that had too many unsettling elements.

Ryce was gone when I walked in, but Fergus Cameron was there, talking to the captain. The two men appeared to be engaged in lively reminiscences, and there was no evidence of the animosity that I'd been told existed between them. Fergus's presence had apparently given the captain a further lift, for there was color in his face and a new brightness in his eyes.

The captain saw me first. "Come in, come in, Hallie. I hoped you might join us. Fergus has been telling me what's turned up on the beach. He and I are going to work together to see that it's properly preserved."

"Is it really one of those rocket boosters that was set off when you were working on Operation Bumblebee?" I asked.

Fergus shook his head. "I don't think so. There are markings on it that indicate that it was an earlier launching from another site. But now it belongs to Topsail—a gift from the sea."

The captain spoke dreamily. "The building where the rockets were assembled is still here, and thanks to our Historical Society and others, it's been saved from use as a nightclub, or from being torn down. Cape Canaveral got all the glory, but we here on Topsail were an important part of the beginning of space science."

Fergus looked at his watch. "I must get along, Nick. I want to see about arranging a place where our find can be properly stored. Maybe in the Assembly Building. It's too big for most places."

"Take Hallie with you and give her a little history," the captain suggested. "You're the one who can tell her about the Assembly Building."

"I would be delighted to have Mrs. Knight along," Fergus offered, "if you care to go."

I would rather have stayed with the captain, but it was out of my hands. I went out with Fergus Cameron to his Jeep and climbed in. Once we were on our way, an unexpected sense of anticipation filled me. Operation Bumblebee was long in the past, yet I felt the tug of all that history in the making. Susan would have loved what was happening. I watched for the landmarks I was beginning to know, suddenly realizing that I hadn't thought of Paul for hours. That was a good sign.

8

⟞———————⟝

Again we drove past the concrete towers, and Fergus Cameron told me more about them. "Photographic equipment and cameras were positioned in those towers. They were spaced at the precise intervals that would enable them to track the missiles. Launchings are more spectacular now, but this was the start of what eventually put a man on the moon."

I could hear the pride in his voice. He had been a very young man when all this was happening, and the events on Topsail must have fired his imagination. Whatever life had dealt him since, he still remembered the early days with an excitement the years hadn't dimmed. As he went on, I listened, liking him because of that young man who was very much in evidence even after all these years.

"The towers were constructed rigidly, with

concrete pilings sunk twenty feet in the ground, so nothing could jar the cameras."

He explained that in the beginning all the tower windows had been covered with plywood in order to protect the equipment inside. "Some of the plywood is still left, though most of the windows are bare and open for winds to blow through."

No distance was great on Topsail, and a few miles south we took a right turn onto a road that led directly to a wide, low building, with a roof that sloped gently forward from a center ridgepole. A porch ran across part of the front of the building, and there were steps on each end leading up to the door.

"At present they open the building to the public only by appointment," Fergus said, turning the Jeep into a parking place. "On certain days tours are conducted so that people know what they're seeing." As we got out and walked toward the steps, he told me more about this historic place.

"The rockets were made somewhere else and brought here to be assembled. Then they were taken on dollies across to the oceanside to the launching pad. That pad is part of the basement of the Jolly Roger motel now. The walls of this main building are reinforced, and copper grounding and lightning rods are built into every corner. We were so afraid of a fire, because of the explosive nature of the propulsion materials, that we did everything we could to protect it. Some pretty big storms blow over the island, and a lightning strike would have been disastrous. Only one tower has been lost to the sea. All the others have withstood a great many storms, and so has this building. There's been only a little damage to the roof now and then."

As we went up the steps of the porch, music drifted out to us—a dreamy, minor-key tune from the past. "Song of India." It was unexpected and seemed out of place, but Fergus only smiled.

"I can guess who's in there," he said as he opened the unlocked door. We stepped inside and he put a hand on my arm, warning me to be quiet. The vast room was as brightly lighted as a stage, and what I saw seemed so strange that I felt an eerie prickling at the back of my neck.

The room that had once been used for the assembling of rockets was so enormous that it took up most of the wide building. The floor was concrete and constructed to hold the great weight of the rockets. Dozens of droplights hung from the high ceiling and all had been turned on. At the back of the room was a decorated counter that must have been used as a bar in some previous incarnation.

I took all of this in at a glance, my eyes held by the figure of a woman who made a dramatic focus in the center of the floor. Carlina Cameron held our attention as though she moved in a spotlight. Loose garments floated around her in multilayers of sapphire and yellow, with flame-like slashes of scarlet seemingly setting her afire as her supple body moved. Her long black hair, hanging loose down her back, stirred as though with a life of its own, lifting and hovering about her shoulders as she drifted in slow motion. Her expressive arms reached out before her as though she were moving in a sensuous dream. She seemed totally unaware of the room around her; unaware of us.

I looked at the man beside me and saw that he was completely entranced. Carlina wasn't dancing, exactly, just moving dreamily to the exotic music. One of her slow turns brought her directly opposite us, and she stopped abruptly, jarred from her dreaming. For an instant a flash of something—uncertainty, perhaps—crossed her face. Then it was gone, and she ran toward her husband, smiling. The music moaned to a stop as the tape ended.

I had never seen Carlina smile before, and her full beauty dazzled me. If she could look like this today, what must she have been like when she was young? Or was the spell of enchantment she cast more powerful in her maturity? The sight of her seemed to burn in an intense reflection in Fergus's eyes.

Nevertheless, the moment of enchanted beauty was gone. She seemed almost embarrassed as he bent to kiss her cheek.

"What are you doing here?" she asked.

He seemed to shake himself free of her spell before he answered her matter-of-factly. "There's been a find on the beach—something from an old rocket launching. I wanted to see if it can be safely stored somewhere here. Nick suggested I bring Mrs. Knight along to see the building."

"You've seen Nick?" Her surprise was clear.

"It's a long story," he said. "I'll tell you later."

Carlina was no less enchanting when seen close up. *This* is what charisma must be, I thought. She belonged in the center of a stage, and I wondered why she had given it up.

She turned to look at me with her luminous green eyes. "How are you enjoying Topsail Island, Mrs. Knight?"

I said I'd found it fascinating, and she smiled her approval. Nevertheless, I sensed a self-consciousness, as though our having discovered her dancing troubled her.

"What are you up to?" Fergus asked.

"I was just thinking—imagining. It always

helps me to visualize as I move." She looked at me. "We're using the Assembly Building as a community center now, and the school Dulcie attends has asked me to help them put on a pageant here to celebrate spring."

As she went on discussing her ideas with Fergus, I found myself wondering about the rivals he and Nicholas Trench must have been. And I wondered about the captain's wife, Anne, who had suffered because of other women. Unfortunately, I knew what that was like.

While Fergus moved about, considering places where the metal object from the sea could be placed, Carlina and I trailed after him, and she began telling me how effective Susan had been when they were raising money to save the building.

"When she put her heart into something, Susan could accomplish wonders. We all miss her."

I snatched at the opening. "What do people on the island think about Susan's disappearance? There must have been a lot of talk—theories?"

She nodded vigorously, her black hair rippling on her shoulders like silk. "There are all sorts of theories, but not one of them has led anywhere."

I looked at Fergus. "Do you have a theory?"

He seemed to hold himself stiffly as we spoke

of Susan. "She belonged to a generation I don't understand. She could do wonderful things when she wanted to—she certainly loved her grandfather—but I never thought she treated her father very well."

I could believe that of the Susan I'd known, but his answer had no relevance to what had happened to an attractive young woman who had disappeared one night without a trace.

"Let me show you another mystery," Carlina said. "Something less disturbing."

She ran across the wide floor to the nearest wall, her floating garments once again showing glints of flame under the sapphire and yellow. A broom leaned against a wooden panel, and she brought it back to us, her every movement graceful and arresting. She must have been a marvel on the trapeze.

Fergus smiled again, watching her.

"Dulcie is lucky to have a mother who understands about magic," I said, as enchanted by this interesting woman as he was.

"Listen!" Carlina commanded, and thumped the end of the broom on the floor. The sounds were loud, but without resonance. She moved here and there, still thumping, until she neared the door. Suddenly the floor gave off a hollow, echoing sound.

"Do you hear that?" she cried, her layered

garments fluttering with rekindled excitement. "There's emptiness down there. I can even trace the shape of the space. It must be a room— though there's no door into it. What do you suppose it is?"

"Now, now you're building something from nothing," Fergus said. "The rockets used to be lowered to ground level, before they were rolled to the launching pad. There's been no use for that space, so I suppose someone who was using the building blocked it off. It hasn't any meaning." He turned to me, smiling. "Carlina would like to make a mystery out of it with her thumping broom."

Carlina's excitement subsided under her husband's teasing. "I need to get back to the school," she said. "I'm glad you dropped in, Mrs. Knight."

"I'm glad I came, too. This is a fascinating place."

When we went outside, I noticed that the spell had dissipated with the magic. Fergus walked me to his Jeep and saw me into the front seat. Then he walked with his wife to her car and stood talking to her for a few moments before he came back to me. "Corey Orion told me that your wife was once with a circus," I said as he got into the Jeep beside me. "No wonder she's so colorful and interesting."

He put the Jeep into gear. "I'd think twice about anything Corey tells you. He has a great imagination. He and Susan made quite a pair, and I can tell you, they both enjoyed creating disrupting escapades."

We followed the road where it ran along a stretch of maritime forest and I looked out into the tangle of trees.

"Do you mean that Carlina was never in a circus?"

"No, actually, in that case he told the truth. But he probably elaborated on the story. Even though Carlina was good on the high trapeze, she never liked circus life. Her mother and father were both performers, but she grew up wanting something else. She wanted what she has now."

It seemed to me he was protesting a bit too much, and I thought about what Corey had also told me—that Nicholas Trench had been in love with her, too. And Nicholas must have been a dashing figure in his day.

"How did you meet Carlina?" I ventured.

The Jeep had been running smoothly, but a spurt of gas fed too suddenly made it jump ahead. So my question had caused a reaction.

"As it happened, it was Nick who introduced me to her."

But Fergus had won out. Because Nicholas already had a wife? Poor Anne, I thought, with a rival like Carlina.

"I understand that you and the captain worked together on Topsail when Bumblebee was begun."

"Yes. We became close friends, even though he ranked as a captain in the navy and I was only an enlisted man. What he wanted to accomplish and my scientific talents brought us together. The news I had for him today about what was found on the beach took us back to a time when we worked as a team."

The way Fergus's big hands grasped the wheel told me he'd had enough questioning from me. I was silent until we reached the two houses near the sound. I thanked him for showing me the Assembly Building and got out of the Jeep.

When I ran upstairs I found the door to my room open, though I had left it closed. I walked in to find that Corey Orion had placed the desk chair in the middle of the floor and was sitting astride it, leaning his arms on its back as he studied a painting of Anne's that he'd turned face out from the baseboard.

I let his intrusion into my room pass without comment and went to stand behind him.

"What do you see?" I asked.

Corey glanced at me, unsmiling. "Of all the work she left behind, this one of Anne's has always interested me most. What do you make of it, Hallie?"

I studied the painting. It was an acrylic, but not one of those in which she'd vividly re-created her anger. Nevertheless, it conveyed strong emotion. A long, narrow space seemed to tunnel deep into infinity. I was reminded of the tunnel I'd seen in my amethyst vision—though this tunnel seemed more menacing. Looking at the beiges and browns she'd used was like look-ing down a tube—into what? At the far end—if there was an end—a watery light glimmered and swirled, as though in a vortex. As I stared into this illusion of depth that was really only a flat surface of canvas, a dim figure seemed to emerge—like the hazy figure in my dream. I sensed the artist's feelings that had created the painting. The emotions were a blend of sadness and depression—and perhaps fear.

"She called it *Corridor*," Corey said. "It really grips you, doesn't it? It conveys something frightening that gets away before I can grasp it."

"It's no more a happy painting than the oth-ers," I said. "But the feeling in it is different. It's as though she was giving up."

He shook his head. "She wasn't like that. She didn't give up. That vortex at the heart of the painting seems to promise darkness, oblivion.

Not the bright, spiritual light that's supposed to come with, say, a near-death experience."

I shivered and he looked at me again. "There's something terribly unhappy about it. Maybe even prophetic."

"Prophetic of what?"

He stood up, went over to the painting, and once again turned it to face the wall. Somehow he looked more uncertain than I'd ever seen him.

"Who *are* you, Corey Orion?" I asked.

That must have startled him, for he gave me half a grin—smiling from just one corner of his mouth. That mouth that had been made for kissing. "What do you mean, who am I?"

"Maybe I mean *what* are you? Every time I see you, you're different. Sometimes you seem as young as a teenager. Other times you're older and serious—and strange. I keep wondering what you're thinking about behind whatever face you have on at the moment."

He laughed out loud, mocking me. "Haven't you found me out yet? I'm not real. I'm a painter's trompe l'oeil—a trick of the eye." He made me a courtier's bow, with a full hand gesture and outstretched leg—theatrical and totally out of character.

I wondered impatiently if *he* knew who he

was. Why was it necessary for him to put on these faces, play these games?

When he spoke again his tone had changed and he sounded gentle and apologetic. "Don't mind me, Hallie. Let me make it up to you for all my nonsense. I'd like to take you for a boat ride in the morning. You might as well have some fun while you're here."

Nothing much escaped Corey. I couldn't have been more surprised by this invitation, and he seemed to be serious about wanting to take me. But I still needed to solve the puzzle *he* presented. I had a feeling he had known Susan better than anyone else and, if he wanted to, could tell me things about her life in North Carolina that might lead me in the right direction.

"All right," I agreed. "I'd enjoy going out in your boat. What time do you want me ready?"

"Early. Say eight o'clock down on the dock. Don't eat breakfast. I promise we won't go hungry. Okay?"

"I'll be ready," I said. He went off quickly, as though I might change my mind, and I wondered why this seemed so important to him.

As the door closed behind him, I realized that Corey had taken with him something almost electric that seemed to touch the air around him. The room was suddenly quiet, and the vision of Anne Trench's depressing paintings was sharp in my mind. I knew how she had felt. Angry and sad and helpless. The pain struck again, and was worse than anger. How was I to get through this? What did other women do to stop the hurting? Anne Trench had painted, but there was no such outlet for me. At least the boat trip with Corey tomorrow morning would be a distraction. Though I wondered what he was really up to. Nothing about Corey was simple and obvious.

I reminded myself that it was time to report to the captain and tell him about my trip with Fergus Cameron to the Assembly Building. Perhaps I would even tell him what had happened with Carlina. How did he feel about her now? The question wasn't one of idle curiosity. I didn't want to hurt him, but there was so much he hadn't told me. How much of Susan lay deep in what he really felt that had made him bring me here?

9

The captain was not in his room, nor was he out on the deck. When I walked to the rail and looked over, I saw that Mrs. Orion had wheeled him onto the long dock that stretched into the water below the house. How she'd gotten him there I had no idea. I hurried down a flight of outside steps and found that a gradual and well-laid path of wooden planks wound from house to dock, so that wheeling his chair would have been simple enough, once it was at the lower level.

I walked along the dock toward them, and Mrs. Orion turned to shake her head despairingly. "He *would* want to come outside, though I didn't think it was a good idea."

"How did you manage to get his chair down here?"

She waved a hand toward the house. "There's

an elevator inside. The captain had it installed when his legs began to give out."

He looked over his shoulder as she spoke, and gestured me toward a bench that had been placed near the end of the dock. When I sat down, he spoke to me with new life in his voice.

"You saw the Assembly Building, Hallie? I haven't been out there for years. How did it look?"

"I don't know how it's supposed to look, but it seemed clean and well kept. Empty." I paused. "Except for Mrs. Cameron. She was there."

Sitting on the bench, with the dock railing behind me, I was on eye level with the captain. I saw him flinch at Carlina's name and then widen his eyes to stare at me.

"What was she doing there?"

"She was moving about—a sort of dancing. She said she'd come there to think about a pageant she's helping Dulcie's school to put on at the Assembly Building."

"I suppose Fergus is still besotted after all these years." There was scorn in his voice.

I preferred the word *enchanted*, but I didn't say so. "I wouldn't know," I answered carefully.

A sadness touched his eyes, and he closed them, perhaps to hide whatever he might be feeling. "Fergus and I both came to regret building houses that forced us to live so close together. Of course, he wasn't married to Carlina when he built his house. He brought her here later."

That would have been hard for everyone, I thought—including Anne Trench, with whom my sympathies lay.

"Perhaps you'll be friends again, now that he's come to see you," I suggested.

The captain scowled at me. "I wouldn't have taken you for the sentimental type, Hallie. Go on back to the house if you're going to talk nonsense. Fergus and I will never forgive each other for anything."

I stayed where I was and said nothing. I was sorry about his bitterness, but perhaps he had received his own due punishment for his treatment of his wife.

Out on the water a large white cruiser was gliding smoothly past, though the rolling waves left in its wake were far-reaching and anything but smooth. There was almost a violence in the way they pounded the pilings clear under the dock. I felt sorry for any small boat caught in those swells. Someone on the deck waved, and I waved back. The sound was part of the Intracoastal Waterway, which ran behind the barrier islands and offered passage to boats traveling up and down the coast.

The captain watched the cruiser as it made its way south. His scowl was gone, so perhaps he regretted his sharp words. I let them hang in the air without response, and studied the near shore below the house.

A narrow dirt road followed the edge of the sound, and bushes rose along the shore, growing out of water that changed its levels with the tides. Back a little way and on a slight elevation the captain's house stood out among surrounding trees. Behind it, almost hidden by twisted growth, the Cameron house was barely in view. They were indeed close neighbors to have kept up a feud all these years.

"I don't think I'm especially sentimental," I said finally. "But it seemed to me that Mr. Cameron was glad to have a reason to break the ice between you."

"He didn't even crack it," the captain said. "What did he say to you?"

"He told me how the Assembly Building was used in the beginning. I'm glad all that history is being preserved."

"When we were living it, we didn't think of it as being history. I suppose that's true of every generation, and it's why things get lost."

"Carlina also told me that Susan had been active in raising money to help the Historical Society."

The captain looked sad, as he always did when Susan's name came up. "She was in her own

room in my house when she disappeared. That's
one reason why I never swallowed the police
theory that she'd gone off somewhere on her
own. Have you been thinking about what happened to her, Hallie?"

"There's nothing to take hold of. I can't see a
direction of any kind. I'm sorry, but there doesn't
seem to be any way I can help. I shouldn't stay
any longer."

"You haven't even got your feet wet. You
can't give up so soon!"

I had a feeling that I was floating in space—
undecided about what to do with my own life
and unable to help the captain. I couldn't think
clearly about anything.

He was watching me. "You're pretty mad at
your husband, aren't you?"

He'd almost read my thoughts. "Why wouldn't
I be?"

"Women!" he said scornfully. "They never understand the men they marry."

I didn't want to understand if he meant that
men had the privilege of roaming because of
their hormones. I had hormones, too, but I'd always directed that energy toward one man.

Mrs. Orion had wandered back toward the
house while the captain and I talked, but now
she turned and came toward us. "Do you think

you could manage the captain's wheelchair, Mrs. Knight? I need to get back to fixing supper. Unless you want to go in now, Captain?"

He didn't, and I told her I would manage.

She went off, and the moment she was out of hearing, the captain reached out to take my hand. It was an affectionate gesture that surprised me.

"I didn't bring you to Topsail to accomplish the impossible, Hallie. I've been sizing you up, and Susan was right about you. As I told you in my letter, you're to be included in my will."

When I started to shake my head, he stopped me. "Don't say anything—just listen. When she was away at school, Susan wrote me letters. She talked about you often—about her gratitude to you, her affection. She never made friends easily, any more than I did. We were both loners. So it was special when you became her friend. You pulled her out of serious trouble more than once, and you gave her good advice."

"I'm afraid she didn't always listen."

"She listened to you more than she did to me. I'm grateful for the friendship you gave her when she most needed it."

"She was like a younger sister. I never had much family, so Susan gave me something, too. She needed me. I'm sorry that we drifted apart during those last few years before she disappeared. I suppose we each had our own lives and—"

He broke in with that growl in his voice again. "She could have had a good life of her own if she hadn't fallen in love with the wrong man."

I knew nothing about this, and I waited. I'd never cared much for any of the men Susan dated. And I'd never thought she did either.

He didn't follow up on who the man was, and it didn't matter now. "Richard Merrick knows what I want, and he's making it happen, though he's not happy about it. Not that how he feels matters in this case. Before Susan disappeared, most of my money was going to her. In my present will everything is being left to my son. But I've been put off with Ryce ever since he married Louise. I won't cut him out now, but he'll only get a bequest. And there are other bequests. The rest of it will go to you."

I couldn't grasp what he was saying. Money wasn't high on my list of what was important in life. I needed enough to take care of myself—especially now. But I had always managed before Paul, and I would manage now, even though it would mean looking for a new job so I wouldn't be working in the same office with my estranged husband. To become suddenly wealthy and acquire all the responsibilities connected with money didn't appeal to me.

"How can I make you see that I don't want this?" I said.

"You can't. My mind is made up. At first I planned to make certain conditions that you would have to decide about, but now that I've met you, I'm waiving those. I've known you for only two days, but I already wish that Susan could have been more like you. This is the only way I can show my gratitude to you and give my money—Susan's money—to someone she would have wanted to have it." She'd have hated to see it in Louise's hands through any inheritance to Ryce.

I was overwhelmed by his generosity, but at the same time there was something in his eyes that I didn't like. I couldn't help wondering if gratitude and Susan's possible desires were the only reasons behind this action. Perhaps more than anything else, this was his own slap at Ryce and Louise.

"I'll talk to Mr. Merrick," I said. "I'll find out how I can refuse this."

He smiled at me benignly, perhaps not really believing.

"What you're willing me is enemies," I said.

"You'll deal with them."

He was beginning to make me angry. "Did Susan have enemies? Did she deal with them?"

He looked suddenly stricken, but before anything more could be said, a loud clanging reached me from the deck of the house. Mrs. Orion was ringing the captain's brass bell. He waved a hand in response and looked at me.

"If we don't start out for the house right away, Mrs. O will be down here in a flash. Can you manage my chair?"

I released the wheel brakes and turned him about. The chair rolled easily from the dock to the plank walk, and he directed me to where the elevator was located on the lower storage floor. After going up to the deck level with a little wheezing and jerking on the part of the machinery, I wheeled the chair out to where Corey and—surprisingly—Dulcie were sitting at the outdoor table. I left the captain at the deck's railing where he could watch the boats on the sound and went to help Mrs. Orion. Corey came with me, and so did Dulcie.

"We have a guest," Corey told me, grinning.

"I invited myself," Dulcie announced cheerfully. "Dad and Mom are having a big row and I hate that. I don't know what they're fighting about this time, but I don't want to be there until it's over. Mrs. O said I could stay for supper."

I could imagine that both Fergus and Carlina

had tempers, but he had seemed so adoring as he watched her dance. Where had the trouble come from?

We helped Mrs. Orion carry food to the table, and she wheeled the captain to its head. Corey set down the centerpiece—a great bowl of potato salad, made with hard-boiled eggs and homemade mayonnaise. Assorted cheeses and rye bread filled out the supper, and we sat down to eat with smiles on our faces.

The meal was cheerful until Corey spoiled our mood. His attention had been caught by Dulcie's words about her parents' fight, and he began to ask questions, even though his mother frowned at him.

10

The captain and Dulcie were clearly old friends, so I realized that Dulcie's remark about their families not speaking had been a momentary fantasy.

"Let it go, my boy," the captain said, putting a halt to Corey's curiosity about the quarrel between Fergus and his wife.

Dulcie, freed from Corey's questions, began talking excitedly about the school pageant and her mother's plans.

"She's making me a costume out of some of her old circus things, so there'll be spangles and everything! I'm going to be a bareback rider."

"What will you do for a horse?" Corey asked.

When he talked to Dulcie, he could be at his most appealing. This was the aspect of his character that I liked best. Who would he be, I wondered, when we went on his boat trip in the morning. At least Corey Orion was never dull.

"Mom is having a horse made for me in Wilmington—out of papier-mâché, but over a form that will be strong enough to hold me. There'll be a saddle like a little platform that I can stand on and do some easy dance steps. The horse can't move on its own, but she thinks maybe he can be pulled along."

Thanks mostly to Dulcie, supper was a lively meal. Mrs. Orion seemed pleased with the captain's progress, and was even willing to give me a bit of credit. Not until we were finishing our meal with Dulcie's favorite pecan ice cream did a long silence fall upon us. The sun had set in the western sky and a big moon was rising out of the water. A lighted cruiser came into view and music drifted toward us. Even Dulcie was quiet, watching. A salmon pink glow stained the water, and I was suddenly aware of the great continent that stretched between me and California. Where was Paul now? Did he know that I'd left our apartment? Would he even care or wonder about me? This was self-pity, and I tried to rouse myself from the indulgence. Whatever happened, I would find a way to deal with it. Other women went through this and I would recover. Of course I would.

Music continued drifting up to our high deck

from the cruiser—a recorded voice singing the "Habanera" from *Carmen*. Dulcie listened eagerly.

"My mother loves that song!" she cried.

Carlina would, I thought. Corey had called her a gypsy, and the word seemed to fit.

Then, suddenly, Dulcie was crying. She made no effort to wipe away her tears, but cried openly like a small child.

Corey put a hand on her arm. "What's the matter, kid?"

"I—I don't want to go home tonight!"

The captain had wheeled himself to the rail to watch the sky and the passing boat, but now he turned back to the table. "You don't have to go home," he said.

Unflappable Mrs. Orion took charge. "If it's all right with your mother, Dulcie, you can stay here for the night—the way you used to sometimes. Tomorrow's Saturday and you can sleep late. I'll phone your mother and ask her if you can stay with us."

The captain's focus was on Dulcie. He returned to what she'd said earlier. "What is it? What's happened with your parents?"

For a moment she looked at him, hesitating. Then she spoke in a low voice. "I don't want to be there when they're fighting. They scare me."

The captain was clearly troubled. "Do they fight often?"

She shook her head. "Mom thinks she's getting old and isn't pretty anymore. She told me so one time. When she doesn't feel pretty, I guess she doesn't act pretty. Dad says she puts up a wall—and that makes him mad." Dulcie turned to me, suddenly entreating. "Can I stay in your room tonight, Hallie? Susan used to let me sleep in her room. Corey can bring in a cot—can't you, Corey?"

"Sure," he said.

"I'd like that," I told her quickly. I would be glad to have someone in my room to draw me away from all those things I couldn't bear to think about. "Do you want to go home and get your overnight things first?"

Dulcie shook her head. "They might make me stay." She looked at Mrs. Orion. "I used to wear one of her big T-shirts when Susan—" She broke off, and I thought her tears would start again.

Mrs. Orion nodded. "I know just the thing for you to sleep in, and we have a fresh toothbrush in the bathroom cabinet. I'll bring them to Mrs. Knight's room."

"Well, that's settled, so you can come and help with the dishes, Dulcie," Corey said cheerfully.

I offered to help, too, but Mrs. Orion shook

her head. "We have enough extra hands. Stay with the captain."

He rejected that idea. "I'll go to my room now. Good night." He stopped his chair as it moved away from me. "I'm glad you're here, Hallie. I'll see you in the morning."

"Corey is taking me for an early boat trip on the sound, but I'll look for you as soon as I get back."

Dulcie, halfway to the kitchen with her hands full of dishes, turned around eagerly. "Can I come, too, Corey?"

"Not this time, kid. I'll take you soon. Promise."

She accepted this with reasonable grace and hurried off with her plates. The captain, however, had paused again. "Where are you going, Corey?"

He answered airily, "Just down the sound. If Hallie likes birds, there are a few to see."

"All right," the captain said. "But don't keep her out too long. We have matters to discuss."

I suspected that he disliked any interference with his own plans for me, but it was out of his hands. I was glad to have an excuse to postpone any more talk about his will. As soon as possible I would see Richard Merrick and ask him to convince the captain that I wanted nothing to do with his money.

The captain wheeled himself off to his room and when the others had gone, I stood for a few moments longer at the rail. A breeze stirred the leaves of live oaks near the house and swept across the deck. Darkness was settling in and I could see stars coming out in pinpoints against the sky. The air had turned suddenly cool, and it was time to go in. Another boat must have passed because waves slapped roughly at the pilings of the dock.

Back in my room, I picked out one of Susan's books on gemstones and sat down to read. The index indicated that there were several pages on amethysts.

Their color, the text said, could range from pale violet to the deep purple valued by royalty to signify nobility of rank. Bishops of the Catholic Church still wore amethyst rings. It was a stone whose powers were considered to be spiritual, and it could give an intensity to dreams if placed near one's head at night. Amethysts had long been used for healing, and it was a stone that granted healing power to the wearer. It could also affect the intellect and result in clearer thinking. Apparently amethysts were strongly connected with the life force and could increase the intuition. I closed the book. Nothing about the stone was alarming.

I reached for the heavy geode and held it on

my knees, where I could look into the purple
peaks and facets at the heart of the stone. I'd left
my door open and wasn't aware that Dulcie had
come in until she stood beside me, her solemn
attention on the rock I held.

"I don't think you should get too close to
that," she said.

I smiled at her. "Why not? I've just been reading about the wonderful properties of the
amethyst."

"Susan knew a lot about crystals and gemstones, and she told me that amethysts have a
dark side. They stand for purity, but if someone
with bad wishes comes near the stone, the bad-
ness in the person could grow and hurt other
people."

I didn't know if this was one of Dulcie's fan-
tasies, intended to alarm me. "I don't think we
have to worry," I said. "We aren't bad people, are
we?"

Her grave look troubled me—as though she
wasn't sure how good we were. I touched the
sharp points where the purple cluster seemed
about to burst from the heart of the stone. Deep
in shadow, the royal color turned almost black. I
moved the stone into the light, and a surprising
streak of flame seemed to flash out of the deep
color, vanishing in a moment.

Dulcie saw it, too. "Once Susan showed me

the fire. That's the stone's secret. It only lets you see it once in a while." She broke off, studying me intently. "Hallie, do you think it's bad to have a secret?"

"Maybe that depends on the secret. On whether or not it would hurt other people. I suppose most of us hide some things we don't want others to know. But I don't think that's bad."

She looked relieved, and I wondered what secret young Dulcie was keeping.

Corey arrived with the cot and set it up while he bantered back and forth with Dulcie. Mrs. Orion followed with bedding and Dulcie's sleep-over things. While she was making up the cot, I returned the geode to its place as a bookend.

"Your mother says it's fine for you to stay," Mrs. Orion told Dulcie.

The girl looked relieved, as though she'd half suspected a summons to return home at once. "How did she sound?" she asked.

"Maybe a little excited. But not upset or angry. I expect everything will be fine in the morning. I'll bring you some hot chocolate before you go to sleep."

"The way you used to do," Dulcie said, smiling.

When we were alone, she went to stand at the window, where she could look down into the clearing. The yard light was on, and so were lights in the Cameron house.

Dulcie spoke softly. "He loves her such a lot, but I think he's still jealous because the captain knew her first."

"That was a long time ago," I said. "Your parents do love each other. I saw that today."

To draw her away from sad thoughts, I told her about the discovery on the beach, and the way her father had come to see the captain. She seemed happy about that and wanted to know every detail. When we'd finished talking, she yawned and went into the bathroom to get into a big old T-shirt of Corey's that Mrs. Orion had found for her.

When she was ready for bed, she picked out a book from the bookcase and settled down on the couch to read. But there was a restlessness in her tonight, and after a few moments of turning pages, she put the book aside and went to one of Anne Trench's paintings that leaned against the baseboard, facing the wall. She turned the painting around, and I saw that it was the one that had interested Corey—the long, dark tunnel.

"I wonder what she meant by that picture," I said.

Dulcie didn't hesitate. "She was painting the Pirate's Pit."

"What's that?"

"It's a bad place, Hallie. You don't want to know."

She turned the picture around and then tucked herself under the blanket on the cot and plumped up her pillow.

In a few moments Mrs. Orion brought in a tray with two cups of hot chocolate on which marshmallows floated. Dulcie sat up and we sipped in companionable silence. Mrs. Orion watched for a moment and then told us good night and went away.

Later, after I'd put on a nightgown, I returned to hear Dulcie breathing softly across the room. Her presence had seemed comforting, but no sooner did my head touch the pillow than the aching inside me began all over again. I'd rather be angry. Anger was better than hurt. But now it wouldn't come. I seemed to be enveloped in a great sadness that was quiet and very deep—not at all like the rage Anne Trench's brush had brought to life in those slashes of wild color that were now hidden against the wall.

❦

When I got up the next morning, Dulcie was still asleep. I dressed quietly and went out on the deck. Looking over the rail, I saw that Corey was already on the dock waiting for me. I ran down the outside steps and across the planks to join him.

Fog had drifted in over the dunes from the ocean, and wisps of it still hid the water. But the sun was up and the mists would soon burn away. Corey helped me into the boat, and I sat down beside him. He started the outboard motor and I felt a thrill go through me as we planed and began to skim over water that in no time was a shining blue in the sun. In a few moments we were past the south end of the barrier island of Topsail and I could look out to the open sea. White-crested waves were rolling in from the Atlantic, and when Corey cut the motor and let us drift for a few moments, I could hear the strong, repetitive voice of the ocean.

The marshes were alive with birds—white egrets, graceful in the air; herons moving on long, wobbly legs; scores of shorebirds hunting for food. We went on, skimming past ospreys already piling sticks for nests where there was any sort of structure.

Plexiglas kept most of the spray from my face as the boat cut through the water. Still, I didn't mind a little wetness, and I felt exhilarated as we flew across the sound just ahead of a cruiser that would have rocked us with its wake. This feeling of being alive was something I hadn't experienced in a long while. It was as though we moved in another dimension where ordinary human problems couldn't touch us.

Though sandbars changed constantly with rising and falling tides, Corey knew his way, and in less than ten minutes he cut the boat's speed as he moved in toward a small island. Most of it was covered by wild growth, but at one end, set high on a dune out of reach of water and shifting sand, stood a single house.

"Where are we?" I shouted over the diminishing sound of the motor.

He shouted back. "Cabbage Island—right on ahead."

The tiny island seemed to float low on the water, with that single rising dune at one end.

Corey's mood this morning seemed to be one of barely suppressed anticipation, which made me wonder again what he was up to. He cut the motor entirely as we neared the shore.

"Used to be a farm family lived out here," he told me. "They sold their cabbages to stores on the mainland, but that's all long gone."

The house was old and weathered—its gray-brown timbers had lasted a long time. The porch looked rickety and so did the steps that led up to it, but smoke rose from the chimney, and a bright Mexican blanket had been hung over the porch rail.

"Does someone really live here?" I asked.

"Just for now. She only rents. She likes the isolation, and I bring her supplies and keep track of her. She has a cellular phone, so she's not out of touch."

I was curious about the house and the woman, but Corey was busy nosing his boat into the low, sandy shore, and the house was lost from sight behind a screening of live oak and scrubby pine. He drove the bow into the sand and dropped an anchor in the water. Then he threw a second anchor over to catch high in the sand. Whatever the tides did, the boat would stay where he wanted it.

I got out on the narrow strip of beach and Corey quickly started ahead of me up a path that ran through tall beach grasses and sea oats.

"Come along," he called back to me. "She's waiting for us and she'll give us breakfast."

The house loomed above as we climbed into the open, and now the roar of the ocean could be heard again, the sound rising and subsiding endlessly. Corey reached back to catch my hand, pulling me up steps that led to the weathered porch.

"I suppose she has a name?" I asked a bit tartly, annoyed with his games, his way of keeping me in the dark.

"Yes," he said as we climbed the steps. "She has a name. It's Anne Trench."

11

My reaction was mixed. There was the shock of surprise, laced with annoyance at Corey. Yet underneath my surface response, excitement stirred, mixed with both anticipation and uneasiness.

Corey looked irritatingly pleased with himself. "She wanted to meet you, but she didn't want me to let you know ahead of time. Perhaps she thought you might not come. No one on Topsail knows that she's here, and she wants to keep it that way for now."

We moved along the narrow porch and Corey rapped on the door. "We're here, Anne," he called out. While we waited I could hear the deep pulsing of the ocean.

The door creaked open, and Susan's grandmother stood in the wide opening. She was tall and slender, with silvery hair drawn into a mound on top of her head. Her skin seemed smooth, with surprisingly few wrinkles. Perhaps, with time, she had arrived at a state of serenity. The eyes that watched us were wide and intent, their color an odd tawny brown. She wore a patchwork skirt over tweed trousers, and had on Mexican huaraches. I thought she looked considerably younger than the captain, though older than Carlina. Her makeup was carefully restrained—only a touch of rose petal on her lips, accented by the black slash of her eyebrows, where no gray had been allowed to show.

The hand she held out to me was elegant, with long fingers that had stayed flexible—a workman's fingers, with no nail polish. Her handclasp was as warm as the smile that brought beauty to her face. At once I felt welcomed and set at ease. Clearly, she had already captivated Corey, who had relaxed into a natural, unmannered state that I'd yet to see him in.

"Come in," she said, and drew us through the doorway into a room that was as warm and welcoming as Anne Trench herself.

She might be living in this ramshackle house for only a short time, but she had brought with her a few possessions to make it hers. Mexican rugs of primitive design covered the cracked boards of the floor. A decorative straw hat with a wide brim hung on the wall, its band of yellow ribbon hanging down. A few pieces of furniture were heaped with cushions in clear, strong earth colors. The fireplace really worked, and a wood fire burned energetically, sending sparks up the chimney whenever a piece of wood fell in the grate. I had grown cold out on the water, and the fire-warmed room added to my feeling of comfort and ease. Anne Trench's presence was as magical as those paintings of hers that I had seen, but far more tranquil and reassuring.

I looked around the walls for more of her work, but crumbling wallpaper had not been hidden with the new paintings I might have expected.

She took my jacket and gestured us to a small table set before the fire. Three mats in an Aztec design of green and white and brown marked our places. She served us papaya, delicious without being iced. Hotcakes made from spelt flour had been kept warm on a wood-burning stove, and she went outside to draw a crock of butter from a pool near the end of the porch. Coffee had been brewed the old-fashioned way in a big granite pot—a little bitter, but just right to take away my chill. We drank it without cream or sugar. Corey made toast by spearing slices of bread on a long fork and holding them to the fire. On a small table behind us an oil lamp with a glass chimney added its own glow to the fire-light, brightening the room. The air had been scented with some herbal potpourri set in a bowl on the back of the stove.

Unexpectedly content and relaxed, I sat facing the fire, and as I watched the flames, I felt enveloped by the spirit of the woman who had created this mood. She could have no idea how much I'd needed this, just as I had no idea why I was here, or what she wanted of me. I knew only that it didn't matter. She would tell me when she was ready.

When she asked about the captain, I told her what little I could, and she sighed deeply. "I'm sorry he is so ill." Then she straightened in her chair to smile at me again. "Susan told me so much about you, Hallie, that I feel that I know you."

"I don't understand why she never mentioned you," I said gently. "She only talked about her grandfather."

"That was what I asked of her. I didn't want anyone else in the family to know that she and I were seeing each other. I didn't even want my son to know. Susan was the member of my family with whom I had the most in common. I was a rebel, too, when I was young, so we understood each other, and the years between us didn't matter."

"You haven't stopped rebelling," Corey said approvingly.

"These days," she said, "I'm afraid it's a rather gentle rebellion."

There had been a time when she had suffered a terrible fury, and I wanted to know about that. How had she dealt with it? How had she come to this time of tranquillity?

"Has Corey told you that they've put me in your old room at the captain's house, Mrs. Trench?" I asked. "It's the room where Susan stayed when she was home, and she filled one wall with your paintings."

"What paintings? I took most of my work with me when I left."

"But not all," I said. "These are abstracts that you must have painted when you were terribly upset."

She looked at me blankly for a moment. "Do you mean that violent outpouring I created in only a few weeks, and then left behind because I never wanted to see them again? I knew Nick would find them—I wanted him to find them—and throw them away."

"He tried, but Susan saved them all," Corey said. "It was a way of keeping you with her."

"Not a very pleasant side of me. I got rid of a lot of what I was feeling in that miserable time by pouring it into those paintings."

"And you really got rid of it?" I asked.

Her tawny brown eyes seemed to sadden. "No. I'm afraid not. But I was able to stop being angry and to stop blaming either myself or others."

Again I wanted to know more, but I couldn't ask questions while Corey was listening.

"There is one painting that made me curious," I said. "Corey told me you called it *Corridor*. Dulcie Cameron said it was the Pirate's Pit."

Corey was eating his second helping of hotcakes, but he set down his fork as though he'd suddenly lost his appetite.

Anne Trench stared at me and the warmth went out of her face. "Yes. I remember that painting. It was one that had to be painted. I always thought of the pit as a corridor, and I tried to capture its mystery on canvas."

"What is the Pirate's Pit?" I asked.

She put a dab of honey on her last bite of toast and settled back in her chair. "There are stories of hidden pirate gold all up and down the East Coast, most of them false. It wasn't gold those highwaymen of the sea hoarded—they did a fine business in all the goods they captured from sailing vessels—but the stories of gold buried on Topsail Island persisted. These stories appealed to two partners who moved onto the island to dig in a large, curious hole they'd found. They convinced others that gold was there. Investments were made in the project, and serious digging began. But in spite of digging to a great depth, nothing in the way of treasure ever surfaced. Then one night the two took the money that island people had advanced and disappeared, leaving nothing but a pit that seemed to have no bottom. Over the years people threw all sorts of things down there, including large objects that simply disappeared. The sinkhole never filled up. Anything that was dropped into it vanished. The idea of the hole fascinated me, so I painted my own impression of it. Not very successfully, I thought, so I left the painting behind when I went away. Susan must have rescued it with all the others."

"I saw it for the first time today," I told her. "It made me feel a little dizzy, as though I were really looking into a long, deep tunnel that led nowhere. Yet you put a light at the end of it—why?"

"I don't remember now. I suppose it needed the light as a focus—to give the painting emphasis and depth."

She raised her hands in dismissal. "Perhaps I

was getting a bit metaphysical by that time. It's all so long ago."

"Where is this Pirate's Pit?"

Anne Trench looked startled. "Why, it's right there on the property behind the Trench and Cameron houses. You haven't noticed it?"

"There's nothing to see," Corey said abruptly, and I wondered at his tone. Later perhaps I'd ask him to show me the pit. Though somehow I didn't like the idea of that bottomless hole so close by.

I changed the subject to something more pleasant. "Do you still paint?" I asked Anne Trench.

"Do I still breathe?" She folded her napkin and stood up. "If you're through with your breakfast, perhaps you'd like to see what I'm doing these days."

Corey and I followed her to where a curtain had been hung across a doorway on the far side of the room. She went to draw it aside so I could step past her into a space that she had turned into a studio. Several canvases were stacked against the wall, and an easel stood near window light, with an unfinished beach scene that suggested Topsail. A bare wooden table held a jar of clean brushes, a palette with daubs of color, rags that smelled of turpentine. Again the walls were empty except for one startling painting.

I went to stand before it. A young woman in gypsy dress held a ribboned tambourine over her head. She danced with her graceful back to the viewer, looking over one shoulder—a look both mischievous and inviting. Masses of dark hair lifted from her shoulders as she moved—just as I had seen. Her skirt blazed with color, and a short green square jacket topped her white blouse.

"Carlina Cameron," I said softly.

"I don't suppose she looks like that anymore. I painted from memory—to get her out of my system. It's rather good, don't you think?"

"It's marvelous," Corey said. A word I hadn't heard him use before. "And sometimes she looks like that even now. I'll bet Fergus would buy it from you."

"It's not for sale."

I liked Anne Trench's quiet assurance. She knew who she was, knew her own worth, so that destructive emotion had no place in her life today.

There was no point to my pretending I didn't know their history, so I dared to ask a question. "Was Carlina the reason behind all those angry paintings?"

For a moment something less tranquil looked out of her eyes, and then she shrugged lightly. "I suppose she was. It's hard to remember."

But she had said that she'd painted this to get Carlina out of her system. I said nothing more, and she relaxed a little as though from sudden tension.

"I wanted to see if I could paint her without anger—and I did."

Again, if Corey hadn't been there, I might have asked more questions. What I wanted from her was something I could apply to my own life. But I went in another direction.

"Why did you want to see me, Mrs. Trench?"

"Let's go back to the other room," she said.

Corey came with us. "I'll take care of this stuff. You and Hallie sit and talk," he said as he began to clear the table.

The room had no real sofa, but a wooden frame with a spring mattress had been heaped with multicolored cushions, and Anne Trench waved me onto it. She sat at the opposite end, placing a large cushion against the wall to support her back.

"I wanted to see you because of Susan. You must have known her better than anyone else during your years in college and for several years after."

"We were good friends, yes. But sometimes I've wondered if I ever really knew her. Especially since I've come to Topsail I've wondered."

"That's what makes people interesting.

There's always one more mystery to solve in any relationship."

"I don't think I like such mysteries."

"Life doesn't ask us to like them, does it?"

Out of my own pain I asked a direct question. "How did you get over what happened with Carlina?"

She was silent for so long that I was afraid I had offended her. Then she returned my question with one of her own. "So it's happened to you, too?"

It was easy to tell her. "Yes. I'm running away. You ran away, didn't you?"

"I had too much pain to stay any longer."

"Without pride we become doormats."

"Only if we have doormat temperaments. I don't have, and neither do you. I can see that clearly enough."

The ground under my feet was growing unsteady. I had to get onto something safer. "Does your son know you're here?"

"Not yet. Though I may change that soon. I haven't wanted Louise over here giving me advice."

I smiled. "Would she dare?"

"She doesn't know how to deal with me. I'm afraid I've made life difficult for her and for Ryce. I miss Susan. Somehow we were always the same age. We saw into each other and we loved what we saw. And we accepted what we didn't like. I want her back and I know that's not going to happen."

"How can you be sure she's dead?"

"I would know if she were alive."

"Will you see the captain while you're here?"

"What could we say to each other now?"

Nevertheless, she *had* come, and the captain's illness might have something to do with the fact that she was here.

"Of course, you knew Fergus, too—even before Carlina came into the picture?"

"Yes. I always liked Fergus. Though he used to put up a guard around his feelings. I'm sure he thought himself inferior to Nicholas at one time. Their ranks were so far apart, though as far as Nicholas was concerned, that made no difference once they began working together. Fergus has a brain that makes him most people's superior."

"At least he married Carlina," I said, and could have bitten my tongue.

She thought about that quietly, not taking offense. "The trouble was that Fergus believed that he was Carlina's second choice. It's a wonder the marriage ever lasted."

"I think they really love each other."

"Mmm. I wonder if that's enough."

I wondered, too. Apparently it wasn't.

I returned to the subject of Susan. "I always hoped she would find a man she could really care about."

"She did," Anne Trench said. "But she didn't trust herself. She saw her grandfather's and my example. And she saw the mistake her father had made in his second marriage. So I think she was afraid."

Corey dropped a knife he was drying. I'd forgotten his presence and I looked toward him in time to catch the flicker of some emotion in his face, though I wasn't sure what it was. When he caught my eye he picked up the knife and wiped it energetically. But I'd seen a glimpse of something. Was Corey the "wrong man" Susan had fallen in love with? Or was he still shaken by the presence of another man in Susan's life, a rival?

"We'd better get back," Corey said abruptly.

Our leaving seemed suddenly arranged. Corey held my jacket for me, and Anne Trench came with me, her hand on my arm. "Please come see me again, Hallie. Will you do that?"

"I'd love to, if Corey will bring me."

"Corey will bring you. Just don't talk to Nicholas or anyone else about this."

Telling Nicholas—or the others on Topsail— was the last thing on my mind. She came out on the porch with us into the warming morning and watched as we went down to the boat. As we drew away far enough from the small beach, I looked back and waved. She stood in the doorway with firelight behind her—a bright figure in her patchwork. I envied her the peace she seemed to have found. She knew exactly how she wanted to live. And she had her work to sustain her. I would certainly come again. But I wanted to see her alone and I needed to find a way to get here by myself.

Corey and I made no attempt to talk on the noisy trip through the sound. Not until he'd tied up at the captain's dock and helped me out of the boat was there quiet enough for speech.

"Thank you for taking me to see her," I said. "She's a remarkable woman."

"She's definitely that. We've become friends because of our love for Susan."

There was no comment I dared to make, and we walked along in silence until we reached the house. Then he stopped beside me and I knew he wanted to talk, though when he did, he looked across the water and not at me.

"We were going to be married," he said. "We were ready to risk it."

"Risk it?"

"Everyone was against us, except my mother. Especially Louise. And she influenced Susan's father. She felt I wasn't good enough for Ryce's daughter."

"What about the captain?"

"He wouldn't have opposed Susan's wishes for long, and he pays no attention to Louise. She thought I was after the money. Knowing how the captain felt about Susan, she could see him cutting Ryce off. Especially if we had kids—which we both wanted."

We'd reached the entrance to the house and I put a hand on his arm. "Thank you for telling me. I'm sorry. Sorrier than ever that Susan is gone."

He stared at me strangely for a moment. "Wait a minute, Hallie. I want to show you something."

I went around the house with him to the clearing in the grove of live oaks between the two houses.

"It's over here," he said.

I followed him to an overgrown area with a circular wire fence around it. "That's it," he said.

I knew what he meant. There was nothing to see beyond the fence but a dark circle where the earth seemed to disappear into a hole. This was the infamous Pirate's Pit.

"That's where she went," he said. "I *know*. I know it inside me, though I haven't any proof. There's a feeling about this place. She'll never be found, and we'll never know for sure, but I have had dreams and I—" He stopped, visibly shaken.

I shivered, though not only because of his words.

He looked at me now, straight into my eyes, and I felt the intensity of his emotion. All the boyishness, the seeming lightheartedness, had gone out of him. I was looking at a man who was still suffering deeply—and who put on a masquerade to hide his feelings.

"I think this is why Anne painted a hazy figure at the end of her *Corridor* painting," Corey said. "Maybe it was even a glimpse of the future."

Much as it frightened me, how could I believe any of this? He saw the question in my eyes and turned away abruptly, disappearing around the house. I moved back from the wire fence and walked over to the road that led to the beach. I was shaking and I couldn't bear to go inside now, or to see anyone. I felt shocked clear through. Horrified.

I was hardly aware of my own movements until I reached the steps to the gazebo that led over the dunes. I ran up them and down the other side. I kicked off my sandals and walked barefoot where the sand was wet and dark and didn't slide under my feet.

I don't know how long I walked, letting white surf curl over my feet as it flowed up the shoreline. Once I stopped with my back to the ocean and looked along the high stretch of houses be-

yond the dunes. At intervals wooden steps sur-
mounted the piled sand and dropped down to
the beach. I walked on aimlessly, and horror
walked with me. I knew it would be a long time
before I could shake off this terrible feeling. It
was possible that Corey's instincts were right,
and this was what had happened to Susan's
body. I dared not let my mind dwell on the details of what might have occurred. Walking
helped, and that was all I could manage for now.

At the top of the steep steps over the dunes
were platforms, sometimes with benches. Near
the place where I walked I saw a man sitting on
one of the benches, looking out over the ocean.
The sudden pain of recognition gripped me,
stabbed through me. Once more I saw a man
who looked like Paul. From a distance the resemblance was so strong that I started across
loose sand to get a little closer. Behind me the
imprint of my feet waited to be filled in by the
next surge of water.

As I approached, the man stood up and
turned to go down the far steps to the road. He
looked so much like Paul. He moved like Paul. I
ran across the sand and up the steps. I had to see
him more closely—foolish though that might be.
But by the time I reached the platform where
he'd stood, the man had gone down the other
side and disappeared. I sat on the bench to catch

my breath. I was shaking again, but for another reason. If only I could have seen him closely enough to be sure—to dismiss my fantasy.

But of course I was sure. Paul didn't know where I was. I hadn't yet written to tell him. I must get myself under control. I *must*. I made my way back to where I'd left my sandals and returned to the captain's house.

12

⟡━━━━━━━━━━⟡

I had gone down to the beach in an attempt to deal with what Corey had told me about the Pirate's Pit. I'd been shocked, unbelieving, frightened. But walking on the sand hadn't clarified anything. Then I'd seen the man who looked like Paul, and that glimpse had pushed me to the edge of an emotional cliff. By the time I got back to the house, I was sick and trembling.

I went first to my room and sat in the chair Corey had left in the middle of the floor. Lined up against the baseboard, Anne Trench's paintings seemed to mock me, even though I saw only their backs. I reminded myself that *she* had thrown them away. Painting them had freed her to some extent. Now I must find a way to free myself, as she had done. Yet all I could see when I closed my eyes was Paul's face. Not as I'd last seen it when he'd left me to my anger and disappeared, but the way he used to look at me—valuing me, loving me as no one else ever had. But that was something I could never recover. Somehow I must get myself in hand and stop seeing Paul in other men.

The reason I was here on Topsail was because of Susan. And now Corey had told me something so terrible that I could not let it pass. As long as I remained here—and perhaps for the rest of my life—I was going to be haunted by the image of Susan's body lost down that deep black hole. What *had* happened to her? How did she die? This was what must occupy me now.

I knew I ought to go see the captain, but I was in no state to talk to him. I couldn't tell him about Anne and the house on Cabbage Island, and I could never tell him what Corey had said. Yet he would certainly sense my state of mind, and I neither wanted him to worry about me nor probe into my confusion.

What I needed to do now was to find Corey and discover what lay behind his belief that Susan had disappeared down the pit. I couldn't accept that it was just a feeling, an instinct. But when I pushed myself out of the chair, the amethyst geode drew me as though to a magnet. I put my hands on the deep purple heart of the stone and closed my eyes. Clarity of thought was one of the attributes amethyst was supposed to convey.

Breathing deeply, slowly, I cleared my mind. Nothing happened except for a dizzy churning. Then, suddenly, across the darkness behind my lids, I could see the flash of a name. The letters were there long enough for me to read them. The name that appeared was *Louise.*

I stared again into the dark lights of the stone and caught that secret hint of flame. Why Louise? From the first I'd disliked her. There seemed to be an artificiality about her that hid something deeper, something that I suspected might reveal the real Louise. Amethyst insight? But I had no idea where to go with what had been given me.

Tonight I would have dinner with her and Ryce, and I would try to see her with new eyes. But first, I had to find Corey.

I found his mother on the deck, resting for once, stretched out in a lounge chair, her eyes closed. Unguarded, the lines of her face had deepened, giving her a troubled look, as though hidden worries had taken over. She heard me and sat up. The lines smoothed out, so that she looked as she always did. Perhaps what I'd read was no more than weariness.

"The captain's having a nap, so don't go in to see him just yet," she warned me.

I was glad he wasn't waiting for me. "Do you know where I can find Corey?"

She hesitated, but must have decided there was no reason not to tell me. "I think he's upstairs in his rooms. Do you know why he seems so upset?"

I told her I didn't, though I could easily guess, and went inside to climb the stairs to a part of the house I'd not been in before. The top step put me into a narrow hallway that ran across the back of the house and appeared to open into several rooms whose doors were now closed. These must be bedrooms that dated back to a day when a number of people had lived in this house.

The entire floor seemed quiet and empty, and I had no idea what to do next. "Hello?" I said tentatively. The silence seemed to deepen, and I wondered if Corey was holding his breath, waiting for me to go away. "Hello!" I called more loudly. "It's Hallie. Are you up here, Corey?"

This time I heard sounds and one of the doors opened. Corey looked out at me without welcome. "What do you want?"

I didn't intend to be turned away. "I need to talk with you. Please."

For a moment I thought he might close the door in my face, but after a few moments of indecision, he stepped back and beckoned me into the first of two rooms. This one, at the back of the house, was his bedroom, plainly furnished with hand-me-down necessities, and without anything that seemed to reveal more about Corey Orion than I already knew. There weren't even any pictures on the walls.

"This way," Corey said, and I followed him through a far door that opened into a big room with windows looking out toward the sound. Clearly, this was Corey's domain. Here I began to have a sense of the man who must spend much of his time here. A long table down one wall held the bits and pieces of the collections he had mentioned. I saw shells of many varieties, assorted sharks' teeth, bits of driftwood, even pieces of colored glass, polished and smooth, that must have rolled in from the sea. I noticed a strong, fishy smell and saw that he had been cleaning shells in which sea creatures had once lived—and died. He waved me toward the front of the room and went to wash his hands at a sink in which more shells were piled.

The morning had turned bright and sunny, and light sent reflected ripples across the ceiling, as I'd seen in the captain's room. This floor was set back from the cantilevered deck below, and I could look across to where Mrs. Orion still lay stretched in her lounge chair near the rail.

Corey joined me, wary and unwelcoming. A

few chairs and a small table had been set before the windows, and he waved a hand in reluctant invitation. I sat in a molded plastic chair, while he took a dark wooden one opposite. A new wariness toward me lighted his eyes.

"I'm not going to talk about it," he said.

My own tense feelings brimmed over. "I'm sorry—I don't want to upset you, but there isn't anyone else to talk to. And I need to talk. I don't think you want me to go to the captain."

He didn't meet my eyes, and after a moment I went on.

"I want to know more about Anne Trench, and why you took me to meet her. But first there's what you believe about Susan. I felt so sick after what you told me that I went down to the beach to try and get hold of myself. I thought that a walk by the ocean would clear my head. I saw a man standing at the top of some steps, a man who looked like my husband, though of course it couldn't have been Paul. He walked away before I could get close enough to be sure. I haven't told you this, but Paul and I are in the midst of a crisis in our marriage. When I got back to my room, I was more shaken than ever, so I got the idea of talking to you—not necessarily about Susan—just to sort things out. Foolish, I suppose. I should just go home and try to figure out my life and forget what I've seen and learned over the past three days. There's nothing to hold me here. The captain doesn't need me." I got up and went over to an open window. Leaning on the sill, I stared blindly at the water.

Corey surprised me by putting an arm about my shoulders in a brotherly hug. "I'm sorry, Hallie. You've never spoken to me about your husband. Now I can see you've had too much thrown at you all at once. Until an hour ago, I'd never told anyone what I think happened to Susan—it just spilled out because you were close to her once. And I'd bottled everything up for too long."

I turned around with my back to the window. "But why? Why do you believe something so terrible happened to her?"

He shook his head helplessly. "I can't tell you because I don't know. I just have this strong feeling that has little to do with reason."

In the face of Corey's unhappiness I tried to pull myself together. "If someone Susan knew did this, then that person must be carrying around a load of guilt. Do you suppose you could tap into it? Have you any suspicion at all about who might have hated Susan that much?"

"I've thought of everyone I know who was connected to her in any way. I've gone over the list again and again, and come up with nothing. Anyone at all could have entered that grove down there when it's dark and never have been noticed. It's not the back windows we look out of most of the time."

"There's a light that burns all night, isn't there?"

"Yes, between the two houses, but its light doesn't reach under the trees."

I moved away from the support of his arm. "She must have met someone down there— someone she knew and wasn't afraid of. Someone who—"

He broke in. "It's no use. I've been down this road a hundred times. Let it go, Hallie. It's not your affair. You might even put yourself at risk. I should never have told you."

"I wonder," I said, beginning to pace slowly across the room, "if it's time to tell everyone— *make* someone worry."

"Stay out of this! I never should have told you," he repeated.

"You needed to talk. Just as I needed to talk. That's why I came looking for you. I didn't want to be alone."

When I sat down again in the hard little chair, I found that some of the tension I'd been feeling had lessened. But I still needed to hear the sound of a voice. "Tell me about you, Corey. Where did you grow up? What was your father like?"

His grin was one I knew. "Distraction? Is that what you want? Stories?"

"It might help. But I'd really like to know."

He stayed where he was, leaning against the windowsill. "All right. I grew up in Wilmington. My father left us when I was ten."

"Were you close to him?"

"I thought I was. He worked for an airline—servicing planes, seeing that everything was all right before they took off. Once he drove me out to the airport so I could see what he did. I could understand that it was pretty important. And then—all of a sudden he was gone. I know my mother and father disagreed a lot—I recall some angry words being spoken. I didn't like it, but I supposed it was what all parents did. After my father left, my mother got a job in a bakery—I remember how hard she worked. She used to come home at night smelling of cinnamon buns." He smiled faintly, lost in the past.

"Don't talk about this if it makes you feel worse," I said.

"It's all right. It feels good to talk. Susan used to listen. After that," he went on, "my mother took her training as a nurse's aide, and we came to live here after Mrs. Trench went away. I was still pretty young. At first the captain was just mad at the world. He wasn't sick then, but he'd had a bad fall that left him with a damaged knee.

He couldn't get around the way he used to, and
he had to have help—though he hated it. Mom
cooked for him, and began to boss him a little.
He accepted us and she became his housekeeper. When he got sick she was the one person
he would let take care of him."

"Was it an affair with Carlina that broke up
his marriage?"

"I suppose. Though I'm not sure. She was
pretty young when she married Fergus
Cameron. The captain used to be a striking-looking man, and I hear he was the sort who was always in charge. I met Anne later, through Susan,
and I liked her right away. I think she likes me,
too—after all, we have Susan in common."
Corey paused. "Now it's your turn. Where did
you grow up?"

I couldn't open up to Corey the way I had to
Paul, but I told him a little. Though he really listened, nothing helped. My sense of loss was
overwhelming me since I'd glimpsed that man
on the dunes. Everything had grown much too
sharp all over again, and I didn't seem able to
push it away.

"What do you want out of life, Corey?" I
asked. "I can't see you picking up jobs as a
waiter forever. Or playing beachcomber. Isn't
there something you want to do more than anything else?"

"There used to be. I made plans with Susan after she came back from college. She was going in with me and we were going to start a restaurant and run it ourselves. Susan would have made the necessary investment, if she could have gotten some of her inheritance from her grandfather. I'd have been good at the management end. I'd have seen to the kitchen and the menus, and she'd have been out in front charming all the customers." He paused, lost in the possibilities, before focusing on me again. "Pipe dreams. Make-believe. We were good at that."

"It sounds like more than a dream. Perhaps it would really have happened. Perhaps it still can. On your own."

His look was wry. "Louise was dead set against the idea. She was always snooty and dismissive, afraid that we'd squander money that was rightfully hers. I suppose she pushed Ryce. Sometimes I wonder about her. Do you think that 'I'm so superior' attitude stems from the fact that she doesn't really believe in herself?"

That was a new way to look at Louise, but I could only shrug. "What about the captain?" I asked.

"He didn't really want us to marry, though he seemed to like me well enough. They all had better plans for Susan. Of course, she would have gone her own way. She wanted us to run off and get married—cause trouble for everybody! I think she hoped that her grandmother would help. Then she . . . disappeared . . . and it was all over."

Corey and I shared a deep pain. Paul was gone for me, as surely as Susan was for Corey. But I didn't mean to live with pain. I meant to get over this somehow. I was stunned that the sight of someone who looked like Paul could throw me so completely. I'd been seeing Paul in other men ever since I left California. But those were only mistakes. I couldn't be sure about this. Obviously I had a lot of recovering to do. Recovery took time. That I wanted it to happen *now* was foolish.

Corey had turned to look out toward the sound, and something must have caught his eye down at the dock. He shouted out the window, warning someone. Then he started down the long room, running.

Alarmed, I followed him down two flights of stairs to the ground, and ran after him out to the dock. Now I saw what had disturbed him. Dulcie was in Corey's boat, about to start the outboard.

"Dulcie!" he shouted, and ran along the dock. "Get out of that boat!"

She looked up at him defiantly. "I can start it. I can run your old boat!"

"You can, but you're not going to. Come up out of there. You're not supposed to go out in any boat unless a grown-up is along. What do you think your father would say?"

"Nobody cares." She made no move to climb out of the boat.

"I'll count to three, Dulcie. If you're not out on the dock by three, I'll come down and throw you in the water."

I was afraid she'd get the motor started and pull away on her own. Perhaps it was the mention of her father that made her give up. She scrambled out onto the dock, her red hair shining in the sun, her expression still defiant.

"What's the matter with you?" Corey looked as though he wanted to shake her. "You know better!"

Dulcie's resistance crumbled. "Maybe if I drowned, they'd pay some attention!" she wailed, bursting into tears.

"I don't think that's very smart," Corey said, squatting down next to her. "You're talking silly. Tell me what's the matter."

She sat down on the end of the dock and swung her legs over the edge. Her shorts were bedraggled and her T-shirt dirty. She hardly looked like the well-dressed little girl we'd had dinner with the night before.

"I can't tell you if *she* listens," Dulcie said, throwing me a doleful look and burying her head on Corey's shoulder.

"Then I'll go in," I said. "You can talk to Corey alone."

Corey shook his head. "You can talk to us both. Hallie was Susan's friend, and she's ours, too—you know that."

I suspected that Dulcie's tears were a little much for him, and he needed me to stay. "I'll sit over on this side," I said. "Then you can pretend I'm not here." I went to the bench where I'd sat with the captain and looked off across the water. A gull soared overhead, squawking noisily.

Dulcie raised her head, upset enough to forget about me as she poured out her troubles to Corey.

"They were still mad at each other this morning. They aren't talking. And they're both mad at me—though I didn't do anything."

"What are they mad about?" Corey asked.

She wiped her eyes with a corner of her T-shirt. "I guess Mom was happy because Dad went to see the captain. She thought she would invite the captain over to our house for dinner, if he could come. That was when Dad got real mad, though I don't see why, or what he was blaming her for. He stomped out of the house and Mom began to cry. When I tried to hug her, she pushed me away and said to leave her alone. All she could think about was *him*."

"They'll get over it," Corey said. "They always do. And it's not a good idea to go out and get drowned just so they'll notice you. That doesn't make much sense, does it? Especially when you know they both love you."

She squinted at him sideways from under her tangle of hair, and I could see the hint of a smile.

"Haven't you got anything clean to put on?" Corey asked.

I stood up. "You're dressed just right for a walk on the beach, Dulcie. Maybe we can find some special shells, or even a shark's tooth." I smiled at Corey. "How about coming along?"

"Sure thing," he said quickly. "Let's all go down to the beach. But first, Dulcie, tell your mother where you'll be. And don't say any of that stuff about her not caring. Grown-ups need to be by themselves sometimes."

She ran off, and I stopped in the house to tell Mrs. Orion where we were going. I wasn't really sure I wanted to return to the beach, but it was like riding a horse: When you fell off, you were supposed to get back on again right away.

13

Mrs. Orion was pleased that we were taking Dulcie down to the beach. "She stayed here with me for a while this morning, but then she said she needed something to do besides moping around. I'll fix a picnic lunch for you to take along. The captain's awake, so you'd better look in on him. Don't mind if he snaps at you. The pain's worse today and that makes him cranky."

I thanked her for offering to fix lunch and went to look into the captain's room. He was awake in bed, and he scowled at me. "You took your time getting back, young lady."

I stayed in the corner of the room beside a window. The way he looked, his face drawn with pain, disturbed me, though I tried not to let him see.

"I didn't know we had a schedule," I said

mildly. "Mrs. Orion is fixing a lunch for Corey and Dulcie and me to take down to the beach, but if you'd rather I stayed with you, of course I will."

His scowl remained fixed. "Oh, go along. You're young—you can't just stay indoors with an old codger like me."

I imitated his scowl. "It's not like you to feel sorry for yourself. Maybe we can make plans for this afternoon. Is there something different you'd like to do?"

His attention had wandered past me and I realized he wasn't listening. His eyes had widened and a flush had come into his face. I turned to find Carlina in the doorway. For once, she wasn't wearing one of her colorful outfits. She had put on jeans and a big shirt that might have belonged to Fergus. Her dark hair hung down her back in a long ponytail, tied with a red ribbon. A puffiness discolored the skin around her eyes, so it was evident that she'd been crying. This was the first time I'd seen her in a state where she didn't seem to care about her appearance. I wondered if she wanted to look her age because the captain was old and sick. Mrs. Orion hovered behind her, uncertain about this unexpected and unannounced visitor. I wondered how long it had been since this woman and the old man in the bed had met.

"It's okay, Mrs. O," the captain said, and Mrs. Orion reluctantly went away.

Carlina Cameron came to stand beside the captain's bed. She hadn't seen me, and the captain appeared to have forgotten I was there. I didn't stir, lest I break whatever spell might have been cast.

For a moment the captain stared up at Carlina. Then he turned his head against his pillow, and I knew how much he hated having her see him as he was now.

"Just go away," he told her. "I don't want to talk to you."

She paid no attention, but took one bony hand of his in hers. His hand stayed limp, offering no response. "Please," she said. "I need your help, Nick."

His silence made it clear that he had no help to offer.

Still holding his hand, she sat down on the bed beside him. "It would be good for Fergus if you two could be friends again. He enjoyed seeing you yesterday. I know that he was glad to use the excuse of what was found on the beach to call on you."

"He can come anytime he wants," the captain said gruffly.

"I told him that it was time that you two got to be friends again and that it would do you both good. I never dreamed he would be so angry with me. He's still jealous, I'm afraid."

"Jealous? Of me? Like this!" The captain's snort was derisive.

Carlina stroked the back of his hand with one finger. "You were always exciting, Nick. I suppose he remembers that. But I love him very much." Her voice broke. After a moment she went on. "He's always believed that he was my second choice, and he can't stand that."

"Was he?" the captain asked. "Was he your second choice?"

I could see her sadness as she returned his look. "No, my dear. You were handsome and exhilarating and married, and Fergus was all the dependable things I wanted in a man. And still want. But I'm not the woman he fell in love with. I know how much I've changed. I thought if you two could become friends again, he could let go of the bitterness. That would be better for him. And for me."

The captain looked up into her face so sadly that it twisted my heart. I had sympathized with Anne from the beginning, and I'd felt angry with Nick, but now I saw his eyes as they rested on Carlina.

"Will you phone him, Nick?" she pleaded. "Ask him to come see you. But don't tell him I was here. As long as he goes on being angry and jealous, life will be impossible for me. And we're both hurting Dulcie. It's terrible for Fergus, too, and so foolish. As though any of us was young anymore. I love him more than ever. But I know how much I've aged and changed, and I'm not sure he can take that in me. His jealousy has been rooted for so long in something that doesn't exist anymore."

The captain stared off into the distance and rediscovered me in my corner. He startled both Carlina and me with one of his best roars.

"What are you doing, skulking around like that?"

I stepped into the light. "I'm sorry. I didn't want to interrupt you, but I suppose I'm eavesdropping."

Carlina's face revealed her dismay. But after a moment of staring at me, the captain roared in a different way—a roar of laughter. When he could catch his breath, he nodded to me. "We'll talk later. I thought you were going on a picnic?"

"I was. I am." I managed to get myself out of the room without looking at Carlina.

Corey and Dulcie were waiting for me. Mrs. Orion had packed our lunch in a basket that Corey was carrying. She handed me a beach umbrella.

"It will be hot out there—you don't want an early sunburn."

Thus prepared, we carried things down to Corey's Ford and drove up the road that led toward the ocean. Dulcie sat between us, talkative again.

"My mother came to see the captain, didn't she? Why?"

I tried to explain. "She would like the captain and your father to be friends again—the way they used to be."

Dulcie nodded, but I could sense the same uneasiness in her that I'd felt before. Something was troubling her, and I remembered what she'd said about a secret. There seemed no way to get her to talk about it, however, until she was ready.

We left the car and went up over the dunes through the gazebo and down to the beach. Corey set up the umbrella and I sat in its shade. The surf sounded a steady beat of rolling and subsiding waves, repeated over and over again. A few birds hopped about at the edge of the water, and there were always gulls, wide-winged overhead, or searching along the sand as they walked about.

Corey left us for a scavenging expedition, and Dulcie went down to wade in shallow surf. In a few moments Corey came hurrying back. "Dulcie!" he called. "The turtles have started!"

She whooped her excitement, sand sticking to

her bare feet as she ran toward us. I got up to join them and find out what was happening.

"Watch it!" Corey said as we came near him. "Don't spoil the tracks."

I stopped before stepping into what looked like a set of bulldozer treads leading up the sand, with a parallel set coming down.

"She's laid her eggs!" Dulcie cried. "We have to find the nest."

As we followed the wide tracks up the beach, Corey explained. "Loggerhead turtles come to Topsail to drop their eggs every spring. The mothers look for what seems to them to be the perfect spot, then they dig a hole with their hind flippers and drop the eggs into it. Maybe a hundred or more. Once she's covered them with sand, the mother goes back to the water. The sun warms the eggs for a couple of months, until the little turtles begin to hatch. Sea turtles are endangered, so everyone on Topsail's beaches goes on alert, and our Turtle Watch starts. There's an organization we can call to report our findings. This is early in the season, so this one's out of sync. I'll go up to the house over there and let them know. The area where the nest is found must be marked so that it can be watched. When the baby turtles hatch, a crew of us turns out to protect them as they start down the beach to the ocean. There are predators who think baby turtles are luscious, and they have to be kept away."

"When the Turtle Watch is on," Dulcie added, "all the people in beach houses keep their outside lights off at night, so as not to confuse the little turtles. The babies can think a porch light is the moon and go in the wrong direction. It's the moon that shows them the way to the ocean."

I liked the idea of community on Topsail. While Corey ran up the steps to the nearest house, I walked along the beach to see if there were any more early tracks. A number of houses that overlooked the dunes were still empty, since the summer season hadn't yet begun. I noted with interest that one of the towers had been incorporated into a home, with an addition built on to it. As I studied this, I saw a man standing at one of the windows, watching me. It was the same man I'd seen before—the man who looked like Paul.

I turned around and walked quickly back to the beach umbrella. This time I'd seen him clearly, and it wasn't just that he looked like Paul: It *was* Paul. I sat down on the sand and pulled up my knees, clasping my hands around them to stop from shaking.

It couldn't be. It wasn't possible. There was no way that Paul could know where I was. I hadn't felt like writing him, but, even if I had, he wouldn't have had time to get the letter yet. My imagination was playing tricks on me again. I must stop this idiotic trembling. But the question was there in my mind. What was I to do if it *was* Paul? I didn't want to see him or talk to him.

After we'd stared at each other for a moment, the man had turned away from the window, just as I was about to turn away from the house, so I hadn't had a really long look. It couldn't be Paul.

"You look funny," Dulcie said, dropping down on the sand beside me.

I drew a deep breath. "I think I'm faint from hunger. Let's start our picnic."

By the time Corey came to join us, we'd set out the cloth Mrs. Orion had packed, and I'd weighted it down from the wind with her metal utensils—nothing picnic-plastic in this basket. Dulcie opened the container of potato salad and doled out pickles onto bright yellow plates. There were sandwiches of thick-sliced ham and cheese, and carefully wrapped slices of apple pie.

I gave my attention to unwrapping a sandwich, while Corey and Dulcie discussed the turtles. I seemed able to eat with a good appetite, which was remarkable under the circumstances. Dulcie gobbled too fast, and before Corey and I were half finished, she was off to play in the surf again. I knew that Corey had been watching me, and that I hadn't hidden my inner upheaval from him. I probably still looked "funny."

"What is it, Hallie? What's happened?"

I tried to speak lightly. "I thought I saw my husband at a window of one of those houses down the beach. But of course that isn't possible."

He asked no more questions, and when the silence between us grew too long, I broke it.

"He couldn't possibly know where I am."

"Do you want him back?"

I shook my head and did busy things with my hands. I had turned away from the tower house, but Corey was looking fixedly over my shoulder.

"I think he's here to see you right now," he said.

Without turning, I knew he was right. Even before Paul spoke, I knew he was behind me.

14

"Hello, Hallie." His voice wasn't like any other man's. I'd always loved those deep, deceptively quiet tones. His voice could cast a spell. He'd always seemed an exciting man to me, and I knew other women found him exciting, too. But since I had been *the* one, I'd trusted him, so when other women looked at him, it didn't matter. I was proud—and foolishly sure.

"I miss you," he said when I didn't respond to his greeting.

I looked up at him then, with pain and anger rising to choke me. I had nothing to say to him. Integrity between us had mattered. I had really believed that. A concept so ... old-fashioned, so easily shattered! Humpty Dumpty could never be put back together again.

"It's important that you talk to me. *Can* we talk, Hallie?" he asked.

Corey took the hint and loped off across the sand, to join Dulcie at the water's edge.

I didn't speak, and he read the answer in my face. At once his own anger rose to meet mine. I glimpsed it in his eyes before he turned away abruptly and strode off along the beach. Even on sand, his walk had a jaunty swing—as though nothing ever fazed him. But I'd seen his eyes, seen the door that had been closed between us. Which was exactly what I wanted.

I stood up and called to Corey and Dulcie. "I'd like to go back now. I promised the captain that I wouldn't be gone too long."

They came toward me together, Dulcie carrying her shoes and socks. At least she didn't put up a fuss about returning. Corey had probably said something, for she looked at me with new curiosity.

"Your face is all red," she announced.

"Just shut up, kid," Corey said softly. "You can help me carry things to the car."

I felt close to tears and angry with myself for feeling hurt. At least I was grateful to Corey for not talking as we carried everything up the steps and through the gazebo to where we'd left the car. For once, Dulcie looked subdued as we got in.

When we reached the house, I went inside at once and hurried to the captain's room. He still lay in his bed, and I could tell that whatever spark of interest Carlina might have lighted in him had been extinguished. He regarded me sadly, without interest.

I sat down beside his bed and picked up a book that lay open on a chair. "Would you like me to read to you?"

"Not now. I couldn't concentrate," he said, waving his hand in the air weakly and letting it drop to the spread as though it was too heavy to stay aloft.

"Captain, I've enjoyed my visit. You and the others have been more than kind, but I must leave as soon as I can get a flight home."

I had caught him by surprise and he looked anxious. I could glimpse the man Carlina had told me needed to always be in control.

"There's nothing you can do about what I intend, Hallie. This is the way it's going to be."

My leftover anger spilled out at him. "You're giving your money to me to pay your son back for marrying Louise. You want to hurt him. You want to make them both suffer."

"That's my right. They deserve whatever I do. Both of them."

"Why?"

He glowered at me in annoyance. "Sometimes I'm sorry that I brought you here. When I was young I had more respect for those who knew more than I did."

"Just tell me something," I said. "If Anne hadn't left you, what would have happened? Would you have stayed married and gone on having affairs with other women?"

"That's none of your business," he sputtered.

"*Would* you have been faithful to Anne if she'd stayed with you?"

At least he'd come to life, and he was still strong enough to hold his own.

"God, or nature, or whatever, didn't create men to be faithful," he responded vehemently. "They were put here on earth to keep the race going. That's why they're driven to females, and it's an instinct in all male animals."

I had to protest. "Not all. Some animals mate for life. And humans are different. Anyway, no other animal has a conscience. Even the *male* animal can know when he's hurting someone he supposedly loves."

"Do you think that's all that keeps two people together in marriage?" He was watching me with new interest. "Don't stand there preaching to me. Sit down!"

I sat, but I didn't give up. "No, I don't think conscience is all there is. What about love? Or don't you believe there's any such thing?"

He sighed. "I suppose it depends on whether the sex drive is stronger than the moral drive. There are all sorts of variables. Love may not come into it at all."

"I don't think you believe that," I said. "Which one did you love—Anne or Carlina?"

Perhaps I'd asked a question for which he had no answer, and I half expected a reprimand.

Instead he spoke quietly, sadly. "I loved them both. And I lost them both."

I could hardly accept that. No woman could accept that the man she loved could love another woman equally. Especially not Anne, I was sure, and certainly not me. I sat watching reflections from the water drift across the ceiling. The house seemed strangely quiet, as though it held its breath. Only my spirit was restless, wounded, uncertain. Unsatisfied.

"Paul is here on Topsail," I told the captain abruptly. "Did you send for him?"

"So that's what this is all about? No, of course I didn't. What does he want?"

"I don't know. Just to talk, he said."

"Of course you know. He wants you back. So what are you going to do?"

"Nothing," I said.

"He'll persist. He values you or he wouldn't have come. He'll make promises, heap coals of fire on his own head—anything to get you to forgive him."

"You don't know Paul."

He went on as though I hadn't spoken. "Then he'll break every one of his solemn promises. That's what nature prompts us to do."

"In that case I don't want him."

He cocked one of his bushy eyebrows at me. "You want him. It's written all over you. And you'll have good times again because he'll be sorry for a good, long while."

I shook my head. "I don't want that sort of relationship."

The captain scowled at me. "Ah, woman! Female virtue!"

"It's not a matter of virtue," I said indignantly. "Nobody worries about that anymore. If he loved me the way I love him—"

"Of course you love him. And as far as he's able, he loves you, I'm sure."

"You're measuring other men by your own standards. Paul's not like that."

"Oh?"

"Let it go." I threw up my hands in defeat, though it was defeat only because I had no more arguments to give him. I only knew how *I* felt. Thinking with my emotions, perhaps, and not with my mind, but for now that was the best I could do.

The captain leaned back against his pillows and closed his eyes. "I'm tired. I'm tired of talking to you about this. Tired of the way you can't face facts. Other animals have better sense. They don't examine what should never be examined. They rely on instinct, and it works for them. But when a man follows his instinct, look what happens!"

I sat where I was in silence. Though I knew he wanted me to go, we weren't through with each other yet. I tried not to think about Paul—and of course, as a result, thought about him all the more. About the way he moved—always jaunty, though not arrogant, just confident—something that had contrasted with my own lack of self-confidence when we met. He had instilled that quality in me, given me courage that I'd never had before. So what was I to do now? One thing—I wasn't going to feel sorry for myself. My backbone would stiffen and I would do whatever it was that I was meant to do. Just as Anne Trench had.

The captain spoke, startling me. "You intend to have dinner tonight with Ryce and Louise and Richard Merrick. That's your plan, isn't it? But I don't think you should go. By this time Richard has probably told Louise what I mean to do with my will. She can be vituperative, and I don't think you need that. Ryce won't oppose me—he hasn't the gumption. But you'll be in for an unpleasant time if you see them tonight."

I answered him firmly. "I want to go. I mean to tell them that I won't have anything to do with your money, and I won't accept it if you leave it to me as you've planned. I'll talk to Mr. Merrick about getting out of this. So Louise should be pleased to have me as her guest."

"Why don't you relax, Hallie, and let an old man do what he wants to do? It won't please Louise if you refuse, because I'll never let her get her hands on anything of mine anyway. There'll be a legacy for Ryce, but not a large one. The rest will be distributed to various societies I've favored over the years. I didn't earn this money myself, though the stock market helped. It was left to me by my father, and I haven't spent recklessly. Ryce will manage, but Louise will probably leave him for Richard—if Richard is foolish enough to take her on. If she leaves, that will be good for my son."

He sounded sad and defeated, but there was nothing I could do to help him, especially when I couldn't even help myself.

"I'll let you know how it goes," I said, and went away quietly.

Dulcie hadn't gone home, but was sitting

high stool at a counter in the kitchen, visiting with Mrs. Orion. She hopped off the stool when she saw me going past. At least she looked more cheerful as she called my name and came to join me.

"Hallie, Dad's gone to Wilmington today, so Mom said I could invite you over to see my room."

"How very nice. I'd like to see your room," I said, happy to accept her invitation.

We went outside and up the steps to the back porch of the Cameron house.

"Hi, Mom!" Dulcie called. "I've brought Hallie."

A voice answered from some distant room, but Carlina didn't appear. "She's been crying," Dulcie said, "so she doesn't want anyone to see her. Now I think she's sad about the captain being so sick."

The kitchen Dulcie led me through was another lovely expression of Carlina Cameron—who had run away from the circus because she wanted to live in a home? Copper-bottomed pots hung where they would catch sunlight and add their own luster to the room. A large round table wore a cloth the color of pale butter, which hung in graceful folds to the floor. Yellow curtains had been tied back to invite the sun. A well-scrubbed chopping board sat beside the sink, and assorted knives hung neatly above it in a rack.

Dulcie noted my interest. "My grandmother came from Hungary, and Mom says when she wasn't too busy in the circus, she loved to cook. So Mom does, too."

Dulcie's room was off a hall that cut through the house toward the sound. Carlina's love of color had been echoed here as well. The bedspread was bright with variegated patches, and matched curtains Carlina must have made. A desk was piled with schoolbooks, and a few dolls lay on a window seat, looking neglected.

Dulcie's interest at the moment centered on a small square platform—perhaps something Fergus had built for her. Behind it, a full-length mirror leaned against the wall.

"Mom said I could show you the dance she's been teaching me," Dulcie said excitedly, "the one I'll do at the pageant when I'm a bareback rider. Sit down over there on the bed where you can watch. I'll put on the tape first."

She turned on a tape player and a lovely voice began to sing in words that were foreign. A woman's voice. The tune was lively and unfamiliar—something that might have accompanied plumed and prancing horses as the ringmaster sent them out to entrance an audience.

Dulcie kicked off her sandals and put on pink

satin ballet slippers, leaning over to wind the ribbons around her ankles.

"Of course it will be nicer when I have my costume. Mom is working on it now. But I can show you what I've been practicing."

The makeshift platform creaked a bit as she stepped up on it. She performed several simple steps in time to the music and I could see that grace was natural to her. The pink shoes lifted in small jumps, and her ankles crossed and re-crossed. The little platform settled into place and stopped objecting. Dulcie's pliés were deep, and her arabesque beautiful, with one arm outstretched and one leg raised behind her in a lovely curve. Not even shorts could spoil the illusion, and I could easily imagine her in a spangled costume.

When she did a small leap off the space that had confined her movements and turned off the tape player, I applauded warmly.

"You're very good," I said.

She shrugged. "I guess so. There's a dance teacher who has a class over in Hampstead, and I go once a week. Mom comes to watch the class, and she says I'm the best. But maybe that's only because she wants me to be the best. Susan used to make up stories about all my famous successes, but that was when I was little. Susan was a pretty good dancer, too, but she never wanted to stick to one thing, so she didn't work at it, the way Mom wants me to work at dancing."

"And is this what you want?"

She looked away from me. "I suppose. Would you like to see something Susan made for me? It was sort of scary, until she explained how it works."

A handsome cedar chest stood at the foot of her bed, and she raised the lid to rummage inside, holding it up with one hand.

"Hallie, would you come and hold the top for me?" she requested.

I held up the heavy lid by one corner and watched her search. In her hurry, she was tumbling everything about, and the cover came off an object that she had packed into the end nearest me. Sunlight caught the glint of purple facets, and I held my breath. For just an instant, before Dulcie realized what she'd uncovered, a match to the amethyst geode in my room was visible. Twin bookends, of course.

Dulcie looked alarmed when she realized that I'd seen what was there. She wrapped it up again hastily, pushed other things on top of it, and continued her search for the small object she finally pulled out of the chest.

I recognized Susan's work. She had loved to create strange little creatures in clay. When they turned out well, she sometimes glazed them and had them fired. This was a finished piece to which she'd given considerable attention.

I let down the lid of the chest and took the object Dulcie held out to me. I didn't mention the amethyst cluster I'd glimpsed in the chest. If she had taken it from Susan's room, that was her affair, and I was sure Susan would never have begrudged her wanting it.

The small ceramic piece I held was one in which Susan had let her imagination go. It appeared to be a demon of some sort, painted emerald green, except for the interior of its open red mouth. The head and face were larger than the body. In fact, the head seemed to be composed mainly of that open mouth, with tiny slivers of fish bone inside, making rows of teeth.

"He certainly is ugly," I said, giving him back.

"He's supposed to be. He's a Trouble Eater. Susan told me he would snap up the troubles that happened to me and just chew them up. But he only worked for a little while. After Susan . . . went away, he couldn't help me anymore. I guess he's just for little kids."

Suddenly she began to cry, a silent, unexpected weeping. She stood with the Trouble Eater in her hands, while tears coursed down her cheeks. Her whole small body cried out for comfort, and I put my arms around her.

"How can I help, Dulcie?"

More tears brimmed and flowed.

"Would you like me to get your mother?" I asked.

For a moment she wept harder than ever, so I knew that suggestion had been rejected.

"I'd really like to help if you'd let me," I said.

She hesitated and then went to lift the lid of the chest again. I helped her hold it as she put away Susan's little green creature. With hands that had looked so graceful as she danced, she fumbled awkwardly with something in the chest. In a moment she lifted out the amethyst cluster, only partly wrapped in an old sweater.

I lowered the lid of the chest carefully and took the heavy geode when she thrust it at me. "Do you want me to put this back with the other one?" I asked her.

She shook her bright head wildly. "No! Don't do that. Put it where no one will ever see it. Don't let my mother know I had it. She's busy now. So just take it away quickly. *Please.*"

Her need to be rid of the geode she must have coveted and taken was so great that I didn't hesitate.

"It will be all right, Dulcie. I promise. I'll hide it away in a safe place."

She came with me to the door, and as I started to leave, she put a hand on my arm. She had stopped crying, but she looked frightened.

"I had to take it! I had to!" she cried, and ran back inside.

I crossed the clearing, and no one saw me as I went up to my room. There I put the amethyst rock, still wrapped in Dulcie's sweater, into a suitcase in my closet and closed the door. Topsail Island, to which I had come to escape my own problems, was proving to be a focal point for trouble.

15

That evening Richard called for me at five-thirty and we stopped for a moment to see the captain before we left. He sat on the deck in his chair, with Mrs. Orion nearby working on a sweater she was knitting for Corey. Her son had already left for his new job at the restaurant.

"This isn't a good idea," the captain said as soon as he saw Richard. "Don't let that woman cut Hallie down."

Richard promised that I would be fine, and got me away as quickly as he could.

"Why doesn't he want me to go?" I asked when we were in his car. "Is it just Louise?"

"Don't worry. Everything will be fine." He sounded cheerful enough. "He's only afraid Louise will influence you in some way he won't approve."

"And Ryce won't?" I asked as we backed out of the clearing.

He gave his attention to driving. "Louise is the one to deal with in that relationship."

I wondered silently about the way others seemed to dismiss the captain's son. When I'd driven back to Topsail with Ryce after lunch the day before, I'd sensed a deep anger brewing in him, something he was unwilling to show. I didn't think he should be discounted as a player in this family's power struggle.

"How is it going at the house?" Richard asked when we were across the bridge.

I didn't mean to give him any details. "All right, I suppose."

"You've seen your husband?"

I stared at him in surprise. "How did you know?"

Richard smiled. "Mr. Knight found an envelope next to the telephone in your apartment when he went back. It had the name of my law firm, and he phoned me. When I said you were on Topsail, he asked me to find him a place to stay on the island—he wanted to fly to North Carolina immediately—so I called a friend on Topsail, and she is putting him up. Mrs. Varidy. He didn't want me to let you know he was here. But when I talked to him on the phone this afternoon, he said he'd seen you on the beach."

There was nothing I could say. I couldn't blame Richard for what he'd done, and a curious sense of elation possessed me. Paul hadn't waited before coming after me. It was as the captain had said—he wanted me back. Still, I couldn't be entirely sure after the way he'd walked off again that afternoon.

"I'm not sure what he wants," I said.

"Are you sure of what *you* want?" Richard asked. He didn't wait for an answer, but reached across and patted my clenched hands. "Relax. I have no business asking personal questions."

I suspected that his work kept him asking all sorts of personal questions, and he was quite used to it.

I turned the tables. "Are you married?"

He made a rueful sound. "Once. A long time ago. Not now."

"Are you ever sorry you and your wife broke up?"

"No, I'm glad we did. Every day of my life. She married again—happily. And I've remained happily free."

Free to pursue other men's wives, I couldn't help thinking.

I had planned to talk to Richard about the captain's will during this drive, but I suddenly felt reticent to bring it up, as though this was not the right time or place to discuss it.

After we'd driven in silence for a few miles, he began to tell me about the house we were to visit.

"Gulls Cove was once a real plantation house. It dates back to the time before the Greek Revival period and all those *Gone With the Wind* columns. It's much more typical of early plantation houses than the grander ones that came later. Beautiful restoration has made it livable, yet true to the original. The grounds are still expansive, though not nearly as large as they once were."

We had turned off the main highway that ran through the Hampstead area and were following a curving road that offered glimpses of the sound. A side road led between gateposts onto a driveway that approached the house. To me it looked large and handsome and impressive. A steep roof of gray shingles sloped forward over a wide front porch. Generously wide steps led up the center, with white railings on either hand.

Louise came through the front door to greet us, her hand held out to me in welcome, though her clasp was cool and quick. She didn't appear to like me any more than I liked her. A rose crepe tunic over black trousers both flattered and concealed her maturing figure. Diamonds at her earlobes caught the light, though she wore no other jewelry except for a jeweled comb tucked into the carefully blond hair she wore coiled at the back of her head.

I had dressed with purpose for this meeting with the formidable woman who was the captain's daughter-in-law. The evening was cool enough for the simple two-piece wool chambray in pale lilac that I'd brought with me from California. A gold locket and chain accentuated the plain V-neck, and I wore gold earrings to match. I'd hesitated about wearing the locket, because it was another piece that Paul had given me, but I couldn't stop wearing what I liked because Paul had been the gift-giver. I would create my own style now, and I could certainly deal with Louise.

We made something of a pair—lilac and rose!

She embraced Richard as though she hadn't seen him as recently as the day before, and invited us in.

"We have a surprise guest," she said as we crossed a narrow hall to the parlor on our right.

I noticed the wide floorboards of another day, the uneven levels of the ancient floors, which were polished to a dark sheen. After I stepped through the parlor door, however, I saw only the woman who sat in a corner armchair, with her son standing beside her.

Anne Trench accepted Louise's introduction as though we hadn't met before, and I played along, taking the hand she held out to me. She gave my fingers a little squeeze of warning, and I smiled and told her how pleased I was to meet her.

Ryce seemed embarrassed by his mother's presence and kept an uneasy eye on Louise. "Until she phoned this afternoon, I had no idea that my mother was in the vicinity," he told me. "Of course, it's wonderful to have her here. Mother knows that you were Susan's friend, Hallie."

Anne Trench looked stunning tonight in velvet trousers that gleamed a rich chestnut brown in the lamplight. A double strand of jade and gold beads was beautifully set off against a pumpkin-colored silk jacket. As it had been that morning, her silvery hair was wound into a mound on top of her head, held with a jade comb, and I noticed that her odd, tawny eyes seemed darker than they had by morning light. Altogether she was a picture of self-assured elegance. Beside her, Louise seemed artificial—someone putting on an act. I wondered again what the act covered up.

Against the wall near Anne's chair stood a small piano, and I perched on its bench to be near her. Richard made an elaborate gesture of kissing her hand—something she accepted with accustomed ease.

Apparently Louise had chosen to cook dinner

herself this evening, and Ryce went out to help her and to get us all a glass of sherry. Richard sat down on Anne's other side and began to ask about her painting. My own surprise at her presence here still left me speechless. From what she had told me that morning on the island about cherishing her solitude there, I hadn't expected her to leave it for a social evening.

Now I had time to look around the lovely room. Gray-blue paneling ran a third of the way up the walls, with light-colored plaster rising to the molding at ceiling height. A huge fireplace, probably once used for cooking, was set into a chimney that I had seen running up the outside of the house. The furnishings were comfortable and simple, reflecting the understated style of a bygone time. The beige pile of a Chinese rug had been carved into magnolia and dogwood shapes at each corner and along the borders.

My interest, however, returned inevitably to the woman who sat straight in a high-backed armchair that would have protected her from drafts in an earlier day. Her artist's hands, bare of rings and scrubbed almost free of paint stains, lay quietly in her lap, though I suspected that tonight the inner woman was anything but quiet. Where I'd sensed tranquillity in her that morning, there was little now. Once, when I caught her eye, I saw a brightness in her face that suggested nervous anticipation. Anne Trench was here for a purpose, and when she was ready she would let us know what it was.

Though the food was delicious, dinner proved to be an uncomfortable meal. A golden brown, roasted chicken, old-fashioned scalloped potatoes, and tender new peas, all served with a white wine that had been chosen with care, should have relaxed us and brought on easy conversation. But no one was at ease, including me.

Though Richard had been placed on Louise's right, her behavior toward him was circumspect, and she made an effort to include Ryce in her conversation. Until the matter of the will was settled, she knew exactly which side of her bread was buttered, it seemed.

Whatever Ryce felt was carefully hidden tonight; he was simply a rather colorless host who kept an eye on the needs of his guests. Once I caught a look of sadness as his eyes rested on Louise, but no anger showed in him tonight.

Not until we were finishing our fresh strawberries and cream, and sipping a fruity liqueur, did Anne place her hands beside her plate and lean forward a little. The moment had come.

"As I've told you, Ryce," she began, "Corey Orion has been helping me on Cabbage Island."

"I don't know why you didn't stay with us," Louise broke in.

Anne continued as though she hadn't spoken. "I like Corey. I'm sure that he and Susan would have married if she had lived."

"Entirely unsuitable," Louise said.

This time Anne seemed to notice—and dismiss her.

Before she could continue, however, Ryce spoke quietly. "We don't *know* that Susan is dead, Mother, though it's likely that she is."

"And you probably never will know, if what Corey believes is true," Anne said.

I set down my small glass carefully. Now I knew what was coming.

"Corey has told me something very disturbing," Anne went on. "He believes that Susan disappeared down that hole near the Trench and Cameron houses that they call the Pirate's Pit."

I held my breath as I looked around the table. As might be expected from a lawyer, Richard's face gave nothing away. Louise looked stunned, and Ryce a little sick.

Anne, sitting next to Ryce, put a hand on his arm. "I'm sorry. I know how much Susan meant to you. But she meant a great deal to me, too, and these strong feelings of Corey's can't be ignored. No one else has come up with a theory. A vibrant, healthy young woman doesn't just disappear into thin air."

"What made him jump to so terrible a conclusion?" Richard asked.

"I don't think we should be discussing such a thing tonight," Louise broke in. "We have a guest present, after all."

"There's not much more to say," Anne told her. "Besides, as Ryce has pointed out, Hallie Knight is an old friend of Susan's. I'm not sure Corey knows why he feels this way. It seems to be a conviction that has been growing in him for a long time. Today he decided to tell me."

So Corey had been back to see her, after our early visit.

Louise shivered—rather a theatrical shiver, I thought. "This is really dreadful. Does Corey think she fell down that hole in the dark?"

"He thinks she was murdered," Anne said, and this time her voice broke. But when Ryce started to speak, she raised her hand. "Corey has a special sensitivity that has led him to this conviction. What he sensed finally became too strong, too real, for him to hold back any longer."

I spoke quietly, taking Anne's side. "Corey told me this, too. Just today. He seemed convinced and I believed him, too."

Louise made a dismissive flick with her fingers. "I would never trust Corey Orion. Is he actually suggesting someone pushed Susan down the pit?"

At the head of the table, Ryce looked pale and ill. He spoke quietly to Anne, ignoring his wife. "I understood why Susan loved Corey, but I was uncertain about her marrying him. I didn't want that, but if they had gone ahead with their plans, I would have backed them. However, this idea Corey has . . . I can't accept—"

"It's pointless to stir all this up," Louise protested. "None of this can help Susan now. Or ever be proved."

Anne turned to look at her daughter-in-law, and I could see the distaste in her eyes. "If what Corey believes is true, it means that someone who is guilty of murder is getting away with it, and is still free. That is something I find hard to accept."

Richard echoed Louise's words. "But why *now*? It's been two years since Susan disappeared."

"Perhaps because Nicholas sent for Hallie and she is here," Anne said, "so everything is surfacing, reaching critical mass. Perhaps someone already feels less than safe and Corey is somehow the recipient of knowledge that person wishes he didn't have."

"The reason Nick sent for Hallie," Richard

said, "is because he decided to change his will. Now he's done it. Except for a small legacy to you, Ryce, everything is to go to Mrs. Knight. And this—"

I interrupted his words. "I've already told the captain that I won't accept this. I don't want anything to do with his money."

"I understand how you feel," Richard said. "But I must go along with the captain's wishes; he'll leave everything to charity if you refuse."

Anne said nothing, but the look she turned on Louise was sharp with amusement. I realized with a start that Anne Trench would like nothing better than to see her son's wife thoroughly unhappy. So, she and her ex-husband had one goal in common.

"You didn't tell me it had gone this far!" Louise snapped at Richard.

For once he seemed to lose patience with her. "He's my client and there's nothing I can do about it. Anyway, I've only just gotten the paperwork done and he insisted on secrecy until now."

The subject of Susan and the pit seemed to have been quickly lost, once Richard had brought up the will.

Anne, at least, had endured enough. She rubbed her forehead above her eyes and spoke to Ryce. "I'm very tired. If you don't mind, I'd like to go up to my room. Mrs. Knight, will you come with me, please?"

Ryce went to help his mother rise from the table, though she hardly needed assistance. "I'll see you upstairs," he said.

She shook her head at him, though not unkindly. "Mrs. Knight was Susan's friend. I'd like to talk with her." I went up with her gladly, relieved to leave all those unpleasant people behind.

"Thank you for not giving me away," Anne said as we climbed the stairs. "I didn't want anyone to know that Corey had brought you to see me this morning."

I wanted to ask her why, but her manner invited no questions. She came up the stairs briskly, belying her own words about being tired. She paused only once to catch her breath, looking down at me on the step behind her.

"I couldn't take any more," she said. "It's as though Susan's loss doesn't count beside money."

When we reached the upper hall, she went to a closed door and opened it. Her bedroom was at the back of the house, and I supposed that by daylight it would overlook lawns and flower beds, perhaps with a glimpse of the sound. The walls were pale blue, the lower paneling a pinky gray. Unusual, but somehow quieting. A graceful four-poster was covered by a quilt with a design of small blue flowers set against a creamy background. A chandelier held china globes from which oil chimneys rose, though the light they gave off was electric.

Anne dropped gratefully into a wing-backed chair and waved me into another alongside it. "Ryce's first wife was responsible for much of the restoration of this house. I wish she could have lived to enjoy it. I wouldn't have come here today, if it hadn't been for Corey. I decided to confront them with what he told me and watch their reaction, though I'm not any the wiser. They all seemed upset—especially my poor son—though of course Richard always hides whatever he's feeling. You probably noticed that he has an eye for Louise—God knows why!"

There was nothing I could say, and Anne went on sadly.

"I feel sorry for Ryce. He should never have been born to parents like Nicholas and me. Susan was a throwback—nothing like her father. She could hold her own, and never hesitated to speak her mind. But of course you know all that."

"I wonder why he married Louise?"

"He was lonely after his wife died. And Louise can be charming when she chooses. She has beauty, sensuality. I just hope she divorces him for Richard."

I felt a little sick. "Aren't there any happy marriages?"

"Things used to be different. A woman raised any number of children, and her job was in the home. She accepted the fact that her husband might have a roving eye, but they stayed together. That was never for me."

"Weren't you happy with Nicholas?"

"Deliriously. For a while. But he always seemed to need more than one woman, and I couldn't put up with that. I couldn't take Carlina. He was more intensely interested in her than he was in the others, even though Fergus was his friend."

"Have you ever been sorry that you left him?"

She rested her head against the back of the chair and closed her eyes. "I missed him terribly at first. I thought I couldn't live without him. But of course I did, and I'm glad of it. I've done much better with my painting since he's been out of my life. Painting has always come first with me."

I felt even more sorry for Ryce, who must have been pushed aside and largely ignored by two high-voltage parents even when they were together. I wondered if that was happening to Dulcie now.

Anne opened her eyes and gave me a sharp look. "I should never have had a child. If it weren't for Susan, I would regret that we had Ryce. Nicholas wasn't much of a father. And I . . . well, I have a good deal to regret. Susan had something of both of us in her—a volatile mixture that probably did her no good. Hallie, are you asking me these questions because of your own situation? Corey told me about your husband showing up on the beach today."

The rush of feeling—longing—that came whenever I thought of Paul was beginning to frighten me. If I gave in to it, there would be all the more pain for me ahead.

"I've let him walk away from me twice," I said. "I think he was ready to apologize and ask me to take him back today, but I couldn't. It would have been on his terms, and I couldn't accept that."

"What happened to drive you apart in the first place? Do you mind telling me?"

Perhaps Anne was the one person I could talk to, and I told her what had happened in California.

"That sounds familiar," she said when I was finished explaining. "I was so angry I could have killed Carlina. But of course I didn't. I painted all those wild pictures instead. In my art I killed them both—over and over. Then I went away, and I've never looked back. Oh, I still loved him, and I did a lot of suffering for a while. But I wouldn't give in to the sort of life he wanted, and I would never have gone back. My painting has been stronger for what I've been through. I believe that I've done better work because I know what pain is like."

"I don't have your outlet. I don't have a talent that consumes me as yours has. I wish I did."

"You have a life. You have work—whatever it is. And there will be other men, as there were for me. There's always that one we never forget, but I haven't been lonely. Now I'm glad to be past all that. I enjoy being alone."

I hesitated and then ventured, "I remember a review I read some time ago about a show of your paintings held in Los Angeles."

"I remember. The critic said my work lacked heart."

"I haven't seen enough of your work to judge," I said. "Were you upset by the review?"

"Of course I was upset. I hadn't learned then to let words flow over me and not stick. Susan made a difference in my life. She helped me to find heart in my work. For a while, at least. You didn't know, but I was seeing Susan frequently all the time she was in college. I didn't want anyone to know because word might reach Nicholas."

"Why should you have cared by that time?"

"Because if he'd known how to get in touch with me, he might have asked me to come back and I might have gone. Then it would have started all over again." She sounded surprisingly wistful. "I wonder if he ever thinks of me—of the way things used to be."

"He does," I told her. "Only today he was talking about you. He said he loved you *and* he loved Carlina. She came over to see him, and I think he still cares about her. So you were probably wise to get away."

"Love that's worth anything can't be divided!" Scorn cut through her words. "Do you know the woman your husband had an affair with?"

"Only by sight and reputation. She's an actress—beautiful, dramatic, lively—all the things I'm not."

"That sounds familiar, too. They marry us for what we are, and then they look for someone who is nothing like us. Or they try to make us over into what they think they want."

Paul had never done that. He had built me up from the beginning, taught me to believe in myself. Encouraged me. Loved me.

Anne was watching my expression. "Let him

go, Hallie. In the long run you'll find he wasn't worth keeping. Besides, how do you know she was the first?"

"It couldn't have happened before, or I'd have known!" I cried.

Her smile was wry. "You *are* an innocent!"

So here was the advice I needed—had asked for. Advice I would certainly take.

"You couldn't look more unhappy," she said. "But that's part of it. And you'll come through— I can see the strength in you. You'll find ways to fill your life. You don't have any children?"

I shook my head. "It would be harder if there was a child. But perhaps it would be better, too. I'd have brought something to love out of our marriage."

Anne made an impatient sound. "Women always think in terms of cute little babies to adore and give themselves to. But the babies grow up into impossible adults with whom we have little in common."

"Poor Ryce." I echoed her words.

She shrugged. "But there was Susan and that was worth everything. I loved her more than I've ever loved anyone. However, she didn't turn out as well as I hoped. There was a wild streak in her that reminded me of Nicholas. Though perhaps she'd have settled down if she'd married Corey."

"I loved her, too," I said gently. "She was the most exciting friend I've ever had."

"And now we're left with the question of what happened to her. Do you think what Corey believes is true?"

I didn't know how to answer that. I had only that moment of Corey's despair to go on. "What if it is true?"

"There's no point in speculating. Unless we can find real evidence about what happened—" She broke off and I had nothing else to offer.

"Why didn't you want them to know we'd met earlier today?"

"It would have hurt Ryce more to realize that I hadn't let him know that I was here, but had asked to see you."

"There must be hurt enough about this change the captain wants to make in his will—a gift I truly can't accept."

"I only wish Ryce would stop holding everything in and tell his father off!"

Just then someone knocked and Anne called, "Come in."

A dour Louise opened the door and stared coldly at both of us.

"Richard wants to know if you're ready to leave, Mrs. Knight. He has a long drive back to Wilmington."

"Of course," I said. "I'll come down right

away." I held out my hand to Anne. "Thank you. May I come to see you sometime?"

She surprised me by leaning over and kissing my cheek. "Anytime you wish. I wanted to meet you because you were Susan's friend. But now I'd like to know *you*. Just think about the things I've said."

I knew I would. Before I left with Louise, however, I remembered something Dulcie had said, and I tossed it out as if in passing.

"Dulcie claims that Susan's spirit visits this house. Have you ever felt anything strange?"

Louise turned so white I thought she might faint. She held on to the door frame, staring at me.

Finally she managed to speak. "Why would she say a thing like that? It's foolish."

Anne commented calmly, giving her a chance to recover, "Sometimes children are closer to other worlds than we are. And Susan's father does live here."

"We mustn't keep Richard waiting," Louise said, and I followed her down the stairs.

Nevertheless, I would wonder more than once why Louise had turned so pale.

16

⟡————————⟡

When Richard dropped me off at the captain's and I came upstairs, I saw no one about. The captain's door was closed, and the screen Mrs. Orion often put up at night was nearby, which meant that Mrs. Orion's cot was in place. She liked to sleep where she could hear any movement he might make.

I went directly to my room and discovered that all of Anne's paintings had been removed during the evening. Since Corey was at work, Mrs. Orion must have done this herself, and I was grateful.

Since I didn't feel sleepy, I put on a robe and slippers and sat down to read for a while. The events of the day were still running through my mind. The very fact that Paul was sleeping not far away in one of those houses on the beach left me unsettled. I needed to take Anne's words to heart and put an end to everything between Paul and me.

But I *had* made an end, hadn't I? I needed to ignore the fact that he was here and manage to get through the next few days before I went home to California. I needn't see or speak to him again. A clean break was the best way. Anne's advice, however painful, was wise and practical.

There was just one thing I wanted to do before I went to bed. I opened the suitcase in my closet, folded back Dulcie's old sweater, and took out the second geode to set it beside the one on Susan's bookcase. It was a mirror image. The markings and shadings exactly matched where the stone had been split apart.

There was just one difference. The rock that held Susan's books upright was sparkling and clean, its violet and deepening purple facets afire in lamplight. Such stones were never scrubbed, or even dusted. They could be restored to luster by dipping in clear water to wash away dust.

The stone Dulcie had taken was dull and dirty, smudged with fingerprints, uncared for. She must have taken it after Susan was gone. By that time no one would have noticed and she could have easily taken it from this room. She must have played with it and she must have soiled it before her conscience told her that she was stealing, whether Susan was here or not. So then she'd wrapped it up and put it out of sight in her chest. Though in that case, why hadn't she simply returned it? Doors were always left open at the captain's house, and Dulcie came and went as she pleased.

There was something wrong here—some puzzle I hadn't found an answer to.

To distract myself, I tried to read one of the mysteries in the bookcase, but I kept thinking about the geode and couldn't concentrate on the story.

Before I gave up and went to bed, I stood again at the window that overlooked the clearing. The light standard was on, and I could see the entire expanse well enough—though not back into the tree shadows where the Pirate's Pit had sucked its bottomless tunnel into the ground. The swing hung motionless and nothing stirred. I couldn't even think about that place without a surprising sense of horror.

I was about to turn away, when movement near the Cameron house caught my attention. Not one person but two lingered in the shadow of the house. A man and a woman seemed to be talking together earnestly, though I sensed at once that this was no lovers' meeting. There seemed to be a tension in the way they stood. I went quickly to turn out my own lights and then returned to the window. Through the opening I caught only the faint whisper of voices, so I could hear no words. After a moment the figures separated, and one ran up the steps to the porch of the Cameron house. I glimpsed Carlina briefly before she disappeared inside. When the man stepped into the open and came toward the captain's house, I saw that it was Corey. Oddly I felt both relieved and a little disturbed. Tomorrow I would simply ask him about what I'd seen.

I lay in bed with the lights off, but my mind wouldn't quiet right away. Bits and pieces of my day persisted in replaying themselves, among them that moment when I'd looked into the amethyst lights and Louise's name had come into my mind as though written on a screen. There had been almost a message of warning there—yet nothing had happened tonight at Gulls Cove to support something so nebulous. There had been only her white paleness at the mention of Susan's spirit.

Before I fell asleep, I saw Paul's face again, the way he used to look at me and hadn't looked for—how long? Had the indications of what was happening been there all along? Had I been too blind to see?

Once more my pillow dampened under my cheek before I finally fell asleep.

When I awoke it was nearly nine, and I felt

drugged and sluggish. A shower woke me up, and I dressed and went out on the deck. Mrs. Orion came from the direction of the captain's room to greet me.

"He's asking for you, Mrs. Knight. Shall I bring your breakfast to his room?"

I thanked her and went across to the captain's open door. He was dressed in his silk gown, again with a scarf tied at his throat. His eyes looked more alive, less sunken than when I'd first seen him.

"Good morning," I said. "You're looking a lot better today."

He waved my words aside. "What happened at Gulls Cove last night?"

I answered carefully, wanting to let nothing slip about Anne. "Louise served us a very good dinner. We talked a bit, and then Richard drove me home. It wasn't very exciting."

"You discussed my will, I suppose?"

"The subject certainly came up. I don't think anyone is happy about it—including me."

"I've signed it," he said. "It's a working will now. You will need to stay here for a little while longer, Hallie, so that you can decide what you want to do and where you want to live."

"My home is in California, and I intend to go back there. Besides, you're very much alive and looking better with each passing day. The money's not anyone's until you no longer have a use for it, which I suspect will not be for a long time. So I'm afraid your will must take care of itself. I've already told Richard that I want nothing to do with it. Give it to your charities, if you need to be so unkind to your son."

"It's not Ryce I'll be hurting. I won't have Louise touching what belonged to me."

Mrs. Orion brought my breakfast of fluffy hotcakes and coffee, and I busied myself with the food.

The captain wheeled his chair close to my table, and his silent attention was too critical to ignore.

"You can't have everything exactly the way you want it," I said at last. "I'm not serving under you, Captain. You can't give me orders and expect me to obey."

"What if I leave everything to Carlina?" His eyes were bright with malice.

"And wreck her marriage completely? Do you think she'll love you for that?"

"I could leave it to Fergus."

"You can leave it to the moon if you like. I'm going to phone Wilmington and find out about a plane home."

"There's someone you haven't considered," he went on, ignoring my plans. "You haven't thought of Dulcie Cameron."

"To leave your money to?"

"No, no, she's a lonely little girl who is some-times neglected by her parents. She's become quite attached to you. Your leaving so soon, so abruptly, will make her feel betrayed all over again. She has already lost Susan."

"Children give and take their affections easily. She's known me for only a few days; she'll forget me in a week."

"You could at least stay for the school pageant she'll be in. She's told me how inter-ested you are in her dancing."

I finished my last hotcake in irritated silence. My business with the captain was done, whether he liked it or not. I needn't listen to his cunning schemes to get me to stay. As far as I was con-cerned, there was no further point to anything he might say.

Not having received the response he desired, he wheeled away from me angrily, and I hoped he had given up. As I might have expected, he had not.

"There's still my other purpose in bringing you here, Hallie," he tossed over his shoulder. "You were supposed to help me find out what happened to Susan. I thought you might bring a fresh eye, a new sensitivity, to what we've all been looking at for so long. After what Corey told me yesterday, I can't just let this go."

It was a shock to think that Corey had risked upsetting this sick old man with his terrible theory.

The captain wheeled himself back to me and saw my face. "It's all right, Hallie. Whatever the truth may be, it's better for me to know than to die without knowing. Corey thinks it's intuition, but I think there must be indications of some sort that took him in that direction. He likes you and he doesn't trust me. I opposed his marriage to Susan, and he's never forgiven me for that. I like Corey, but he'd have been the wrong husband for her. She'd have been a very rich woman and Corey doesn't care about money. They would have grown apart. It couldn't have worked out. He was angry when he told me—almost as though he blamed me for her death."

"That doesn't make any sense," I said.

This outpouring had tired the captain and he slumped in his chair. All the lines in his face had deepened.

"Help me," he said.

I raised my hands in protest. "I'm not able to help myself, let alone anyone else. I'm an outsider here, and I have no idea about what might have happened. There's no thread to pick up, nowhere to start."

"Start with Corey. I think he's been afraid to explore his own suspicions. Now I gather that he's telling everyone in order to get it into the open, hoping someone may betray something. Pool your efforts. Murder doesn't happen in a vacuum. It's committed by a person who has friends, confidants, enemies. Someone close to this person knows something. During my years in the navy I had to track down problems that were caused by men under me. It can be done. I'm too old to make the effort now, but you can be my eyes, my legs. Please, Hallie. My wits are still working."

I hadn't the heart to cut him off with another refusal. "Let me think about it," I said reluctantly. I was the one who had thought everything should be brought out into the open, but now that so much had been, I'd begun to feel alarmed. What the captain had said about murder was true.

"Don't call about your plane yet," he said.

I promised that I wouldn't call today, and asked if he wanted me to get Mrs. Orion to come and help him.

He shook his head. "Not now. I want to be quiet for a while."

I picked up my tray and carried it out to the kitchen. Mrs. Orion was working at the sink and she looked around at me.

"He's all right," I told her quickly. "He just wants to be alone for a little while."

She nodded, but when I started away, she stopped me. "Could I talk with you for a moment?"

"Of course," I said, though there was nothing I wanted to discuss right now with Mrs. O.

"Let's sit out on the deck." She led the way outside, and I had the feeling that she didn't want to be overheard, though who was around who might hear her? She pulled chairs into the shade and we sat down next to each other. I wondered if she wanted to discuss Corey's theory, but she had something else on her mind.

"I want to talk about Dulcie Cameron, Mrs. Knight," she said. "I'm very worried about her."

I was both relieved and concerned, and I settled down to listen.

17

Mrs. Orion picked up her knitting and began working, watching her needles as she talked. "I can't help but notice how unhappy and lonely that little girl is," she said. "I know her mother loves her—Carlina is always arranging for her to do whatever she wants—but Mr. Cameron has been a difficult man for all the years that I've been here. Perhaps this is none of my business, but I think both Mrs. Cameron and Dulcie are afraid of him at times."

"I've had the same feeling," I agreed. "But I don't know what can be done."

"It's his black Scottish temper. I'm sure he loves them both and he would never willingly hurt them when he's in his right mind. Dulcie hasn't any friends her own age nearby until the summer people come. And I don't know how she is with children at her school. Susan was always good to her. She never talked down to her, and she knew how to make life seem exciting. After Susan . . . went away, Dulcie changed. She's not as open and friendly as she used to be. What I thought—" Mrs. Orion looked at me, hesitant now and apologetic. "What I thought was that you might be her friend. Maybe take her some- place interesting. Give her something to look for- ward to. Just be someone she can talk to."

"I'll do what I can," I said. "But, as you know, I don't expect to be here much longer. I've had the feeling that something specific is troubling Dulcie, but she doesn't know me well enough to talk to me, so I can't ask her questions. Perhaps Corey could take us on a boat trip while I'm still here." I didn't mention Anne Trench, since I didn't know what Corey had told his mother about Anne. "Anyway, I'll do what I can."

"Thank you, Mrs. Knight." She got up, clutch- ing her knitting to her chest, and walked to the railing, where she could look out over the sound. She spoke without turning around. "Corey says he told you what he believes about Susan."

"Yes—he seems to be telling everyone. Did he give you any reason why he thinks this?"

"No. I don't think he has any. Sometimes my son seems much younger than his years. He holds in his feelings, and he won't open up and talk to me."

Though Mrs. Orion herself seemed to be opening up more than ever, her manner made me uneasy, and I wondered what *she* might be holding back.

"Did you want Corey to marry Susan?" I asked.

She startled me by bursting into tears. "I wanted it as much as Susan and Corey did! I would have loaned them money to run away and make a start somewhere else. In fact, they were already making plans when she disappeared, plans the captain didn't know about. He wasn't fair to Corey—or to Susan, either."

"What about Susan's father? Couldn't he have taken her side?"

Mrs. Orion's dismissive expression told me what she thought of Ryce. "Louise didn't want Susan to marry! If Susan had married and had children, the money would have all gone to them!"

For a few moments she had nothing more to say. Then she began to muse aloud. "It's a funny thing—about Mrs. Louise Trench. You know, her family lived around here and they weren't much. Her father drank a lot, and Mrs. Trench's mother left him and took her little girl away. I knew them back then. They must have had a pretty rough time, so the daughter grew up wanting to be somebody else. I understand that what little family she had are gone now, so she needn't own up to them. Of course, she was a beauty, even as a little girl, and the way she looked attracted the wrong sort of man—that is, until she met Mr. Ryce. The captain didn't want his son to marry her, but for once Mr. Ryce went his own way. More's the pity. I suppose I shouldn't be telling you all this. I'd only meant to talk about Dulcie."

What Mrs. Orion was saying came as some surprise, since Richard had told me that Ryce believed that Louise's family had come from the north and were well-to-do.

Mrs. Orion folded her knitting to indicate that she was through talking. She excused herself and returned to her work in the kitchen, leaving me with a new picture of Louise—a confused picture that indicated untruths on her part. If her family had lived around here, why wouldn't Ryce know? Perhaps he did and didn't care? Her early life had probably made her grasping and formed her into the woman she now was.

For the rest of the day I mostly marked time. Corey didn't appear and Dulcie remained indoors. I had nothing more to say to the captain, and I didn't return to his room. I had no wish to go down to the beach again, for fear of seeing Paul, so I was left with time on my hands and too many busy thoughts.

Mrs. Orion suggested I might take a walk,

which sounded like a good idea. After a light, early supper alone on the deck, I borrowed her Chevy and drove to the south end of the island, where I would get out and walk. She had told me that Serenity Point was a wonderful place to watch the sunset—she'd done it many times herself.

Any sort of activity appealed to me. I followed a central road, driving slowly so as to look at the rows of houses on both the soundside and oceanside, which fascinated me with their variety and individual colors and shapes. All of the houses were different until I reached the end of the island, where a few condominiums had been built, with the joined structures looking exactly like one another. Where the pavement ended, I left the car and walked over rough grass and uneven ground.

The tide was out and the sandbars stood free of water. Gulls moved about, picking up whatever they could scavenge, or flying in low swoops over the land. Several pelicans flew past—a pinky brown, far more graceful in the air than on the ground. There were little shore birds, too, though I didn't know their names.

It was the sky that enthralled me most. Fluffy white clouds wore pinkish trimmings, while toward the west yellow streaks had been painted up the sky. The reds of sunset were gathering near the horizon, and to my delight I saw that a moon was rising, pale but still visible in the fading light. Sunset and moonrise at the same moment!

A strong wind blew in from the ocean, bringing with it the sharp, salty smell of the Atlantic and the voice of the surf, which sounded louder than ever. I felt braced and a bit more courageous. Of course I could meet whatever lay ahead, even when it came to Paul. For the moment there was nothing I needed to do. I could simply breathe in the wonderful sea air and let the peace of the scene around me take over. I could just *be*. The vanishing rim of the sun and the rising, humpbacked moon reminded me that the universe went on sublimely and small human woes were not its center.

Feeling completely free and alone, I raised my arms and turned about slowly, almost dancing— as Carlina had danced in the Assembly Building. Then, as I turned, with my eyes wide open, I saw that I wasn't alone, after all. Not far away a woman was walking in my direction. She was tall and slender, dressed in jeans and a bulky sweater with reindeer prancing across its front. Her short black hair was curly, so the wind hardly ruffled a lock. She was striking rather than beautiful, and the entire look of her was so familiar that I recognized her at once in the sunset glow—even at a distance. I was startled to find her here, of all places, since my long acquaintance with her was entirely on a television screen.

She saw me and called out, "Isn't this heavenly!"

When she reached me, she held out her hand and I took it warmly. "You're Brenda Wilshire," I said.

"Yes. And you're Hallie Knight."

It wasn't surprising that I should recognize her, but I didn't understand how she could know who I was.

She must have read my expression, for she laughed—a musical, familiar sound. The series she'd starred in was the only soap opera I'd ever watched.

"I know who you are because Topsail's pretty small," she said. "Especially during the off-season. I grew up here and Susan Trench was my buddy for years. Once we were even in love with the same boy when we were in our teens, though I'm afraid Susan won out. She would have married him, I expect—if she'd lived."

Corey, I thought. "You sound as though you're sure she's dead."

"I saw Corey today and I know he believes that, so I'm up on what's going on. He told me that Captain Nick sent for you."

My brief state of exuberance disappeared and I shivered in the ocean wind.

"You're cold," Brenda said. "Look—I'm staying with my aunt in one of the beach houses. How about coming back with me for a hot drink and some talk?"

I accepted with pleasure, and we returned to where she had left her car near Mrs. Orion's. I was still astonished that she knew Corey and had known Susan. I didn't want to let her out of my sight.

As I followed her car back along the central road, I thought about what I knew of Brenda Wilshire. For years she'd played slightly villainous roles, always trying to take the handsome leading man away from some lovely, innocent young heroine. *Round We Go* always had a good story line, and once I'd even written an episode for them, though Brenda Wilshire hadn't been in that one. Recently I'd read some unpleasant scuttlebutt about her. She'd thrown one too many of her famous tantrums, and had been dropped from the show only a few months ago. Rumor had it that she was having trouble finding another job. I knew how hard it could be for an actress in television. Gossip always flourished around the famous, what was said often exaggerated out of all proportion to the truth. And I knew that because her face was identified with one role, it might be hard for her to get another job. I liked her immediately, and was happy to be following up on this chance acquaintance.

I hadn't paid much attention to where we were heading, because I'd been simply tailing her car, but when she pulled up before a house on the oceanside and I drew in beside her, I looked out my window with a sense of shock.

The house she'd stopped in front of was the one built as an addition to one of the towers. I had seen it from the beach when Paul disappeared into it. This was the last house on Topsail Island that I wanted to enter and I didn't know what to do.

18

renda was waiting for me on the ramp that led to a door at the side of the tower house. When I was slow about following, she called out to me, "Come on, Hallie. This is it."

There was no way out unless I explained what I had no intention of explaining. I left my car and stood for a moment looking up at the house I had seen from the beach—the addition to the tower was a full-sized house in itself. I followed Brenda up the side ramp to the second-floor entrance. Inside, I was introduced to Mrs. Meg Varidy, Brenda's aunt. Paul was nowhere in sight, and I began to breathe evenly again. He was probably out and I needn't worry.

The living room was large and bright, with an opening into the tower at the far end. I need only relax and enjoy this unusual setting.

Mrs. Varidy wore comfortable-looking slacks and a blue shirt. Her manner was friendly as she recognized my name and shook my hand, remarking that she knew the captain. No one mentioned that Paul Knight was rooming here. I hoped they wouldn't make the connection.

"Do you like hot chocolate?" Brenda asked. "I'm off anything stronger just now. That's what got me in trouble with the studio. One scotch too many."

I'd seldom met anyone more open and unself-conscious. If Paul would just prove to be somewhere else, everything might be fine.

"We'll be up in the tower room," Brenda told her aunt. "If Mr. Townsend comes in, ask him to join us. And whistle when the chocolate's ready, dear. I'll come and carry it up."

Townsend! I was climbing steps that wound up steeply for two flights, with a small square room at each level. Somehow I went through the motions of climbing, of admiring the last room at the top that Brenda told me she'd annexed for herself as a child. Apparently her parents had divorced when she was small, and she'd come here to live with her aunt. We had that in common, but Mrs. Varidy was nothing like the aunt whom I'd been forced upon. I looked out each of the four high windows from which all of flat Topsail could be viewed. It was a little like looking at a relief map. I could see the long stretches of the maritime forest, the rows of little houses, the beach and ocean on one side and the sound on the other. All the while the name Townsend was running through my mind. Townsend was my maiden name and I felt thoroughly upset that he had used it.

As soon as I sat down in a somewhat battered armchair, I managed to find my tongue. "Mr. Townsend?" I repeated.

"Yes. Paul Townsend. He's a great guy." Brenda plumped up faded green cushions on the sofa and curled her legs under her. "I had dinner with him last night at the Soundside restaurant. I like him, though he's a bit mysterious about why he's come to Topsail. Richard Merrick arranged with my aunt for him to stay with us a few days, and Paul and I seemed to hit it off right away."

I examined my surroundings carefully, silently. This must have been used as a family room at one time. The furnishings were comfortable and old, and there was a game table and a corner bookcase, well packed with books with bright jackets. A braided, oval rug covered part of the floor, and where there was wall space between windows, pictures had been hung. They were all professional glossies of Brenda Wilshire—smiling wickedly, scowling, always enticing. There were even two old magazine covers that featured her distinctive face—not beautiful, but arresting.

All this I managed to take in, my hands clasped in my lap so they wouldn't betray me by shaking. New anger with Paul was beginning to rise in me, and I knew it couldn't be stopped. I'd have to vent it quietly.

"Mr. Townsend is not Mr. Townsend," I said evenly. "Townsend is my maiden name, and Paul is my husband, Paul Knight."

Brenda unwound herself and sat up. "Oh, gosh! I have put my foot in it, haven't I? Now I can understand why you've looked upset ever since I mentioned his name. I never guessed, and for once Topsail gossip didn't cover our visitor."

There wasn't much I could say, and she went on after a moment.

"Look, Hallie, if you'd rather not stay here, we could go somewhere else."

I smiled a little too brightly. "Of course I'll stay. I'm glad we've met, and I hope we can talk about Susan. What was she like as a little girl?"

Brenda was clearly relieved to shift the focus from Paul, and she began to talk about the young Susan I had never known, though the nature of the child seemed to match what I knew of the woman. Susan must have been spunky, mischievous, rebellious.

"She was always full of schemes," Brenda said.

"After the captain's wife left, and Corey came with his mother, he and I became faithful followers with Susan as our leader. I know you've seen something of Corey since you've been here. He's told me a little about you. You seem to have made quite an impression in that house."

I said nothing, waiting for her to go on.

"As kids, the three of us were inseparable." She spoke in a musing voice, remembering. "We used to put on little shows on our own. We didn't need an audience. Of course, Corey was always the hero and I was the leading lady, but Susan made a wonderful villain and later on I used to copy her mannerisms on television. She even scared *us* some of the time. Nobody ever knew what she was going to do next. And she could get mad—could she ever! Her ups and downs kept us going."

I added a memory of my own. "I envied her for her independence and her lack of fear about anything. She never cared what anyone said or thought."

"I know," Brenda said. "I've heard her sass the captain, and he never even scolded. Only her grandmother could manage her."

"In college, Susan even leaned on me a little," I told her. "We were about the same age, but I always felt years older. She thought I was the sensible one, and I think she needed a steadying hand in her life. I'm glad I could give her that for a little while. Apparently she talked to her grandfather about me, which is why I'm here now."

"I always liked her grandmother," Brenda said. "In some ways Anne Trench and Susan were a pair. They were both rebels. I used to feel sorry for Susan's father sometimes—he was so out of it. He didn't even seem related to those two women, yet he was the captain's and Anne's son, and Susan's father. Though once when I was poking fun at him, Susan told me to lay off. She said he could be pushed just so far, and then watch out! So I avoided criticizing him after that."

As she talked, something of the young Brenda, the woman I imagined she'd been before becoming famous and successful, seemed to shine through. Her look was one I'd seldom seen on TV—open and young. "You know, we even had a secret meeting place that the grown-ups didn't know about. Or at least I don't think they did. I wonder if anyone goes there anymore. Of course, this was after Anne had moved away, and Corey and his mother had come. That's when we became a team. Ask Corey to show you our secret room sometime."

Footsteps sounded on the steep, circular stairs to the tower, and I froze.

Brenda jumped up. "I didn't want Aunt Meg to bring up our cups. She hates these stairs."

She ran to look down and then threw up her hands, stepping back to let Paul carry up a tray with three cups of fragrant hot chocolate. He set it down on the game table and spoke to Brenda.

"I thought I'd join you," he said. "If you don't mind." He didn't look at me, though he knew very well that I was there.

Brenda brought a steaming cup over to me. "I'm sorry," she said under her breath.

Paul carried his own cup to the sofa and sat down, with Brenda settling herself at the other end. She made no innocent pretext of introducing us.

"Am I crashing a party?" he asked.

I knew very well that no one ever minded when it was Paul Knight who did the crashing, and I said nothing in response.

After a moment, Brenda looked at me and jumped up. "Oh my God, there's something I need to tell Aunt Meg," she announced and clattered off down the stairs.

I didn't want to be alone with Paul, but there I was. As I sipped foamy chocolate, burning my tongue, I felt trapped and completely helpless.

"Hallie," he said in that voice that had always mesmerized me, "you can't keep running away from me forever, you know."

"I'm not the one who has run away," I told him. I stirred dark liquid and watched the steam rise.

"I'm sorry," he said. "I'm sorry about every-thing."

Sorry is such an easy word. "I'm not," I told him flatly. "I needed to find out. It had to happen sooner or later, didn't it? Though it's hard to get used to, when I thought you were someone I knew. How many were there before Carol?"

That was *my* hurt striking out, echoing Anne's words. I didn't really believe it had happened be-fore. And yet—why not? What did I really know about Paul Knight, after all?

He flushed so darkly, looked so angry, that I thought he might get up and walk out again. At least there was satisfaction for me in making him angry. I wanted to hurt him, as I'd been hurt. He stayed where he was, however, crossing his knees as though he meant to settle for a while. One long-fingered hand hung loosely over the arm of the sofa. I remembered his hands touching me gently, lovingly. When he rubbed the bridge of his nose, the gesture was achingly familiar.

"What do you want me to do?" he asked.

When I answered, I was pleased with my voice—smooth as silk, unemotional. "I'll be here on the island for a few more days. When I go back to California, I'll pack up my things and find a smaller apartment. And I'll look for a new job, so we needn't meet at the office. Will that suit you?"

He'd always been good at hiding his feelings when he needed to. His quick anger with me was under control. I could see him push it back. "If that's the way you want it." He still made no move to leave, but sat looking at me in that remote way that told me nothing.

I set my cup down on the game table too firmly, so that chocolate spilled over the rim, and stood up. The tower room was small, but it seemed a mile wide as I walked to the stairs and descended. Brenda was standing beside her aunt's chair, and she came toward me at once.

"I can't tell you how sorry I am. I never dreamed—"

That word again! People were always being sorry. Still, I couldn't help but notice again what a striking-looking woman she was—just the sort of woman Paul would find attractive. Why hadn't I minded before? Why had I been so gullible and trusting?

"It's not your fault," I said. "You didn't know me, or anything about me, or you wouldn't have led me into this."

I said good-bye to her aunt, and Brenda walked me out to my car. "If he hadn't come to us under that other name . . ." she said.

"It's all right," I told her. "I've had a chance to make things final. I needed that."

She looked doubtful, hesitant. "Hallie—tell me. Was it a good marriage?"

"I thought it was," I said. "I thought I had a wonderful marriage. We couldn't have been more in love, more compatible—" I broke off because I was protesting too much.

She patted my arm as I got into the car. "Then everything will work itself out. Don't do anything rash. Do you mind if I phone so we can set a date to meet again?"

"Of course," I said. "I'd like that." Though the truth was I wasn't sure I would. After all, I'd freed them both to get together, if they liked.

As I drove away, I looked into the mirror and saw her standing there on the walk to the tower house. In the highest windows of the tower no one stood watching me go.

Brenda's words echoed in my mind. *Was it a good marriage?*

Well, was it? Suddenly I wasn't sure.

19

When I'd parked Mrs. Orion's car at the captain's house, I didn't go upstairs at once. The last daylight had faded, and the big, lopsided moon had the night to itself. A hazy radiance bathed the clearing, except for that one terrible spot lost under the trees. A spot that drew me. No one was about, and I went to stand near the wire fence that kept the careless away from the pit.

Of course, there was nothing to be seen, only a black circle in the ground that was darker than anything around it. Weeds and vines grew to the edge of a mysterious emptiness. I could hear nothing in the darkness around me, except wind in the trees that reached up past windows of the captain's house.

A voice spoke at my elbow, startling me. It

was Dulcie, who seemed to have a way of appearing without warning.

"What do you suppose happened to the things that went down that hole, Hallie?" Her words were hardly more than a whisper.

I hoped the question was an innocent one. Surely Corey wouldn't have told this child what he believed.

"I don't know," I said. "I'm not the right person to ask."

"Corey says things that fall down there could wind up in the sound, or even in the ocean, but nobody's ever found the place where the pit might empty out. I know Susan went down there."

"Did Corey tell you that?" I asked, shaken.

She shook her head vigorously. I couldn't catch the bright color of her hair in the moonlight, but I could catch ripple and movement. "Oh, no! I had a dream that told me. In the dream Susan came out here in the dark and fell into the hole."

"That would be hard to do, considering there's a fence around it."

"It would have been easy then. The old fence was sagging in spots. It's only been fixed up since . . . since . . ."

She faltered and I caught her up. "Since when?"

"Since after I told Dad about my dream. He said it was a dangerous place, and he fixed the fence himself."

"After Susan disappeared?"

I could see the way her eyes widened as she stared at me. "I don't remember. Maybe it was before."

"Then your dream couldn't be true, could it? It was just a dream."

"It was an amethyst dream—and they're always true. Susan told me that. She told me that when I wanted to find something in a dream, I should put amethyst near my head and ask a question before I go to sleep. I told you that."

"Is that why you took the geode—so you could use it for dreaming?"

She looked frightened, and I knew she was going to do her disappearing act again. I spoke quickly.

"Wait, Dulcie. How would you like to go on a boat trip tomorrow?"

"Where to? Cabbage Island?"

So Dulcie knew of Anne's presence. "Would you like that?"

"To see Susan's grandmother, who painted all those pictures?"

I nodded. "But she paints differently now. I'll phone her and see if it's all right to come."

The plan seemed to please her. "That would be fun. I'll come over early."

"Not too early. Let's say nine o'clock?"

"Okay," she said. "See you then." And she ran off.

I went upstairs into a quiet house and encountered no one until Mrs. Orion heard me and came out from behind her screen.

"I was taking a nap," she said. "I think it's going to be a hard night."

"Is he upset?"

"He's usually upset about something, and that makes the pain worse. But he's been fretting a lot this evening. Mostly about you." Her look was critical.

"I'm sorry," I told her, and winced at the sound of the word.

"Did you have a good walk?"

"Yes—I went out to the end of the island, as you suggested. I saw the sun set and the moon rise at the same time. It's a beautiful spot. I also met someone out there—Brenda Wilshire. It seems that she knew Susan."

Mrs. Orion didn't look pleased. "I remember her very well. She was a wild one when she was younger. And I didn't think she was always a good friend to Susan."

"She told me that she and Susan and Corey were together a lot after you moved here."

"That's right. Those three didn't have many other friends on the island. When they got into their late teens, they . . . oh, never mind. It's all so long ago. Good night." She turned away so suddenly that I wondered what thought had spooked her.

When I went into my room and turned on a lamp, the quiet welcomed me. Over here, near the sound, where the island was wide, the crashing rhythm of the surf couldn't be heard.

I refused to think of Paul. I didn't want to think at all. I dipped into one of Susan's books on crystals and found it interesting enough that I could force away thoughts about myself. When I finally went to bed, though, I was at the mercy of my own imagination. *Was it a good marriage?* Brenda had asked. Was a union that was taken for granted a good marriage?

I remembered the beginning, when we'd had so much to tell each other. Our days together were filled with discovery and a wonderful, fresh excitement. Was that what Paul wanted to find again with someone he didn't know everything about?

If I'd allowed him to talk to me on the beach, what would he have said? Never mind that. What had happened had happened. Explanations, apologies—none of that would help. Trust had been broken, and without trust in a marriage, there was nothing. So I must do as I'd said. I would pack up my belongings in the apartment, pack up my life, and find a new place to live, a new job. And then what?

Life without Paul?

It must have been two o'clock by the time I finally got to sleep, only to have a terrible dream grip me. I was sinking into quicksand, and there was no one around to help. In a few moments I would sink below the surface and I would be suffocated. I couldn't cry out. Though I struggled, I couldn't make a sound. I could only sink helplessly.

Of course, no dream, however dreadful, destroys the dreamer. I woke up drenched in sweat and calling for Paul. No one heard me. No one came.

For a few moments I lay in my bed trembling, and then I began to talk to myself—calming words to reassure me. I told myself that I was fine, and that Susan hadn't died the horrible death I'd just imagined. My own words, spoken aloud, repeated again and again, started to have a soothing effect, calming me.

I had no idea how the Pirate's Pit had figured in Susan's life, but the conviction was strong in me that she hadn't died there. Others had their convictions, but I had mine. I left my bed and went to where the amethyst cluster stood on the bookcase. I picked up the bookend and placed it on the table beside my bed. *I* could do with an amethyst dream. From what I'd read, they might be vivid, but they were not destructive.

I slept. And I dreamed. But in the morning I couldn't remember anything I could use.

It was a beautiful day, so I put all thoughts of Paul out of my head and concentrated on the pleasure of taking Dulcie to see Anne Trench. As soon as I was wide awake, I phoned Anne. She was pleased with the idea of our coming over, though first she wanted to know how I was getting along.

"I was concerned about you at Gulls Cove, Hallie. After you'd gone I had doubts about whether I should have given you my strong feelings on life and marriage. No one should advise anyone else when it comes to such matters."

"It's all right," I said. "I appreciated your advice, though of course in the end I'll do my own thinking." Which I'd certainly done, hadn't I? So now I had to get on with my life.

Corey was sitting at the table eating breakfast when I went out on the deck. The morning was lovely and clear—warmer, with spring in the air. I could hear that the birds were happy about that. A trip over to see Anne Trench suited

Corey just fine, so we finished breakfast together, with his mother in and out of the kitchen as usual, refusing help.

I told Corey about meeting Brenda Wilshire, and he seemed to approve.

"She's great," he said. "I've always liked her a lot. We try to see each other whenever she comes home. And, of course, right after Susan disappeared, we stuck together."

"What do you mean, stuck together?"

"Well, we were closer to Susan than anyone else, so when the sheriff was convinced that she was really missing, we were asked a lot of questions—along with everyone else who knew her well. All the questioning was rough on Brenda because she had been pretty mad at Susan around that time. Other people heard them quarreling."

Mrs. Orion brought out her own coffee and toast and sat down beside us. "They used to fight over everything," she told me. "I always felt that Brenda knew something about Susan's disappearance that she wasn't telling."

Somehow, the words she was speaking didn't ring true, and when I looked at her, her eyes avoided mine.

"I doubt that, Mom," Corey said. Then he seemed to consider something further he wanted to say to me. "I told you, didn't I, that Susan was writing a letter the last time I saw her?"

I nodded.

"Well, I didn't tell the whole truth. The letter she was writing was to her grandmother. An envelope addressed to Anne was found on Susan's desk. The letter itself never turned up."

I was more interested in the quarrel between Susan and Brenda. I sensed, however, that I would get a lot more out of Mrs. Orion when she was alone. I knew her answers to my questions would be much franker without her son around.

We were still sitting at the breakfast table when Dulcie appeared, dressed in clean shorts and a T-shirt, with a sweater tied around her waist. Her red hair was neatly combed and caught up with a green spangled clasp—Carlina's touch, of course—that matched her lively eyes. All these were signs that her mother was in charge again. The fact that Dulcie looked happy made me more sure of this.

We left soon after in Corey's boat. Dulcie and I took the two seats in the stern, with Corey ahead of us at the wheel. Dulcie had brought a large brown envelope with her, and she held it carefully in her lap, without explaining.

The sound was a shining blue this morning, like the sky, contrasting with verdant greens to the west along the shoreline, where pines and live oaks grew wild. Dulcie squealed with delight as the boat planed for a few moments before settling down to skim over the water. Spray rose, flying past us, and a white wake frothed behind.

Since we were crossing the sound, Corey didn't need to follow the buoy markings of red and green that indicated the channel. He knew his course and avoided the constantly changing sands that could pile up as the sea took away sand from the north and deposited it at the south end of the island, piling up in one direction what it stole from the other.

Again the wind and a sense of flying across the water were exhilarating, and my spirits rose. For this little while I was free.

In a few minutes we reached Cabbage Island and I could see the house perched on its high, safe place. Corey beached the boat on the sound side of the island, away from the sea, but when Dulcie and I jumped out onto sand, Corey stayed in the boat.

"Aren't you coming with us?" I asked.

"Not this time. You'll be fine now, and I'll be back for you in a couple of hours. I want to catch Brenda while she's still on Topsail."

"I don't think she's going anywhere," I said, and then added a question before he could get away: "Did you know that my husband is staying at Brenda's?"

He grinned at me. "Sure. I saw him go into the tower house yesterday when we were on the beach."

Dulcie missed nothing. "If that man who was talking to you yesterday is your husband, why aren't you together?"

Corey rescued me. "Don't ask personal questions, Dulcie."

She made a face. "Why shouldn't I? You always do."

He waved a hand at us and pushed off.

As Dulcie and I climbed toward the house, Anne Trench stepped out into the sea wind to wait for us, her patchwork skirt blowing around her legs.

To my surprise, Dulcie suddenly pulled back, holding her brown envelope close to her chest. "Maybe I'll go down and wait for you by the water."

"What is it? I thought you wanted to meet Anne Trench."

She held up the envelope, shielding her face from the sun. "I changed my mind."

"I won't go without you. If you won't come, we'll both go back to the beach and wait for Corey, but that could be for a couple of tiresome hours."

"Do come up," Anne called to us. This morning she wore jeans under her patchwork skirt, her working smock topping the other layers. She'd drawn her silvery hair back with a green ribbon so that it hung free.

Dulcie lowered the envelope and whispered to me, "She's a real famous artist, Hallie. I don't know what to say to her."

Dulcie's shyness was totally out of character and therefore touching.

"Just let her do the talking," I advised. "You needn't say anything unless you feel like it."

Though not altogether reassured, Dulcie came with me up the porch steps.

nne recognized Dulcie's shyness, if not its cause, and spoke casually as she took us inside.

"I'm glad to meet the daughter of Fergus and Carlina Cameron. I used to be a neighbor of your parents, Dulcie. Though that was a long time ago, when I lived on Topsail Island."

Dulcie recovered her tongue. "I know. Lots of the captain's stories are about you. He can tell real good stories."

Anne winced but continued to smile. "Don't believe *everything* he tells you. He loves to make things up. Or he used to."

"I guess he still does."

"Are you hungry, Dulcie?" Anne asked.

I explained that we'd had breakfast, and Anne smiled at Dulcie. "Well then, I'll just get us a mid-morning snack of milk and cookies. Oatmeal cookies, still hot from my stove. Come in and sit by the fire."

Once more, the small room seemed to glow in the firelight—perhaps because of Anne's presence. After two cookies and a glass of milk, Dulcie relaxed.

Anne and I talked for a few moments about how beautiful the morning was, and how blue the sound looked under the sky. Then she turned her attention to Dulcie and the envelope she fidgeted with.

"Have you brought something to show me?" she asked.

Dulcie shook her head and folded her hands over the envelope on her knees.

"You like to draw pictures, don't you?" Anne said.

"Well—yes. But I'm not very good."

"Neither was I in the beginning. I'd like to see what you've done. Susan used to brag about your talent as an artist."

Dulcie shook her head. "I was little then. I can do better now."

"Of course you can. So show me."

She patted a place beside her on the makeshift sofa, and Dulcie sat down hesitantly. I'd taken the armchair I'd been comfortable in before, and I watched what was happening with interest.

For a moment longer Dulcie hung back. Then she surrendered the envelope to Anne. With fingers once more stained with paint, Anne slipped out several sheets of drawing paper and spread them on the low table. Firelight flickered, catching the vivid acrylics. I was startled to see what they were. Dulcie had covered the five sheets with abstract forms in raw, angry color.

Thoughtfully, one by one, Anne studied the paintings. "These are really very good, Dulcie. You've used your imagination in choosing colors and forms, but I wonder if you were really angry when you painted them."

"I can get mad," Dulcie said, sounding tentative.

"Most of us can. But I have the feeling that you might have been paying too much attention to old paintings of mine that I thought had been thrown away. I think that's *my* anger on the paper, and not really yours."

"I didn't copy!" Dulcie cried. "I made all that myself."

"Yes. I can see that. You took inspiration from what I'd done. That's why I said these were very good—you made them yours. At least partly. Of course, that's what artists do in the beginning. We borrow from other artists who excite and inspire us. That's how we learn to draw and paint. That's how writers learn to write. Then, when the skill begins to feel natural, we go our own way and do our own thing. Would you like to see what I'm painting now, Dulcie—now that I'm not angry anymore?"

Dulcie's eyes were shining and she didn't need to put her feelings into words.

Anne showed the way behind the curtain into her studio. I followed and watched Dulcie look around, as though every splotch of paint, every bit of muddle on the work table, pleased her. But I was remembering two days ago.

"I thought you wanted to be a dancer, Dulcie."

She cast that idea aside with a wave of her hand. "That's what my mother wants. It makes her happy if I try. And I really do like to dance. It's just not what I *want* to do. It upsets my mother that I like to paint."

Anne's eyes met mine over Dulcie's head and she grimaced.

"I remember your father," Anne said gently. "Your mother married a wonderful man."

"Dad thinks she wanted to be married to the captain. I heard him say that to her once."

The words, spoken today with such calm acceptance, disturbed me. Their daughter saw far more than her parents realized.

Anne acted as though she hadn't noticed anything amiss. "Come over here," she said. "I'd like to show you something."

The gypsy portrait of Carlina had been taken down from the wall and placed on an easel. Carlina, tambourine raised, looked over her shoulder—as tantalizing as she might have seemed as a young woman.

Dulcie stood before the easel, enchanted. "It's my mother, isn't it? A wonderful picture of my mother!"

"I'm pleased that you recognize her," Anne said. "I painted it from memory, so I couldn't be sure I'd really caught the way she used to be."

"This is the way she'd *like* to be," Dulcie said wisely. "She thinks she's old because of some wrinkles and gray hairs, but inside, this is what she's really like. Oh, I wish she could see this. Then she'd know who she is."

Anne picked up a cloth and covered the painting. "It's not finished. I don't know if I'll ever finish it—and I'm not sure she'd like it anyway. It belongs to a past that I can hardly remember. Would you like to see some of my other work, Dulcie?"

"I'd love to!" Dulcie cried, and I knew that Anne Trench had worked her special magic.

I left the two of them to talk about painting, and wandered back to the firelit room. Anne was the one who gave it *presence*. Without her, it was only a lifeless, shabby room, in spite of the fire that still flickered in the grate.

I picked up a cookie to munch on and went outside to stand at the porch railing. An egret was down in the marsh darting its head about. Beyond it a small white boat like Corey's moved in toward the island. Suddenly I realized it was Corey, with Brenda Wilshire beside him!

The boat disappeared behind a dune, and a few minutes later I heard the motor rev up again and watched the little boat head back out. A moment later, Brenda came into view, climbing toward the house. She saw me and waved, and I waved back, even though her coming here made me uneasy.

As she reached the porch, she explained. "I bullied Corey into bringing me over as soon as I learned that Anne Trench was here. I remember her from when I was a little girl and was terribly in awe of her. Besides, this was a chance to see you again."

"That's nice of you to say. I enjoyed our visit last night. Tell me, though, where did Corey go off to?"

"He had some errands he needed to run, and since I wanted to come here, he dropped me off and went on his way. He promised to return in an hour or so."

She seemed cheerful, her own woes put aside. I kept feeling that I knew her well when this came only from having watched her on a television screen.

Anne had heard the boat, and she came out on the porch to welcome Brenda with an outstretched hand.

"I haven't seen you in person since you were a child, but I've watched your work many times on the small screen. And I've kept track of your career. Corey told me you were back on Topsail, so I'm glad you've come to see me."

"It's good to see you, too. I hear about your shows and see your work in different museums. I'm glad things have gone so well for you."

Anne smiled and looked at me. "You should have seen Brenda and Corey and Susan in their mischief-making heyday!"

Brenda's dark eyes were bright with memories. "We weren't very original back then. We called ourselves the Three Musketeers, Susan, Corey, and I. It's hard to believe that Susan can't be here with us right now."

I thought about what Corey had said—that Susan and Brenda hadn't parted as friends.

Anne brought us in out of the wind to where a little warmth still radiated from red embers.

"Dulcie's busy," Anne said to me. "I gave her drawing things and a place to work, and she's settled in. She's a very bright, gifted little girl."

Cookies were passed around, and apple-cinnamon tea was offered instead of milk. Brenda, like everyone else, seemed enchanted in the presence of Anne Trench.

"I've always wanted to know more about the early days on Topsail," Brenda said to Anne, "when Operation Bumblebee was in effect. Were you here then?"

"I was and I remember it well. I was about twenty and working as a secretary over at Camp Davis in Holly Ridge. Nicholas was a young ensign, not long out of Annapolis, and he was the best-looking man I'd ever seen. You could have combined the looks of several movie stars of that time and not equaled Nicholas Trench. Of course, I fell for him—hard."

"Did you know Fergus Cameron then?" I asked.

"He was around, but I didn't pay much attention to him. Of course, he was Nicholas's friend, but he reminded me of a young stork. He had long legs and an awkward way of moving. But he was a *brain*. He changed a lot as he grew older, and of course eventually married Carlina. Everybody thought she was too young for him, and that she'd never stick to marriage after her colorful life, but she's apparently done all right. Especially since she's the mother of a child as delightful as that little girl in there. Thank you for bringing Dulcie to see me, Hallie."

I smiled and nodded, but Brenda and I were silent, not wanting to interrupt any memories of a past time that Anne might share with us. As her gaze rested on the glow that remained of the fire, she began to tell us story after story of that time, painting for us in words. She made me feel the excitement that all those young men and women must have experienced, taking part in a secret plan that would be vitally important to their country. The war aroused a patriotism that hadn't faded into the cynicism that would come later.

Anne's eyes were dreamy as she remembered. "We had a good time, along with all the hard work. It *was* exciting, and Nicholas was exciting. I've never known anyone so alive with energy. And he had so much of the unexpected about him. He was never dull, and I simply let him sweep me along on waves of exuberance."

Listening, I was reminded a little of Paul. He had been the exuberant one in my life. And I thought sadly of the old man in bed in the Topsail Island house—the spark of life fading in him, the vigor long gone. But it was illness, not age, that had done this. I'd heard him rally to roar at Mrs. Orion, or anyone else who displeased him, though listening to Anne, I wished I could have known the young Nicholas Trench.

"Did you know Carlina then?" Brenda asked.

I glanced at her, wondering how innocent a question that might be.

Anne didn't seem to mind. "Not then. We all got to know her much later. Things had closed down on Topsail, but Fergus and Nicholas and I had decided to stay and build year-round homes. One day, years later, Carlina popped up from nowhere. Or not nowhere, really. She'd left her circus in Florida and was dancing in nightclubs throughout the Southeast."

The storyteller seemed to return abruptly from her time travel and looked up at us. "But that was then, as they say, and this is now. I've made the life I wanted for myself. I've been trying to create a new relationship with my son, but we haven't much in common. It's not his fault or mine that I cared more about Susan than I do about her father." Her words had taken a slightly defiant turn.

"I cared about Susan, too," Brenda said softly. "I've never forgiven myself for parting with her on such bad terms. But of course I couldn't know that I'd never see her again."

Anne spoke quietly. "You were too much alike, weren't you? There was always tension, competition."

Brenda shook her head. "You'll have more perspective than I ever did. Maybe it was like the song—looking for my best friend, looking for myself, lookin' too hard . . . I'm not sure Susan cared enough about our friendship, while I cared too much."

"And now?" Anne asked.

I began to wish she wouldn't push Brenda, but Anne took the privilege of age and did as she pleased.

At her question, Brenda jumped up and went to look out a window toward the sound, her back to us. "I don't care a lot about anything anymore."

This was growing uncomfortable and I tried to rescue Brenda with a question. "Will you be here for the show Dulcie's school is putting on in the Assembly Building?"

"I expect I will. My phone hasn't been ringing off the hook with offers. I'll volunteer to help, if they can use me."

"Did you know that Louise is going to sing?" Anne asked me.

This was a surprise and I shook my head.

"She has a lovely voice. If there had been any money when she was young, she might have trained for the stage. Ryce loves music, so it's one of the things that brought them together."

"That old Assembly Building is full of history," Brenda added, not listening to us. "Susan and I heard a lot about it from the captain when we were growing up. Then you went away, Anne, and the Orions came. That gave us Corey."

The way she spoke his name made me realize that Brenda and Susan may have shared similar taste in men. It was natural that she and Corey Orion might be attracted to each other in Susan's absence.

Brenda still had her mind on the Assembly Building. "Anne, did you know about the hollow place under the floor near the front of the building?"

"I recall that there was an underground tunnel that ran under the road and was used to carry the missiles down to the launch sites, so I suppose there are remnants of that space down there. It would sound hollow if someone thumped from above."

Brenda nodded. "That's it. Corey and Susan and I found a way into that space. We partitioned it off and it made a lovely secret meeting place. We smuggled some old furniture down there and fixed it up so it was comfortable. I suppose the grown-ups knew about it, but they let us alone." She turned to me. "I haven't seen that room in years, Hallie. Maybe Corey and I ought to introduce you to our special place. I expect some of Susan's stuff is still down there."

"I wonder if you should," Anne said quietly. "I mean, do you want to dig up old ghosts? Somehow I don't have a good feeling about that place. All that missile launching was exciting, but it was a bit spooky, too. I always wondered what might be coming back at us from out there."

Brenda shrugged her words aside and glanced at her watch. "Corey will be here pretty soon, so perhaps we should walk down to where he'll bring the boat in."

"I'll help Dulcie put things away," Anne said. "Then I'll send her down to join you." We parted with promises to come again.

I sensed that Brenda wanted to talk to me alone. As we followed the path through the grasses and sea oats, she gave me a sidelong glance. "I usually don't meddle in other people's affairs," she said.

Since that remark usually prefaces an effort to meddle, I stiffened, ready to resist whatever she meant to say.

"When Paul and I had dinner the other night, he gave me a pretty good picture of what's going on with you two. He didn't give me your name, so I had no idea who he was talking about—that there was any connection between you. I think he wanted someone to listen—which is what I did. It's always easier to talk to a stranger than to those you know well."

"True confessions?" I asked.

"It wasn't like that. It's just that I know how angry you must feel. I've been there. My own marriage cracked up years ago. But anger carries too high a price—I've found that out. Look—I'm not trying to play Cupid. It's just because I messed up myself that I'm talking like this."

I had nothing to say on the subject of Paul, and Brenda must have recognized that. We'd reached the stretch of sand where Corey would beach his boat and we sat down on a log to wait.

"I suppose Louise is still around?" Brenda said idly. "How are things working out for her with Ryce?"

I shrugged. "I'm not sure Ryce is happy. Louise seems to pretty much just look after herself."

Brenda nodded, watching a cruiser glide past down the waterway, big and white, creating those great rollers in its wake that small boats had to watch out for. Tiny crabs burrowed in the sand at our feet, darting sideways, absorbing to watch. I leaned over to pick up a delicate sand dollar half embedded near my feet. It was perfect, without a crack or blemish.

Brenda looked out at the green shore across the sound. "I knew Louise a long time ago in New York, when we were both models for a big agency. I was only eighteen. She was at least ten

years older than me, maybe more, and very successful. I thought she was the most beautiful
woman I'd ever seen. They only used me because
I had a different sort of look. I never reached the
peak she did as a model, nor did I expect to. I
was really trying to get into stage work or television, but I think all that Louise wanted was to be
a model."

Though somewhat taken aback by this information, I wasn't completely surprised. I could
imagine how cameras must have loved Louise
when she was young.

Brenda sighed. "I haven't seen her in years. I
knew that she'd married Ryce Trench, of course,
but our paths haven't crossed when I've come
back to the island. She was more than beautiful
when I knew her. She was a vital, happy person,
always helping other people."

This startled me. "I'm afraid she's changed."

"That's likely enough, considering all that
happened to her. I felt very sorry for her at the
time."

"Oh?" I said, brushing sand off the paper-thin
shell in my fingers.

Her sigh was a little deeper this time. "I suppose her bad luck was mostly her own fault. I
went to see her a couple of times while she was
in prison."

The sand dollar cracked in my fingers and I

threw the pieces away. Brenda caught my shocked look.

"Uh-oh! If Louise has kept quiet about what happened in the past, I'd better shut up. Anyway, here comes our transportation."

Corey's boat was heading in toward shore, but he wasn't at the wheel. Fergus Cameron nosed the little craft in toward the beach and turned off the motor so that it drifted, eventually running its bow into the sand. Then he threw over an anchor, climbed out, and walked toward us.

21

I was stunned by the sketchy information Brenda had dropped about Louise, but for now my attention was diverted by the surprise of Fergus's appearance. As he walked toward us, I remembered Anne's remark that he had reminded her of a stork when he was a young man. There was still something of that quality about him as he moved his long legs a bit stiffly.

He nodded to me, but his focus was on Brenda. "Hello. I didn't know you were back from New York."

"Hello, Fergus," she said. "If you've come for your daughter, she's up at Anne's. That's a fine little girl you and Carlina have produced."

"We think so," he said, and started up the path past us. "I told Corey I'd pick you all up because I wanted to see Anne while she's here."

Brenda looked after him and then got up from the log. "Come on, Hallie. I wouldn't miss this meeting for anything."

There were a hundred questions I wanted to ask about Louise, but that would have to wait. I followed Brenda as she hurried up the hill.

Since Fergus, with his long strides, was well ahead of us, I spoke to her softly. "What's up? Why are you so interested in Fergus seeing Anne?"

"There was a blowup the last time they met. Anne was angry with Carlina and Nicholas, and she spilled everything out in front of Fergus. He defended his wife and told Anne off pretty harshly."

So he had defended her—but what had he believed?

When we neared the house, Anne came out on the porch with Dulcie, to watch our approach.

Fergus climbed the steps ahead of us and held out his hand. "You're looking well, Anne."

She took his hand without hesitation, smiling warmly. "It's been a long time, Fergus. How are you?"

"Getting old. Only you and Carlina manage to go on looking young."

Dulcie came running up to her father, holding a tote bag as well as her big envelope. Anne must have supplied her with art materials and packed them up for her. Dulcie set down her things and hugged her father, then looked over her shoulder at Anne.

"Can I show him?"

It took Anne a moment to realize what Dulcie was referring to, and when she did her expression turned doubtful.

"*Please,*" Dulcie pleaded.

"All right," Anne said. "Come in the house, Fergus."

Brenda and I were included in Anne's sweeping gesture and we all went through to the studio. This time it was Dulcie who ran to remove the covering over the painting of the gypsy.

Fergus went to the easel and studied the portrait. "This is remarkable," he told Anne. "It's a generous portrait, considering all that—"

"That was a long time ago," Anne broke in. "I probably wasn't fair to Carlina or to you. Nicholas was the one I was angry with."

Brenda and I watched, absorbed in the little drama being played out between these two.

The stiffening was still there in Fergus's tall frame as he spoke. "Nick was to blame. Always. But Carlina could never help playing the coquette. You've caught that perfectly in your portrait."

"Ah, the wonders of memory," Anne said lightly. "I didn't even have a snapshot to work with. I expect that she's a very different woman now. Just as I am someone else."

Fergus continued to study the portrait, silent now.

"You stayed married," Anne said. "I suppose that's an achievement these days—though it wouldn't rate as that for me."

I sensed the uneasiness in Fergus. "Perhaps we've been together too long to ever change. Don't take this the wrong way, but maybe it's better if you don't see Carlina while you're here."

"I shan't look her up, if that's what you mean. Though surely there's been enough water under the bridge. Those overwrought emotions would be pretty hard on us these days."

That might be, I thought, but Anne didn't know that Fergus was still quite capable of exploding over the past.

Dulcie was showing Brenda the contents of her tote bag, and Brenda was properly admiring. Then she looked around at Fergus, with the winning smile I knew so well from TV. "I ought to be getting back. I promised my aunt—"

"Of course," Fergus said. "We can leave right away." But he didn't move toward the door at once, his focus again on the painting. "Would you sell this to me, Anne?"

She hesitated. "I'll think about it."

She came with us to the top of the steps and watched us head down the path. When I turned back to wave, I saw that her face was sad, as though filled with bittersweet memories.

Again Fergus's long legs took him ahead of us, and Dulcie, at peace now with her father, trotted along beside him. I was glad of the chance to speak privately to Brenda. Unexpectedly, I had made up my mind about something, surprising myself.

"When we get back to the island, may I come with you to your aunt's house?" I asked her. "I want to see my husband."

She smiled cheerfully. "Good idea. We've given him the tower room to work in, so he's probably up there reading page proofs or something."

I had made my decision quickly, impulsively—in a sense, without consulting myself. But now it was done and the confrontation I'd been putting off was about to happen. The prospect frightened me a little. This time sparks were going to fly, and that was what I wanted, wasn't it? A confrontation. No turning away, but speaking my mind!

Once we were on our way, however, anxiety began to build in me. Was this really a good idea? I began to panic, wanting only to turn back.

When we reached the soundside dock near Brenda's house, Fergus secured the boat and we stepped out. As I waved good-bye to father and daughter, I asked Dulcie to tell Mrs. Orion that I was going to visit with Brenda for a while and would be back later.

Brenda said nothing on the short walk to the tower house, and I tried to suppress my rising doubts. When we got there she looked up at the top floor.

"There's a window open," she said, "so he must be there. Go on up. My aunt and I will stay out of the way and you can have him to yourself." When I hesitated, she gave me a shove. "Just do it," she said. "You'll know what to say when the time comes. Though sometimes maybe we just need to listen."

I could feel a pulse beating in my throat, and I only remembered the warnings Anne Trench had given me. When we went inside, I left Brenda to explain to her aunt, and hurried toward the stairs to the tower. My feet sounded on the bare boards, so Paul was certainly warned that someone was coming. When I reached the top step, I stood still and looked around.

He was sprawled in the one armchair, his glasses sliding down his nose, so that he had to push them up every little while. That familiar gesture. He seemed deep in the pages he was reading, and for a moment he didn't look up, though I knew he could only be pretending that he hadn't heard my approach. Finally he took off his glasses and stared at me—a look that was hardly welcoming.

I went up the last step and dropped onto the sofa opposite his chair. "Talk to me," I said. "Please talk to me."

His look softened, and thankfully he didn't remind me that he had been trying to do just that. Words didn't come easily to him now, and I braced myself against hearing that he was sorry, that it wouldn't happen again, but when he spoke, that wasn't what he offered me.

"I've had to do some thinking, Hallie. I've been thinking about what matters to me most, about what's worthwhile in life and what isn't, and I know one thing: I'm not like my father."

The pulse that had been beating so hard in my throat quieted. Paul's father had been something of a Don Juan, and his mother had suffered in a marriage she'd simply endured.

"I've hurt you, and I've hurt myself," he went on. "I made a stupid mistake. I won't excuse myself or ask you to forgive me or any such nonsense. I just want you to know that I value what we've had between us more than anything else in my life. I've had a taste of doing without you, and I don't like it. Maybe we've been taking too much for granted about marriage, and I hope that can change."

He went to stand at one of the high windows that looked out over Topsail. I sat so still that I hardly breathed.

When he continued he didn't turn around. "I've seen how hurt and angry you've been, and nothing is worth that to me. I've been angry and hurt myself, though not with as good a reason. Maybe this is something new for us. Not a turning point. A growing point? Away from patterns we've become fixed in? Once in a while maybe you could come with me to some of those Hollywood parties you hate. And I'd like to stay home more than I have and get to know you again. To know myself. We've lived together for eight years, but I'm not sure we understand each other as well as we did in the beginning."

I knew very well that he was right. Something between us had slipped away and we hadn't noticed.

"It's not gone," I said. "I love you. I don't want to lose you, even though I don't—" I paused, stepping back before I said the wrong words.

He smiled, the old, loving smile that I had missed so terribly. "Will you have dinner with me tonight, Hallie? I tried out the Soundside with

Brenda and her aunt, so now I can show it to you."

"I'd like that." I went to stand beside him at the window and he put an arm around me. It felt right—exactly the way it should feel.

"I have a lot to tell you," I said. "I need your help."

He kissed the top of my head and then under my chin. When he found my mouth, the kiss lasted a very long time. My heart was thumping wildly and I put my arms around his neck so I could hold on tight, yet even there in his arms, wanting to be held, wanting a great deal more, an undercurrent of uncertainty lingered. I was afraid of being happy too soon. I didn't want to be hurt all over again, yet how was I to trust him as I had before?

He sensed my slight withdrawal and stepped back, releasing me. "Let's give it time. Let's not make promises we might not be able to keep. First there's mending to do—for both of us. I've rented a car, so if you like, I can drive you back to the captain's now."

He was right. My emotions were so raw, the hurt so fresh, that I still had a tendency to shake, and I knew we needed a quiet time apart in order to find our own way.

"That will be fine," I said. "I'd like you to meet Captain Trench, and I want him to meet you."

We went down the tower stairs to find Brenda alone. She simply smiled at us, not needing words.

On the drive I told Paul a little of what had been happening. He knew of my college friendship with Susan, and how fond of her I'd been. In the last few years I'd almost forgotten what a good listener Paul could be, perhaps because I hadn't talked to him enough lately to remember. The enemy of love was to take for granted.

There was only time to tell him a little of the story, though. Corey and the Pirate's Pit would have to wait. And so would Louise—who was still an enormous question mark.

When we reached the house, Mrs. Orion met us.

"This is my husband, Paul Knight," I said. "Paul, this is Mrs. Orion, the captain's housekeeper. Do you suppose the captain could see us for a few minutes?" I asked her.

She looked pleased, and with a fair amount of surprise I sensed that I'd somehow made it into Mrs. O's good graces. She didn't disapprove of me as she had at first.

The captain was sitting up in his chair watching television when we reached his room. He gave us a long look and then used the remote to turn off the set.

"You're Hallie's Paul, of course," he said, and held out his hand. Then he looked at me. "You're a smart girl. I knew that from the first minute I saw you."

Paul had a way of making friends. There were no strangers in his life, and he sat down and began to talk about the towers and what he had learned of Operation Bumblebee. The two men were quickly at ease with each other, so I left them to get acquainted and went to my room. Once the door was closed, I had another shaking spell. I hadn't known that all this emotion was bottled up inside me. The only feeling I'd been willing to accept was anger, and there was still a part of me that wanted to stay angry—a negative aspect that I would have to deal with. For the first time I could see that anger was an indulgence that I had enjoyed. That had to stop.

All I was sure of now was that Paul had come back to me—at least for the moment—and that I wanted him. I couldn't see any further than that. Hollywood and all those stunning women were still out there, but now I would try to be more active in his life, just as he would need to be more active in mine.

Someone tapped on my door, and Mrs. Orion came in smiling—not her stiff, tentative smile, but something warmer, and supportive.

"This is a big house, Mrs. Knight. If your husband would like to move his things over here, I can fix a nice room for the two of you upstairs."

I hesitated only a moment. Paul was right—we needed to give ourselves time. The state of affairs between us was still unsettled. Our physical need for each other mustn't be allowed to take over, not until we knew how to be together in a new way.

"Not just yet," I told her. "We need a little time."

She nodded in understanding. "He'll court you, and that's the way it should be."

Court. What a lovely, old-fashioned word.

Mrs. Orion went on, "Dulcie came home with her father looking happy. Thank you for taking her out this morning. Everything seems fine now."

Seems was the key word. I wondered how certain anyone could be of anything. I had *seemed* to have a good marriage, hadn't I?

By the time Paul left the captain's room, I had steadied myself and was waiting for him on the deck, where he came out to join me.

"I like the captain," he told me. "I'm glad I had a chance to meet him."

He didn't kiss me again, but his eyes were warm, appreciating me. I hadn't had that from him in a long while, and I was ready to bask in the return of this old feeling.

We parted until evening, when he would pick me up at seven for dinner. There was still an awkwardness between us. We were two people who hoped we would mean a great deal to each other for a long time to come, but weren't entirely sure of it yet.

When he'd gone, I stood at the railing looking out over the sound. I didn't want to see the captain right away and listen to him talk about Paul—perhaps even give me advice—so I decided to sit on the deck and read.

Just then I noticed that Corey's boat wasn't tied up to the dock where Fergus would have left it. I looked around, curious, and saw it out in the channel, turning in toward Topsail. Corey sat behind the wheel, with Anne Trench beside him. She could only be coming here to see the captain, I realized with amazement, and a new concern held me as I watched Corey pull into the dock.

⟋⟋⟋⟋⟋⟋⟋⟋⟋⟋⟋⟋⟋⟋⟋⟋⟋⟋⟋

22

*C*orey helped her out of the boat, and Anne stood on the dock looking up at the house with grave, searching eyes. It must have been a very long time since she'd seen it. When she found me there on the cantilevered deck, she raised a hand in greeting. However, she didn't move at once toward the house.

Corey was busy lifting something out of the boat, and I saw by the shape of it that it must be a painting. I could guess what it was. Anne must have brought her portrait of Carlina. So perhaps there would be two meetings now—one with Fergus and his "gypsy," and one with the captain. Or at least, so I hoped.

Anne made a picture herself there on the dock, with the water of the sound glinting behind her in the sun. An osprey that had been perched at the end of the dock flew away with a great flapping of wings, and for a moment she stood watching him go. She wore slim gray trousers and a green pullover with a woven yellow pattern. Above the rolled neck her head rose proudly, silver hair hidden under a green scarf. Instead of a handbag she held a small tote.

She spoke to Corey, perhaps instructing him about the painting, for he carried it out of sight into the lower area of the house. Again she looked up at me, but this time she called out, "Wait, please."

Never in anything she'd done in the short time I'd known her had she seemed indecisive, but now I could sense her uncertainty. She had left this house in anger and never returned until now, when the captain was old and sick, which might not please him in the least.

I waited for her at the top of the stairs. Mrs. Orion had seen what was about to happen, and though she'd never met Anne Trench, she knew who she must be. She came to stand beside me, gripping the railing as though she needed it for balance.

"This will upset him," she whispered. "I'd better warn him first."

"No," I said. "Just wait."

Anne came up the stairs briskly and at the top she held out her hand. "You must be Mrs. Orion. I'm Anne Trench. Susan told me about you and

what a great help you've been to the captain.
May I see him now?"

Mrs. Orion was still doubtful. "I'll go and ask,"
she said.

Anne put a hand on her arm. "No, please. He
might refuse to see me. But I think the time has
come to mend old injuries."

Mrs. Orion gave in reluctantly, and Anne
turned to me. "Come with me, Hallie. I don't
want to face him alone."

The hesitance I felt in her was surprising and
somehow touching. That a woman as strong as
Anne Trench could be unsure of herself and vulnerable was somehow reassuring. Vulnerability
was allowed.

When we reached the captain's door, she
stepped back so that I could go in ahead of her. I
had no idea what to say or do. "There's a—a visitor to see you," I managed.

He wheeled around in his chair and stared
past me at the door. She came into the room
with her head still held high, chin up. She'd taken
off her scarf and her beautiful hair was piled on
top of her head as usual. The last time the captain had seen her it would not have been silver.
The word for Anne Trench was *gallant*, I
thought. The captain's amazement was clearly
evident, but whatever she might be feeling, Anne

went to stand close enough to touch him if she wished.

Her voice was soft when she spoke. "It's been a long time, Nicholas. I think we're old enough now to forgive each other. Do you suppose we can do that?"

He had hated to have Carlina see him as he was now, but with Anne it didn't seem to matter. More than a love affair lay between them. Once she had been his wife.

"I was a fool," he said. "Hello, Anne."

She took the hand he held out and bent to kiss his cheek lightly. "So was I. But there wasn't anything else I could do at the time. I was too young and angry. I was beyond reason."

I knew I should go away and leave them alone, but I was mesmerized by the scene unfolding before me.

"I should never have let you go." The captain's voice could still rumble, but now the thunder was subdued. "If I'd gone after you, I might have brought you back."

She shook her head. "By that time it was too late."

"I saw the paintings you left behind. They told me how angry you were, and how much you cared. When I saw them I knew how much I cared, too. Unfortunately, pride was more impor-

tant to me in those days than love. I'm no longer
proud, as you can see. But now we've grown into
strangers."

"Perhaps we can still be friends," she said gently. "May I sit down and visit with you for a little
while?"

I felt tears come into my eyes, and I went
quickly away and left them alone. Anne didn't
need me now. If he had loved two women, his
love for each had been different. Carlina would
have given him bright excitement. She did that
even now. But Anne was gifted with depth,
heart, understanding. Carlina had been a young
man's love. Anne was for the years. So much had
been thrown away by two angry people. That
mustn't happen to Paul and me.

Mrs. Orion was hovering when I came out,
and I nodded reassuringly. "It's all right. They
just need to be alone for a while."

Corey had come upstairs. "What a day! How
are they doing?"

"I think they're becoming friends again," I
told him.

"That's a relief. I worried when she phoned
me to come after her and bring her here. I'm
glad it's going okay. She's given me a job—she
wants me to take the painting she did of Carlina
to Fergus. How about coming with me? This
should be interesting."

I was curious about what Fergus's wife would think of the gypsy Anne had painted, and I went with Corey downstairs to pick up the portrait. I suggested that he phone first, but he didn't think it was necessary.

After we crossed the clearing to the other house, Dulcie met us at the door, with her father close behind.

"Mrs. Trench would like you to have this painting that you admired," Corey explained.

"Come on in," Fergus said, and turned to call his wife. Carlina came at once, with no inkling of what was in store for her.

"Apparently Anne Trench has sent us a gift," Fergus said.

Dulcie knew what was in the package and danced about excitedly. "Open it, Mom!" she cried. "I know what it is, and I know how much you'll like it!"

But Dulcie was wrong. When the wrapping was off and the painting had been propped up where it could be seen, Carlina looked at it for a moment and then burst into tears. Fergus reached for her, but she backed away almost angrily. "I don't look like that anymore!" she cried. "I haven't looked like that for years. She was only mocking me when she painted it. I know how I've changed."

Fergus regarded her in amazement. "Don't be

foolish! We're all what we are now, but we're also what we were then. When I look at you, I can see the gypsy dancing. Don't you know that? But you mean much more to me now than you ever did then. That's why when you think too much about Nicholas, I go a little crazy."

I nudged Corey. "Come along. We'd better get back."

Only Dulcie noticed when we left, and she came after us, happy and talkative. "My mother tells me stuff sometimes—about how old she looks. She thinks my dad only cares about that. So when she pulls away, he thinks she doesn't love him anymore. Hallie, how can grown-ups be so silly?"

Out of the mouths of babes! *I* could learn from Dulcie.

Corey said he'd wait down at the boat until Anne was ready to leave, and Dulcie went with him. When I got back inside, I was just in time to see Anne come out of the captain's room. She stopped to speak to Mrs. Orion and they both looked grave. I waited for her a little apart, and then we went downstairs together.

"I didn't realize how ill he is." She spoke sadly. "I'll come every day for a while. I've brought him two books that I hope he'll read. He doesn't have to take this. There are ways out."

I didn't know what she was talking about.

"I wish someone else was looking after him, instead of Mrs. Orion. Or at least spelling her."

That surprised me. "Mrs. Orion seems devoted to him, and she gives him the best of care. She even protects him from anything that might upset him. Don't you like her?"

"I expect she does a very conscientious job, but she encourages him to be ill. Besides—oh, I wish I knew what's wrong. I get the sense that Mrs. Orion is a very frightened woman. I hope her negative energy isn't something that might hurt Nicholas."

The last thing I would have suspected of Mrs. O was that she might be afraid of something. "Why do you think that?"

We'd reached the dock and were walking toward the boat. She put a hand on my arm, so that we stopped before we reached Corey and Dulcie.

"I'm not sure, but she was uneasy when we spoke—worried. Perhaps you can find out what it is that's frightening her?"

Corey helped Anne into the boat, and Dulcie followed. "I'm going to ride over with Corey," she called up to me. "He'll bring me right back."

The boat roared into life and moved out across the sound, cutting the water into two waves of white foam. Anne had tied the scarf around her head again, her face framed in color.

I watched until the boat disappeared around a jutting of land as it turned toward Cabbage Island.

When I went upstairs Mrs. Orion was waiting for me. I tried to see her with new eyes, but she looked the same as ever to me, and I shrugged off Anne's words.

"How is the captain?" I asked. "I hope that seeing Mrs. Trench was good for him."

"He's gone to sleep, and that's a good sign. It means he's relaxed. He hasn't been sleeping well lately. By the way, you have a visitor, Mrs. Knight."

The way she spoke the words alerted me to her disapproval. I looked into the long living room and saw Brenda waiting for me.

"Don't you like her?" I asked Mrs. Orion.

The housekeeper frowned. "Like or not like isn't up to me. I only know she wasn't good for Susan—or for Corey, either."

She walked off and I went to greet Brenda, surprised to see her so soon after I'd left her house.

"Can we talk?" she said, and cast a look toward the deck where Mrs. Orion was sitting down with her knitting.

I led the way to my room—a room Brenda knew well, since it had been Susan's after her grandmother left.

She didn't sit down, but moved about, as if reacquainting herself with the furnishings. "I'm here because Ryce phoned me, Hallie. He's going to meet me here in a little while." She stopped before Susan's collection of books about crystals, which sat next to the amethyst geode.

"What's up?" I said.

"Ryce wants to talk to his father about Louise, and he wants me there because I knew her in New York."

What Brenda had told me about Louise being in prison had shocked me and left me with questions. "You've told me a little about her, but not enough. What *is* her story?"

Brenda dropped into a chair and stretched widely, as if to delay answering. Then she made up her mind and began to talk.

"Louise has had a pretty bad deal, even though she brought most of it on herself. She fell hard for an actor in New York. He wasn't much good—you don't need to know his name. I'll call him Jack. They had an affair and there was a baby, though they never married. For a little stretch of time I think Louise was completely happy. I saw the baby once—a darling little girl—but she was colicky and cried a lot, and I guess that drove Jack crazy. He'd never wanted a baby in the first place, but when Louise became pregnant, there was no choice—not in those days." Brenda seemed to brace herself before she went on. "Anyway, Louise went out on an errand one day, and when she came back, Jack was gone and the baby was dead. There were marks which meant that he'd either struck her or dropped her. Louise chose to believe it was an accident."

I felt suddenly ill. Brenda shook her head and went on.

"Louise really loved that worthless bum, but if the truth had come out, his career would have been finished, let alone his life. Besides, I think Louise somehow blamed herself. If she had been home, nothing would have happened. So she had to punish herself, and she took the blame and protected him. She was the one to go to prison for what he had done."

I was having a hard time reconciling all this with the Louise I'd come to know.

"Does Ryce know about this?" I asked.

"I don't think Louise would have told him. He's too stiff and proper. I did tell Susan one night when I'd had too much to drink and I've always regretted it. I saw Louise when she was released from prison after a few years. She didn't seem like the same woman who went in—prison had toughened her. She told me she was going back to North Carolina. She didn't have anyone left there, but she was going to marry a rich man and enjoy all the things she'd missed in life. And that's what she did. I wonder if she's been happy?"

I doubted that she had, but for the first time I was sorry for Louise.

Brenda read what I was feeling. "Let it go, Hallie. It's not your problem, but you wanted to know." She touched the purple facets of the amethyst. "There used to be a pair of these. What happened to the other one?"

I hesitated for a moment. Then I went to my suitcase in the closet and lifted out the heavy rock to bring it to Brenda.

"Dulcie had this one in her room. I'm not sure why, but she asked me to keep it for her."

Brenda carried the geode to the window so the facets would catch the light. "It needs to be cleaned. You only need to immerse it in water to clean it, you know." She looked more closely. "And it's been damaged. Three of the central facets are broken or cracked."

I hadn't noticed this in my haste to put it away. Now I went to stand beside Brenda and saw what she meant. The central crystals were dulled, their sharp edges blunted.

"It must have been dropped," Brenda said.

I looked into the amethyst's depths and a thought came into my mind, a thought so disturbing that for a moment I couldn't speak it aloud.

"What is it? What do you see?"

"Could this rock have been used as a weapon?"

She understood. "Do you mean could it have killed Susan?"

"I don't want to think that, but would it have been possible, do you suppose?"

Brenda shook her head. "I doubt it. The rock is too heavy and awkward to use as a weapon." She rubbed a finger over the dull film that marred the surface, but she had nothing more to suggest.

I put the stone away again, closing it into the darkness of my suitcase. I didn't want to think that murder had been connected with so pure a stone as an amethyst. Besides, the ramifications might be too disturbing.

"Why do you suppose Dulcie had it?" Brenda asked.

"I've been waiting for her to tell me, but the very sight of the stone upsets her. She doesn't want to talk about it."

"That seems pretty odd. Maybe you ought to push her a little more and find out. If she knows anything, we'd better learn what it is."

I didn't want to push Dulcie. She had enough problems. If she ever wanted to tell me, I would listen. Besides, I wasn't sure by this time how much I wanted to involve Brenda Wilshire in all of this.

A sudden boom like thunder reverberated through the house, and I felt a tremor under my feet. I looked at Brenda in alarm. "I'm getting spooked! This happened once before when I was holding one of those thunder eggs."

Brenda laughed. "Coincidence. Come on out on the deck."

When we stood at the rail everything was calm. There wasn't a cloud in the sky, and the ground beneath us didn't move.

"Seneca guns." Brenda wrinkled her nose. "Nobody can explain what happens, but it occurs every once in a while up and down the East Coast."

"Sonic booms, perhaps?"

"It can happen when there's no plane activity around. Besides, the phenomenon has been going on for two hundred years. The Seneca Indians were a powerful Iroquois tribe in New York. The Dutch sold them guns, so the story goes that they're still firing them in resentment over what's happened to Indian lands and Indian people. There's even a theory of underwater landslides in the ocean, but no one really knows. None of the seismological stations in North Carolina ever pick anything up." She turned toward the stairs. "Here comes Ryce. By the way, I hope everything's all right between you and Paul, Hallie."

"I'm having dinner with him tonight."

"That's good."

As she left me at the door to my room and started down the stairs to meet Ryce, Corey came down from his upper room, and I caught a look between them. Of affection? Intimacy? It made me wonder. Since I didn't want to see Ryce, I returned to my room and sat down to think about Louise's terrible story. What would a divorce from Ryce do to her now? My instincts told me that Richard Merrick was unlikely to marry again. And Louise, however beautiful, was no longer young.

I touched the amethyst geode and put her out of my thoughts. Seneca guns, Brenda had said. I liked that idea. And the geode was a thunder egg—a gift from the thunder gods. Perhaps it was all tied together. Fantasy, however, couldn't distract me for long. Inevitably my thoughts were pulled back to Paul and what might come of our dining together that night.

For a little while in the tower room we'd seemed close again—as I wanted to be. I wished that old warnings planted when I was young could be dislodged, dismissed. I didn't want to distrust him.

23

⟨ornamental divider⟩

Paul had made a reservation and we were graciously welcomed at the Soundside. The big dining room had a verdant feeling about it, with plants and flowers everywhere. Woodsy green tablecloths and bright green napkins made every table part of a garden. A row of windows along one side of the room offered a view of the bridge and the sound, with low-tide sandbars striping the water.

When we'd been seated beside a window, I could look across a narrow porch and watch the sky glow pink with sunset. After we'd ordered our seafood dinner, I found myself shy and tongue-tied. I was behaving like a young girl on her first date. Perhaps Paul felt something of the same restraint, for at first we didn't look directly at each other. Not that I needed to look again to appreciate how well his tan jacket and brown turtleneck sweater suited him. And I knew very well how I looked—I'd stood in front of the mirror in my room long enough, arranging the draped neck of my delphinium blue dress. My hair shone with brushing, and jonquil earrings added a touch of spring.

"Fill me in some more about Susan's disappearance and the whole situation, Hallie," he said.

This subject was safe, and I told him some of the bits and pieces that I'd learned since arriving on Topsail Island. As we talked, the awkwardness fell away. It seemed right to be here, recounting everything that had happened. Or almost everything. I didn't want to talk about how—in only a few days—I had seemed to lose all that was most important to me. Perhaps now we might earn it back. But I had to step cautiously.

My account was disconnected, but at least it gave him something of the picture. He was especially interested in Louise and what Brenda had said about her being in prison. All the tricky intertwinings of emotion and drive in these people fascinated him. Life and movie scripts weren't really so far apart, and his interest made me uneasy. I finished by telling him the frightening story of the Pirate's Pit and what Corey believed. That shocked him and he lost himself in thinking about what I'd told him.

For the first time since I'd sat down, I began to look around at the other diners. I saw Corey, very proper in his role as a waiter. When he caught my eye he winked. But it was the couple he waited on who drew my attention.

"Don't look now," I cautioned Paul, "but Louise is here having dinner with Richard Merrick."

When you tell people not to look, they usually do anyway. Paul turned his head in time to catch Richard's eye, and the two men exchanged nods of recognition.

"You sound as if you don't approve," Paul said, turning back to me.

By this time I wasn't sure exactly how I felt about Louise. Until now I'd glimpsed only the woman she had turned herself into, but knowing her story, I felt more generous.

"Louise dabbles in real estate, and Richard Merrick is her lawyer. But the fact that he also handles the captain's will makes me uneasy, especially since those two seem attracted to each other. I guess my sympathies are still more with Ryce than with Louise."

"Where do you think Merrick stands?"

"I'm not sure. There can't be much of an advantage for him in getting involved with Ryce's wife."

"She's very beautiful," Paul said.

I bit my tongue, refraining from the wrong remark, and set down my fork carefully before I spoke. "I keep going round and round in my head about all these people and their connections with Susan. Who could possibly have wanted to harm her? I know she could be maddening, and she could fly into a terrible temper when she was crossed, but still..." I had nowhere to go with this.

"I'd like to meet some of your new friends," Paul said. The familiar crease showed between his eyes—a sign that he was puzzling about something.

Suddenly I felt ridiculously happy. Paul was here. He *wanted* to be here with me. And now he would help me sort everything out. This was the way we used to be.

"When we leave here, will you show me this Pirate's Pit you were talking about?" he asked.

Though I didn't want to go near that place again, I agreed.

Our meal had been delicious, and now we were indulging ourselves with the cheesecake we both loved. When Louise and Merrick rose to leave and came past our table, they stopped. Paul rose and Richard made the introductions. I saw Louise's eyes rest on Paul and linger. At once I was on guard in a new way that I'd never experienced before, and I gave myself an inward shake. Paul was an attractive man and his life had always been filled with beautiful women. I needed to regain the confidence I used to have about myself, and about a relationship that no outsider could touch. Only it *had* been touched, and how was I to live from now on with my knowledge of that?

"You must bring your husband over to see us while he's here, Hallie," Louise said, still looking at Paul as she spoke. I glanced at Richard Merrick and caught him watching me with a slight smile. It was a sympathetic look, and somehow reassuring. As though he were saying, *We both know Louise and what she's like. Don't worry. Your husband knows, too.*

As they left the dining room, I looked after them and for a moment I couldn't look at Paul.

"I feel sorry for her," he said. "She's fighting for her life. I expect she's done that for a good many years, and now she's afraid that everything, including the money, is slipping away. You don't want it, but the captain seems determined to give it to someone outside the family. If Ryce should decide that he can't put up with Louise anymore, what would happen to her? I suppose Richard is a straw she's reaching for."

I regarded my husband with love and admiration—and confusion. The confusion was for me. He had always been generous and uncritical, and he was seeing Louise as I would have liked to see her—with generosity.

He held out a hand to me across the table. "Thanks for coming out with me, Hallie. I'm beginning to have a good feeling about *us*." The spell held for just a moment. Then it was he who let it go.

"Perhaps we can pay the Pirate's Pit a visit now."

I took back my hand that he'd been holding. "This isn't a script, Paul."

For an instant I'd startled him. Then he nodded. "That's why I want to meet the rest of the people you've told me about. So they'll be real for me. Then perhaps I can bring some fresh insight to what's been happening. A visit to the pit is part of the reality."

He pushed back his chair, but I didn't move. While we were here in a public place, I knew I must set my foot into dangerous currents.

"Anne Trench advised me not to go back to you. She thinks men never change."

His eyes turned cool, critical again. He could be critical of me, but not of Louise, and I resented that. But then a guardian voice whispered in my mind, *That's because he cares about you.* I agreed with the voice and relaxed a little. We were critical of those we loved because we expected perfection. Foolish but human.

I smiled, surprising him. He picked up the words I'd quoted from Anne Trench. "What you do with your life and what I do with mine is up to us."

More than anything I longed to be with Paul—to walk out of this room with him and into his arms. I wanted to shut out every niggling thought that might keep me from doing that. But even as I smiled at him, I also knew that we could never pick up again exactly where we'd left off. Something more solid needed time to evolve between us. Neither of us knew with certainty how to cross the space that had widened between us, and it was safer to wait.

I thought again of Anne's advice and said, "Perhaps it helps to listen to people like Anne Trench who have been there before us. Even if we don't follow their course. As I hope we won't."

He didn't answer as we rose to leave the restaurant. At the front desk he stopped to compliment the owner of the Soundside, and I knew she was pleased. I remembered how well he did such things, not in any calculated way, but because it was natural to him to appreciate the efforts of others. Paul had always fit in anywhere and been able to talk to anyone. As I watched him with the owner, I could sense part of the answer. He was a gentle man. He never alarmed anyone. He had never liked confrontations—which was what I had tried to force him into. But didn't we all need to take a stand sometime?

As I went outside with him, new confusion began to stir in me. Would I ever be able to see him through that haze of loving admiration that I once had?

The area around the restaurant was given over to businesses and was brightly lighted. We drove south along a darker central road and Paul opened the car windows to let in breezes from the sea. I breathed deeply and tried to think of nothing except the fact that I was with my husband—where I wanted to be.

Nevertheless, when we turned down the side road that led between the stunted, intertwined trees of the maritime forest, I began to dread what we were about to do.

"You can't possibly see anything at night," I warned him.

"I have a flashlight. Besides, it's not just seeing a hole in the ground—it's a lot more."

I didn't know what he meant, but I held back any further objection.

He left the car on the road and we got out to walk past the captain's house, where lights burned upstairs, and I heard the sound of voices. The clearing was dimly lighted by the standard over near the Cameron house, and the Pirate's Pit was lost in deep shadow.

Suppressing my dread, I led the way toward where the wire fence circled the black emptiness in the ground. I wasn't sure what Paul wanted, but I had to go along.

Vines and shrubbery had almost enveloped the sandy earth, and the green tangle showed as Paul played his flashlight around the area.

He pushed his way into the growth nearest the fence, lifting strands of vines with his free hand. We could look up at a space visible between crowding tree branches and glimpse a moonlit sky. When Paul tipped his head back, I could see his face, grave and absorbed.

As he spoke, his voice was low. "This could very well be where it happened."

"How can you say that?" I whispered.

"It's as if there's a haunting in this place. Something terrible has left a stain. Some places can become marked ground, you know."

This was what Corey—and perhaps Dulcie, too—had felt. I didn't want to believe. "What good does it do, even if you think that? How can it lead us to an answer?"

"I don't expect it to. I just wanted to get a sense of the place."

Dulcie must have been watching us from

nearby, for she came over to stand beside us. "That's where I found it," she said. "Right over there."

Paul had no idea what she meant, but quite suddenly I knew. "How did you find it, Dulcie?"

"I saw the purple color shining under the moon. The stones almost winked at me. So I crawled past the vines on the edge of the pit, and it was just lodged there—the rock with the amethyst. I think somebody must have tried to throw it down the hole. Whoever it was didn't see that it hadn't fallen in. It was just stuck there. So I got it out and took it up to my room. I didn't know what it meant, but I was scared, so I hid it in my chest and never showed it to anyone until I gave it to you, Hallie."

"What are you talking about?" Paul asked.

Dulcie suddenly looked frightened and she didn't stay to explain. She ran off toward the house, and I heard a screen door slam.

"Come upstairs," I said to Paul, "and I'll show you what she means."

We went through the open space under the captain's house, then headed upstairs. I was glad to meet no one on the way to my room.

"This was Anne's room originally," I said, turning on a light. "After her grandmother left, Susan began to use it. Mrs. Orion has given it to me. The main bedrooms are upstairs."

He stood looking around as I had done the first time I'd stepped into this room. I knew he noticed the wide bed with its two pillows, but his eyes moved from it quickly. There were no madly colored paintings to hold his attention, and for the first time I saw how bare the walls were. Not that it mattered—I wouldn't be here much longer. The pageant at the Assembly Building was two days ahead, and I had promised to stay for it, but after that I couldn't be sure of anything. Even though I'd enjoyed our dinner together tonight, all the questions about Paul remained. My moments of acceptance that had seemed like clarity were fading.

I went to the bookcase and showed him the amethyst geode. Then I took its twin from my suitcase. He turned the second amethyst cluster around in his hands and saw the damaged facets.

I sat down on the edge of a chair. "This is what Dulcie found caught on the lip of that hole out there. I wondered if it might have been used as a weapon against Susan, but that doesn't seem possible. It would be so heavy and clumsy."

"Yes." He weighed the stone doubtfully in his hands. "There must be something here that we're missing. Have you any suspicion at all?"

I shook my head. "I've gone round and round hopelessly. Corey is convinced that Susan's body went down the pit. But it's only a feeling—the same as yours. If she'd been pushed, she would surely have screamed. But no one heard anything."

"The more I find out, the more questions there are. I'd still like to meet the other actors in this tragedy."

"Perhaps you can. Tomorrow morning there's a dress rehearsal of the pageant at the Assembly Building. I don't think anyone would mind if you came to watch. At least you could meet Carlina. And I'm sure others will be there."

"I'd like to come," Paul said. "Brenda said she was going to attend, so maybe I can come with her. She'll know everyone." He gave the amethyst back to me and picked up its twin from the bookcase, while I returned the damaged geode to its hiding place. Paul was ready to leave.

"Thank you for tonight, Hallie," he said, his tone gentle and affectionate, but he made no move to touch me. We were still uncertain about each other, and I wondered again if the trust we'd once had could ever be recovered.

I thanked him for dinner and knew that I sounded stiff. He said he could find his way out, and I let him leave alone.

When he'd gone I stood for a while staring absently at the too-wide bed I was beginning to hate.

24

The next morning, when I went out on the deck for breakfast, I found Mrs. Orion bustling about, directing both Corey and the captain. She didn't look pleased, and I gathered quickly that she disapproved of a plan the captain had suggested.

It seemed the whole household was going to the Assembly Building to watch the rehearsal. Carlina had suggested it to the captain on the phone, and apparently he'd thought the idea entertaining. He was already up and dressed, and seemed more cheerful than at any time since I'd arrived. Anne's doing, perhaps. Corey was managing his wheelchair.

"We need to be there early if we're to find a good place for the captain to watch," Mrs. Orion said. "If we pick a spot near an exit, he can leave quietly before he begins to tire."

Corey rolled his eyes at me, but the captain's good humor held, and he accepted Mrs. Orion's bossing without objection.

After they'd left, I finished my breakfast and then set off at my own pace. This event wasn't something I needed to show up for at any special time, and I needn't stay longer than I wished. My mood swings of yesterday had settled into something that resembled steady gloom and discouragement. There had been good moments the night before with Paul, but I didn't know what would happen when we returned to California. The thought of Susan deepened my depression, and I had less belief than ever that any answers would be found.

The only thing that lifted my spirits a little was the prospect of seeing Paul that morning if he came to the Assembly Building with Brenda. No matter that nothing was settled in my mind—I would see him. And perhaps when I did I would know how I truly felt.

Mrs. O had said I might use her car again, since they were taking the captain's van, which accommodated his wheelchair. I made the short drive slowly. When I arrived mothers were busy fussing with their children's costumes. There were shrill admonishments not to get dirty, since all this would be repeated the following night for real.

Carlina was very much in charge. She had on jeans and an oversized shirt, and her hair was tied back with a flowered scarf. She looked both excited and worried. Fergus wasn't there, and perhaps that made it easier for her.

Corey had found a corner where the captain would be out of the way in his chair and could see what was happening without being jostled. I discovered Paul at once, and we smiled at each other across the room. I'd hoped that seeing him would clarify something, but I knew even less than I had the day before. He had been commandeered into arranging chairs before the platform and he kept busy at his task. Brenda was bustling about making herself useful, and she waved to me cheerfully.

The most delightful sight was Dulcie, who looked beautiful in a white, gold-spangled tutu, with a wreath of white roses around her head, contrasting nicely with her red hair. When I discovered her, she was sitting cross-legged on the saddle of her remarkable horse. He was, by necessity, a fairly large animal, because he needed to hold the oblong wooden platform on which Dulcie was to do her little dance.

I went over to admire the imaginative creature. His wicked black eyes gave him the look of being about to bolt, and his lush mane, made of green plastic curls, fell over the side of his neck.

His large body was dappled in patches of green and white, and his mouth had been painted lipstick red, with the lips drawn back to show a fierce set of papier-mâché teeth.

"He's really something," I told Dulcie, and she nodded proudly.

"Maximilian's not made of paper, you know. There's a wooden form underneath, so he's strong enough to hold me."

Some small, out-of-control Indians were chasing one another across the stage, before being herded together by a teacher under Carlina's direction. The theme of the pageant was the history of Topsail Island, so Indians were a necessity. Even the towers were represented. Two cardboard forms hid small boys whose eyes peered out the top windows. The towers kept running about—completely out of character.

Several people who knew the captain had gathered around his chair. Even Ryce was there, though I didn't see Louise, who was supposed to sing. Mrs. Orion seemed tense and nervous, and she reluctantly gave up the captain's guardianship to his son, while she went off to rest her feet.

As soon as she could escape Carlina's supervision, Brenda came over to me. "Hi, Hallie. Let's get Corey and Paul and go outside for a few minutes. I want to show you something."

We waved Paul over, and as soon as Corey could get away, the four of us went outside. I still felt a little spacey being near Paul—as though part of me was a young girl falling in love all over again. I had no idea how he felt. He was fitting himself to the occasion lightheartedly, as he always did.

The spark that Brenda could generate was back in her eyes, and she looked mysterious. Corey watched her with obvious delight.

"Of course, we have to swear you and Paul to secrecy, Hallie," she warned. "At least a blood oath!"

"We'll promise to keep our lips zipped," Paul said, falling into the spirit of whatever she was about, and we all laughed.

We went down the central steps of the porch that fronted the wide building, and Corey stood for a moment looking up with satisfaction at the large sign that faced the road.

ASSEMBLY BUILDING
Topsail Island Community Center

"I get a good feeling when I look at that sign," he said. "Better an assembly building for people than for missiles."

Brenda paid no attention. She had scurried around the front corner where low, thick bushes grew, and when a car pulled up to let out more visitors for the rehearsal, she pretended an interest in some distant spot.

Corey grinned at us. "She's never grown up, and I hope she never will."

We joined Brenda and she reached back to pull me into the narrow space behind a screen of bushes. Paul came close behind with Corey, and we watched as Brenda pulled at a board that blocked our way. It creaked open under her hand, forming an opening into a long, dark, descending alleyway.

This must be the childhood hiding place where Brenda, Susan, and Corey had held their secret meetings. Corey produced a flashlight and its beam showed a cramped passageway whose ceiling just grazed our heads. There were cobwebs that Brenda brushed aside casually before hurrying on to another door, which opened into a larger space. She touched an electric switch, but no lights came on, and Corey played his torch beam around the room.

"We're under that hollow place in the floor up there," Brenda said. "Susan found this place a long time ago. I suppose the grown-ups knew, but they let us alone."

Under the roving beam I could see that furnishings had been brought in—a rickety table, a couch, and two dilapidated chairs. Mice, or even something larger, had been at work, and what remained of fabric and upholstery had been finished off by moths. A heap of cushions lay in shadow on the low couch.

Brenda shook her head sadly. "We had it fixed up so beautifully. We painted everything, and we brought swatches of colored cloth to brighten things up. What meetings we used to have! Susan always ran them because she liked to be in charge. Corey and I let her do as she pleased and be what she pleased—queen or empress or president. Whatever."

Corey picked up an old notebook covered with dust and flipped pages under the light. "Susan's writing," he said. "She used to keep minutes until the idea began to bore her."

Paul was poking around, looking into corners. There was something disturbing about this place and I wondered if he felt it, too.

Brenda ran on, sounding sad. "I thought it might be fun to go back, but it's only depressing—a lot of junk. We were so young in those days. I've had enough. Let's go."

She started toward the door, but Paul stopped her. "Wait a minute. Corey, let's have your light."

As he ran the flashlight beam along the couch, we all stood watching, transfixed. What we'd thought was a heap of cushions was a woman who lay stretched out on the couch, facedown. A woman's body. Corey moved gingerly to turn her over and Paul played the light on her face. Louise's eyes were closed and she looked white as death.

Paul bent over, putting his fingers to her throat. "She's alive. We need a doctor or a nurse."

"Go get my mother, Hallie," Corey said. "And somebody call an ambulance. Better find Ryce. I saw him upstairs with the captain. We'll stay here."

I bent over Louise and spoke her name, but her eyes didn't open and she didn't make a sound or move.

"Hurry!" Corey said.

I found my way back upstairs and met Mrs. Orion at the front door. She came down with me, and the sight of Louise sent her into a state of trembling that surprised me. She did what little she could with hands that shook, and said nothing at all.

When the ambulance arrived, Corey guided the men into the dusty room with their stretcher. Ryce had been found and he was visibly shaken. He traveled to the hospital with his wife in the ambulance.

Brenda looked as upset as Mrs. Orion had,

and she refused to stay for the rest of the rehearsal, preferring to wait outside on the steps in the sunshine. Paul and Corey and I followed his mother back to the captain's chair.

"Don't say anything to anyone," Corey warned us. "Let the rehearsal go on, and don't upset the captain."

Mrs. Orion looked as though she was not about to speak at all, and when the captain said something to her sharply, she didn't seem to hear him.

I still felt shocked, but now I was occupied with the question of what Louise had been doing in that place. I had no answer, but the question would keep on nagging at me for the next few days.

Upset as I was, I held on to one handle of the wheelchair for support and simply watched as the rehearsal continued.

We were in time to see Dulcie perform the little dance she'd shown me. She proved to be her mother's daughter and a born performer. I will always remember the picture she made—a red-haired little girl in a white tutu moving gracefully on the green-and-white make-believe horse she had named Maximilian.

Carlina knew something was wrong, but she didn't learn the details until the rehearsal was over. She was as disturbed as the rest of us, but mostly anxious to get Dulcie away before she could hear what had happened.

When he'd assured himself that I was all right, Paul left with Brenda. The captain had tired, so Mrs. Orion and Corey took him back to the house in the van. I followed in the car I'd borrowed from Mrs. Orion. When I arrived at the house, I found that Corey had told the captain what had happened. He'd gone even further and given him Louise's whole story, which Brenda had revealed years ago but he'd kept secret until now.

I wished Corey had been more discreet. The captain was more disturbed about Louise's past than about what had happened to her in the present. Mrs. Orion seemed to have collected herself, and she shooed everyone out of the captain's room so she could get him some quiet. I found myself watching her and wondering what it was that had upset her so badly. What did *she* know about Louise?

Later in the day I was sent in to read to the captain, and I was there when Anne arrived. By now Corey—whatever his motives—had told her everything, too, so no one needed to explain. When I got up to leave, the captain stopped me.

"No, I want you to stay and listen," he ordered, his indignation spilling over as he turned to Anne. "Ryce will have to divorce her now. He'll be well out of a marriage that was a mistake in the first place."

I hoped that Anne would have more sympathy for Louise than the captain did.

She answered him quietly. "If she recovers, that's going to be up to Ryce, isn't it?"

"He'll do what I say! It's time to get rid of that woman."

"I can't say I like her either, but let's wait and see what happens."

At least Anne and the captain were referring to themselves as *us* and *we* again.

When he had calmed down, Anne reached for one of two books on his night table.

"I hope you've had time to look into these, Nicholas," she said.

A gleam came into his eyes. I'm reading that top one—it's pretty arresting."

"I thought you'd think so. By the way, Nicholas, there's a doctor in Wilmington who I'd like to bring to see you."

"I've had enough of doctors! These days they only tell me when I'm going to die—and they've been wrong so far."

She gave him a smile that lighted her face and was reflected in his. "This one may show you a way to live. You've already got what it takes. It's the feisty ones who get well—not the passive ones who give up too easily."

I knew how quickly he'd have dismissed such remarks from most people. But he seemed ready to listen to Anne.

⁊⁌

In the days following, the captain grew visibly stronger, and we could all see the way he looked forward to Anne's visits. None of us went to the pageant, though word came afterward that it had gone very well. The only casualty was a small Indian who fell off the platform and received assorted black-and-blue marks for the tumble. A good sum of money had been raised to further the preservation of the Assembly Building and to support plans for a museum the Historical Society was going to build in its vast spaces.

For the moment, matters between Paul and me were at a standstill. A wariness had grown between us that neither one seemed willing or able to break through. Yet neither of us made a move to return to California.

Louise was still in the hospital recovering from what proved to have been a mild stroke. We still had no idea what she'd been doing in that room, or what had caused her collapse. Ryce spent a good deal of time with her, and I wondered if she was enjoying his attention. Richard Merrick was away and removed from all that had happened.

Corey seemed more worried about his mother than about anything else. "She's got something on her mind," he told me, "but she won't talk about it. She scares me sometimes, since I've never seen her like this. Once, when I questioned her, she just said trouble was coming."

A quiet standoff existed between Ryce and his father for several days and then one afternoon the friction between them came to a head.

It began when I had stopped in to see the captain and found him in bed, with Mrs. Orion standing on one side and Anne on the other.

"I don't need you now," he snapped at Mrs. Orion, and she went away, affronted. Then he told Anne and me in the same voice, "For God's sake, sit down." We sat and he lay quietly for a moment, seemingly exhausted by his outburst. Then he drew in a deep breath, opened his eyes, and began to speak more quietly.

"When I was a small boy, I lived in a world of giants who ordered my life and told me what I could and could not do. Now I'm an old man, and I lie in this bed and look up at more giants, vigorous with life. They tower over me and make me feel the same way—helpless."

Anne reached for his hand. "Not me," she said softly. "I'm only a pygmy, my dear."

He didn't withdraw his hand. "Why did you go away?"

"You know the answer very well."

"It takes so long to learn," he said, his eyes fixed on Anne's face. "Sometimes I think I'm only beginning now."

I kept very still, lest I interrupt the stirring of emotion that was surfacing between these two.

He went on in the same low voice. "When it's too late, maybe that's when we learn that there was a better way."

"Perhaps it's never too late. In the end I suppose we grow and change, or we deteriorate. I'm still trying to grow."

"I wonder if there's any time left for me?"

She spoke with a loving gentleness. "Of course there is, if you make it so. All we have is *now*—if only we can use it."

He sighed deeply and I could see his hand tighten around Anne's.

Just then Ryce came into the room and stood looking down at his mother and father. Another giant, and an angry one. When he spoke I could hear a cold, biting fury in his voice. Finally it was out.

"Louise has told me everything that happened to her when she was young." His eyes moved from one to the other of his parents, and there was no forgiveness in him. "I'm taking her home to Gulls Cove soon, so she can rest and recover."

The captain's face had darkened. "I've heard her story, too, and she's not someone we want in our family. You should divorce her, *now*."

The top heat of Ryce's anger was suppressed beneath ice. "I'm not going to divorce her. She needs me, and I need her. That's something neither of you will ever understand."

I saw Anne's stricken look and knew that she understood very well. Perhaps no one had ever needed Ryce before—not his mother, or his father, or his daughter. All of them had been too preoccupied with their own affairs.

For once the captain was silenced, staring at his son.

Anne bent toward him. "He's right, you know, Nicholas. We both have a lot to make up for."

I slipped out of the room, leaving the three of them to work this out alone. One thing I recognized, with a lift of my own spirits: The captain was not as sick as he had been. He was not merely rebelling against a disease—which he had been doing—but, with Anne at his side, he might really insist on living.

25

⟲───────⟳

U nexpectedly, I went to visit Louise in the hospital before Ryce took her home. I had no wish to see her, but since she'd asked for me, I agreed to go and Ryce drove me in. When we got to her room, she told him she wanted to see me alone, and he kissed her and went away.

She sat in a chair by the window. Her hair, darkening a little at the roots, had been twisted into a severe braid that hung over one shoulder. Her expensive dressing gown belonged to the Louise I'd known before, but nothing else about her resembled the model she'd once been. The only remaining sign of her stroke was a slight hesitation in the movements of her left hand.

Aside from when she greeted me, her tone was absent, as though she spoke more to herself than to me.

"I'm beginning to realize the sort of man my husband is," she said. "He's been here every day. He doesn't mind how I look—he *cares* about *me*." Her voice broke. "I know Nicholas will want him to divorce me because of what happened in the past, but Ryce accepts me as I am now." Her smile twisted wryly. "I wonder if I'm falling in love."

"Why did you want to see me, Louise?" I asked gently.

When she spoke again she seemed like a mixture of two women—the loving one Brenda had known long ago, and the hard, grasping woman she had become. Perhaps she wasn't sure herself which one governed her actions now.

She motioned me to a chair beside hers. "Ryce tells me you'll be leaving Topsail soon."

"I expect so," I said.

"Have you given up the quest the captain brought you here for?"

"Quest?"

"To find out what happened to Susan."

This startled me, so I waited in silence to see where the subject would take her.

She was quiet for a moment and when she spoke her voice was low. "I can tell you who killed her. I've always known, but I've never told anyone."

There was nothing I could do but wait as I

held on to the arms of my chair. She looked almost pleased at the effect she had made.

"It was Mrs. Orion who killed her."

I found that hard to believe, even though Mrs. O had been behaving strangely in the last few days.

I managed to find words. "But why—? What happened?"

"You needn't know the details. You won't want to pursue this. Think what it would do to the captain. He depends on Mrs. Orion more than on anyone else. What would be the use in exposing her? In bringing a woman her age to justice?"

"It matters a great deal to the captain."

Her tone turned sharp. "That can't be helped."

I tried another approach. "Why were you in that room under the Assembly Building? What caused you to have a stroke?"

She didn't want to tell me. To my surprise, she left her chair and walked about the room. "See! I'm quite strong again! Ryce will take me home soon."

"Tell me," I said.

The look she gave me was suddenly helpless, and I knew she couldn't stand up to pressure. She returned to her chair and began to speak slowly.

"All right—I'll tell you this much. Mrs. Orion wanted to talk to me privately. I thought I could frighten her if I got her down to that room where the children used to play. She hates that place."

"Why did you want to frighten her?"

"That doesn't matter now."

"So what happened?"

"She threatened me." Louise's voice rose. "She actually threatened *me.*"

I tried to calm her. "Perhaps you'd better not talk now. I'll call Ryce."

Her right hand reached out and clasped mine tightly. "I'm all right. Don't go."

I tried another question. "How did she threaten you?"

"She said it was time for the captain to know what had happened. I couldn't allow that. Not on top of everything else. I told her that if she opened this up with the captain, I would tell him the truth about her—that *she* had killed Susan. She was furious with me. We were both pretty excited; I have a blood pressure problem—and I got too angry. That's the last I remember until I woke up here."

"Mrs. Orion—a nurse—went away and left you there?" This I couldn't understand. It didn't seem in character.

"That's what she must have done. But if you talk to her, she will twist everything to protect herself. She may do this even if you don't say anything. That's why I wanted you to be warned and on your guard."

"Have you told Ryce?"

This alarmed her. "Oh, no! I couldn't do that. If he were to believe Mrs. Orion's lies, he might easily blame me for his daughter's death. I'm much too vulnerable because of what has already happened to me in the past."

"Brenda told me some of your story."

"She would!"

"I think she admired you. You've given up enough. Ryce will understand whatever you may tell him now."

"I can't risk it. He could forgive me a great deal. But not this."

"What do you mean? You said Mrs. Orion killed Susan. Though I still find that hard to believe."

Louise put her face in her hands. "It's more complicated than you can possibly guess. But I don't see what I can do if Mrs. Orion tells him her lies about what happened. That's what they will be—lies!"

Neither of us had heard Ryce when he came to the door. "What lies? What are you talking about?"

Louise began to cry softly, helplessly.

"You've upset her," he said to me. "Whatever

it is, Louise, we'll take care of it. Don't you worry. Mrs. Knight, I'd better take you back to the captain's now."

I went with him quickly, feeling more bewildered than ever.

He dropped me off at the house, but wouldn't come in. When I went upstairs Dulcie came running to meet me.

"Miss Anne left, in the boat," she informed me, "and Mrs. Orion and Corey went, too."

"Leaving the captain alone?" I asked.

"Mrs. O said I should look in on him once in a while and see if he needs anything. She said they'd be back soon. But I don't know what it's all about and I'm scared."

I tried to reassure her. "Everything is probably fine. I'll stop in to see the captain."

She accepted that and seemed glad to escape. When I went into his room, the captain was in a peevish mood over being "abandoned." I gave him a censored version of my visit to the hospital, but he didn't want to hear about Louise; he wanted Mrs. Orion, and on the double. When I told him that she and Anne Trench had gone off together, and suggested that I stay with him, he grumbled that he didn't want a baby-sitter. So I went outdoors to where Dulcie sat in the swing, pushing herself lazily with one foot.

I decided this was a good time to find out

more about the geode she had found on the edge of the Pirate's Pit. She stopped the swing when I reached her.

"Dulcie," I said, "I wonder if there's something more you can tell me about what happened with the geode you found. If you don't tell me the rest, the wrong person might be blamed for what happened to Susan." This was reaching, but I had to try.

Tears weren't far away, but this time Dulcie didn't run from me. She clearly needed to talk to someone, and I drew her into the shade under the captain's house, where there was a wide, comfortable bench and we could sit together.

"Can you tell me about it now?" I asked gently.

Her need to confide was stronger than her reluctance, and she began to speak rapidly. "I couldn't really see much outside that night—it was too dark. But I think my mother was there."

"With Susan?"

"I don't know. I had a feeling there were two people." She paused and then rushed on. "Susan and Mom were already mad at each other and I know they'd had a fight. I guess Susan loved her grandmother so much that she couldn't stand the captain's liking my mother. One time I heard Susan tell her what she would do if Mom didn't stay away from him. Mom can get pretty mad sometimes, too, so when I heard them shouting at each other, I went away from the house, and I didn't go back until everything was quiet again."

Dulcie stopped, not wanting to go on.

"I can't help if you don't tell me," I said.

She took a deep breath and plunged ahead. "When I saw someone down at the pit that night, I thought it was my mother. I waited before I went down. That's when I found the geode. But I didn't think about what might have happened until it turned out that Susan was missing. The geode had been in her room, so I began to think that my mother had—had—But it's not true, is it?"

She began to cry and I put my arm around her. "No, I don't think it's true at all."

After what Louise had said, I didn't believe that Carlina had gone down to the pit that night.

"I don't think you have anything to worry about," I assured her. "I'm glad that everything seems to be fine with your father and mother, and that Anne is coming to see the captain. I want to find out what really happened to Susan if I can."

She sniffled, and when I gave her a tissue, she wiped her eyes and blew her nose. "I'm okay now, Hallie. I'm glad you're here."

She ran back to the tree and began to swing more vigorously now, and I went upstairs and looked in on the captain, to find him sleeping. As I started across to my room, the phone rang and I answered it. An official from the hospital was on the line, asking for Ryce. She hadn't been able to reach him at home.

"It's urgent that I talk to him," she said.

"He's not here, and I have no idea where he might be," I said. "Is there anything I can do?"

"Mrs. Trench has dressed herself and left the hospital without telling anyone. We must let her husband know."

"If I hear from him, I'll have him call you," I said.

I hung up feeling thoroughly upset. Louise had shown another side when I visited her, but the harder self was still in control, and her running away seemed frightening. Nothing else could be done for the moment so far as Ryce was concerned, but things seemed to be getting out of hand, and suddenly I knew what *I* must do.

I phoned Mrs. Varidy and asked to speak to Paul. When I heard his voice on the line, I kept everything simple. "I need you," I said.

"I'll be there in a few minutes," he told me and hung up.

I waited for him at the top of the stairs, and when he arrived in the promised few minutes, we went to sit on the wide deck overlooking the sound. The spring sunshine was mild and pleasant, the air invigorating. Or perhaps it was just that Paul was with me—that he had come at once when I called him.

I described my visit to the hospital, the talk with Louise, and repeated what she had said about Mrs. Orion. "Both Corey and his mother have disappeared, too, so the captain is alone, except for Dulcie and me. It's as though something terrible is happening just out of sight. Or about to happen, and I don't know what to do."

"There's nothing we can do but wait," he said, and took my hand to hold it gently. "As soon as there's been some unraveling here, though, Hallie, I think we should go home. Together—if you're willing."

I was ready and willing. "I'm not sure what you want for us, Paul. Or even what I want for myself. Except to be with you."

"Perhaps what we both want is for everything to be the way it used to be. But I don't think we can ever go back. Do you suppose we might figure out something for the future if we try?"

"I want that, too," I said. A melting seemed to start inside me—a thawing, a release that let old anger flow away. Perhaps Paul and I could avoid what had happened to Nicholas and Anne Trench so long ago.

"We used to have something important in our

marriage," he said. "Marriages often break up because the couple that married in all that first excitement finds that they don't really have much in common. That wasn't the case with us."

What he said was true. We'd both been interested in so many of the same things. We were friends soon after we met and best friends when we married. And that needn't be lost. A new hope stirred in me.

We had been so focused on each other that we failed to notice the sound of a boat approaching until it drew in below the captain's house. It was Corey, with Anne Trench and Mrs. Orion.

We watched as he got out of the boat and helped the two women onto the dock. Anne looked up and waved, and in moments they had joined us up on the deck.

Mrs. Orion spoke first. She looked pale, and perhaps a little guilty. "Is the captain all right, Mrs. Knight? I needed to leave quickly. Corey was just about to cast off, and Mrs. Trench was in the boat, so I went with them."

"He's fine," I said. "I came home from the hospital a little while ago. When I looked in just now, he was asleep."

Mrs. Orion started toward his room, but Anne stopped her. "Wait until you're calmer. You'll only alarm him now. Everything will work itself out if you'll give it time. You were right to come and talk to me. When it's possible, we'll go and see Louise together."

"When it's possible," I said. "She's left the hospital and no one knows where she's gone. The hospital hasn't been able to locate Ryce."

Mrs. Orion was visibly alarmed by this news. "I don't trust her. She tricked me into going down to that room under the Assembly Building."

"She told me you were there with her," I said, "but she wouldn't tell me what happened."

"That's just as well. I don't know what her version might be, but everyone's got to know the whole story. I told Louise that myself, but she got terribly upset. I shouldn't have left her down there after she collapsed, but I was afraid I'd be blamed and I ran."

I had never seen Mrs. Orion so close to going to pieces, but she sat down, pulled herself together, and went on.

"Please believe me when I tell you that I came to my senses. I *am* a nurse, after all. I was returning to take care of her when you came looking for me, Mrs. Knight. Afterwards, when Louise was taken to the hospital, I didn't know what to do. Until I went to see you, Mrs. Trench, I was still too confused to act. Now I know that everything must be told, no matter what happens to Louise and me."

Mrs. Orion closed her eyes and leaned back in her chair. Corey put his hand on her shoulder. "Hang on, Ma. Nothing's going to happen to you."

I had to say what I did, though I spoke very softly. "Mrs. Orion, did you kill Susan?"

Her eyes flew open and she stared at me—a look that was sad and hopeless. "I didn't kill her, but I helped Louise to conceal what happened. I couldn't stand up to her when she was so desperate."

"You've told me the story," Anne said, "and I believe you've told me the truth. There's nothing Louise can do without hurting herself."

Before Anne could explain, someone came running up the stairs. I turned to watch as Louise rushed out to the deck. She looked frantic, her eyes wild. In her headlong rush she saw no one but Mrs. Orion.

Corey stopped her, blocking her way. Her hand came up to strike him, but he caught it and held it. For a moment she struggled, then collapsed against him.

"I won't go to prison again!" she cried. "I'll kill myself first!"

Anne pulled over another chair and she and Corey helped Louise to sit down. "No one is going to prison," Anne assured her quietly. "Mrs. Orion has told me exactly what happened. If there was blame, it belonged to three people. You and Mrs. Orion—and Susan. Perhaps most of all to Susan. I can understand how frightened you both must have been when it happened. Ryce didn't know your story then, Louise, and you didn't know that you could trust him. You thought the safe life you'd built for yourself was going to collapse, so you went a bit out of your head. I've been there—I know what it's like. But Ryce must be told how his daughter died. You understand that, Louise?"

Louise's strength had given out. She began to cry softly. I looked at Paul, but he could only shake his head. Neither of us spoke.

Again I heard someone running up the stairs, and this time it was Ryce who hurried toward us. He didn't see Louise slumped in her chair.

He began to talk before he reached us. "I called the hospital and they told me Louise had left without a word to anyone. Have you heard—?" He saw her then, where she sat, still huddled over, and he went to her at once. "I don't know why you ran out of the hospital. I would have brought you here if you wanted to come."

She looked at him through her tears and held up her hand to meet his. "I just want to go home to Gulls Cove."

Before he could help her to her feet, Anne

spoke in her firm, calm voice. "Please sit down, Ryce. We need to talk. But first I think the captain must be here to hear this."

Mrs. Orion shook her head. "No! Please! He isn't strong enough. This would be too much."

"He's stronger than you think," Anne replied. "I'll get him. Take some time and quiet down. We need to find an answer to what we do next."

She went off toward the captain's room, while the rest of us waited. Ryce was doing his best to comfort Louise, though he had no more idea than Paul and I about what had happened.

Corey had pulled a chair over so he could sit beside his mother, and was holding her hand. "It's going to be all right," he told her. "You haven't done anything."

"But I have!" she cried. "I have, and there's no way out."

It took Anne a few moments to rouse the captain from his sleep and get him into his wheelchair, and when he was settled into our circle on the deck, Anne spoke to Louise in her gentlest voice.

"Will you tell us about the geodes that seem to have started everything, Louise?"

For a moment it seemed as though Louise couldn't—or wouldn't—speak, but Ryce put an arm about her. "It's all right. Is she talking about the geode amethysts I gave you and Susan?"

Louise nodded silently.

"I bought a pair that were bookends," Ryce said, "but then I thought I would give one to you and one to Susan, since they were each very beautiful and unusual. Susan had been depressed and I thought the gift might cheer her up. So what happened, Louise?"

She roused herself and began to speak. "Susan phoned me and wanted me to let her have the geode you'd given her. She said they belonged together and she *had* to have them. She sounded too excited, and I gave in right away. It was getting toward dusk, but we have a good light on our boat, so I meant to run quickly across the sound, give her the geode, and get back before dark. But when I reached the dock she was waiting for me, and I think she was nearly out of control."

Louise looked up at her husband and he touched her cheek gently. "She could be like that. I understand."

I saw that Mrs. Orion was watching this changed Louise as though she couldn't altogether accept her.

After she'd drawn a deep breath, steadying herself, Louise continued. "Apparently Brenda had just told Susan about my being in prison and what happened in New York. Susan never liked me for marrying you, Ryce, and she was furious because I'd deceived you and hadn't told you all the truth about myself. She was waiting for me at the end of the dock, and the minute I climbed out to give her the geode, she started in on me. She was crazy-wild and she called me terrible names and accused me of all sorts of things I hadn't done. You heard her, Mrs. Orion. She'd brought you down there to hear what she meant to say to me. You told me that."

"Yes," Mrs. Orion said quietly.

So you knew the provocation and why I got angry. I never intended what happened. You would've thought that geode would be too heavy to throw, but when I got mad enough, I threw it at her. It struck her squarely in the face and she went backward into the water. The geode fell on the dock, and in the light from the boat I could see the blood on it—Susan's blood. She died and I am to blame."

Louise put her face in her hands and began to cry again.

"No," Mrs. Orion said. "You weren't to blame—not entirely. I saw what you were too upset to see. Susan was standing there beyond you and there was blood on her face, but the rock didn't knock her into the water. She had her hand up to her face in pain, but she took it down and there was an instant before she stepped backward into the water. I don't think she knew how close the edge was. It happened very fast, but I know what I saw. Susan swam under the dock we were standing on. She probably wanted to hold on to a piling."

Louise raised her head. "You never told me that."

"You didn't give me a chance. You were completely panicked and later you were only thinking about saving yourself."

"I did try to save her. You know I tried."

"Yes, you did." She turned to us again. "When Louise got hold of herself, she jumped into the water and tried to find Susan."

"It was dark around the dock and I couldn't locate her right away," Louise told us sadly. "It was that long scarf she'd wound around her neck that trapped her. A big cruiser had gone by right as she went into the water. It sent waves clear to the dock, so that Susan's scarf got caught in the pilings. I had to tear it loose before I could bring her to shore. You helped me drag her out of the water, Mrs. Orion."

Corey's mother spoke sadly. "We did our best to save her. I knew the routine, but nothing helped. That's when I should have stood up to you, Louise, but you frightened me. You said you'd blame me if I didn't help you."

Louise looked up at her husband, her voice muffled. "I thought I'd killed her and that you'd never forgive me. All I could think of was that I could be sent back to prison again. I made Mrs. Orion help me. I think she was afraid of me by that time."

Ryce quieted her with a soothing hand, and Mrs. Orion went on. "It's true. I helped Louise drag Susan back to the Pirate's Pit. It was dark by that time, and no one had been watching from the captain's house. God forgive me, I helped her put Susan's body down the hole. Then I went back to the dock and picked up the bloodstained geode, and threw that into the hole, too. Louise got a brush and water and scrubbed the dock. Then she went back across the sound and we never talked about any of what had happened again, except once, when she reminded me that I was an accessory and in danger myself if the truth ever came out. But what I knew has been eating at me for a long time, and when Mrs. Knight came here and began to stir things up, I knew I had to talk to someone."

"And you did," Anne said. "You came to me, which was the right thing to do."

The whole grim story had been told. Now the question remained of what must be done in the aftermath. I went to stand beside Paul at the rail, and he put his arm around me.

The captain had been silent through the whole telling, and I saw that Anne was watching him anxiously. The answers had been given—the answers that he wanted.

Ryce spoke first. "What do we do now? Dad, whatever happens, I will stand by Louise."

Nicholas Trench focused on his son. "As a man should stand beside his wife." He didn't look at Anne.

"We have to go to the police," Mrs. Orion said. "There's no other way."

"I'm not sure that's necessary." I knew by the sound of the captain's voice that he was in control again.

"If nothing else, a dead body has been disposed of," Paul said. "Isn't that a crime?"

"Not that I know of. Any law-breaking would be in the obstruction of justice. That's a misdemeanor. But what obstruction has there been? There's no body, and no crime has been committed. My poor granddaughter was apparently the victim of an accident as much as anything else— and in an agitated, almost crazy state of mind. If there was any proof of how upset she was before Louise arrived, it might help."

Mrs. Orion rose suddenly to her feet. "Wait! I have something that I've kept." She glanced uneasily at her son. "Susan was writing a letter earlier that evening. I found it afterward and I kept it. It was addressed to Mrs. Trench—to Anne— but when I read it, I decided not to show it to anyone. There was no need, since Susan was gone. She wrote about how depressed she had been over her life, how unhappy."

Mrs. Orion went off to her room and returned with the letter. Anne took it and read it through with tears in her eyes.

"There's information in there that I didn't want anybody to see," Mrs. Orion added miserably. "She writes about how she isn't really sure she loves you, Corey, or that she wants to marry you. I didn't want you to see what she'd written. I'm sorry now, but—"

"It's okay, Ma," Corey said, patting her arm. "You did what you thought was best."

Anne handed the letter to the captain and he read it through twice. When he was finished he said, "Yes, Susan was clearly in a frantic state when she wrote this. After Brenda told her about Louise, she just about lost control." He paused to contain his own grief, and then continued, "I have a good friend who is a judge, and I'm going to talk this whole thing over with him—as a hypothetical case. I think he'll agree that nothing further needs to be done."

Ryce looked enormously relieved. "Just the same, are we to sweep everything under the rug as though nothing has happened?"

Anne smiled sadly at her son. "I don't think it

will be like that. We'll all carry memories with us, and a good deal of guilt for the rest of our lives."

The captain reached for her hand. "At least we can grieve now as we couldn't before."

Paul had tightened his arm around me. "Guilt doesn't help a lot. It's too late for that. I'm on the outside and there's nothing I can add except from my own life. Maybe all that counts now is what we do in the present."

Anne smiled at him. Then she looked at her son. "Take your wife home, Ryce. We'll be in touch, Louise." Simple words, but they held open a door.

There was a dispersal after that. Anne helped the captain back to his room, and Corey went off to find Brenda. Ryce and Louise walked to the stairs together, and I could see that she leaned on his arm heavily. Of them all, I think Mrs. Orion looked the most relieved—as though the guilt of silence that she had carried for so long had finally begun to slip away.

Only Paul and I were left on the dock, and I looked out over the sound and found myself much too full of emotion for words. A pair of brown pelicans flew past—impossible birds, but graceful in flight. I thought absently of that turtle whose nest was still being protected. In a way I regretted the fact that I wouldn't be here to see the drama of the Turtle Watch when the baby turtles made their way to the ocean. But I *wouldn't* be here—I didn't want to be here.

"Can we go home tomorrow?" I asked.

"That's what I've been waiting to hear you say."

"Someday I'll come back to visit the captain. I have a feeling that he's going to keep on confounding his doctors. Besides, I don't want to lose track of Anne Trench."

"We'll come back together," Paul said.

Together. One of the most satisfying words in the English language. And this time we would make the changes that would make it work. His arms and the way he kissed me told me that.

Postscript from Phyllis A. Whitney

Perhaps you would like to know the titles
of the two books Anne brought to the captain.

I believe in them as much as she did.

Miracles Can Happen
by C. Norman Sheely

Remarkable Recovery
by Caryle Hirshberg and Marc Ian Barash

Guest, Judith, *Errands*
Hailey, Arthur, *Detective*
Halberstam, David, *The Fifties* (2 volumes)
Hepburn, Katharine, *Me*
James, P. D., *The Children of Men*
Koontz, Dean, *Dark Rivers of the Heart*
Koontz, Dean, *Icebound*
Koontz, Dean, *Intensity*
Koontz, Dean, *Sole Survivor*
Koontz, Dean, *Ticktock*
Krantz, Judith, *Lovers*
Krantz, Judith, *Scruples Two*
Krantz, Judith, *Spring Collection*
Landers, Ann, *Wake Up and Smell the Coffee!*
le Carré, John, *Our Game*
le Carré, John, *The Tailor of Panama*
Lindbergh, Anne Morrow, *Gift from the Sea*
Ludlum, Robert, *The Road to Omaha*
Mayle, Peter, *Anything Considered*
Mayle, Peter, *Chasing Cezanne*
McCarthy, Cormac, *The Crossing*
Meadows, Audrey with Joe Daley, *Love, Alice*
Michaels, Judith, *Acts of Love*
Michener, James A., *Mexico*
Mother Teresa, *A Simple Path*
Patterson, Richard North, *Eyes of a Child*
Patterson, Richard North, *The Final Judgment*
Patterson, Richard North, *Silent Witness*
Peck, M. Scott, M.D., *Denial of the Soul*
Phillips, Louis, editor, *The Random House Large Print Treasury of Best-Loved Poems*
Pope John Paul II, *Crossing the Threshold of Hope*
Pope John Paul II, *The Gospel of Life*
Powell, Colin with Joseph E. Persico, *My American Journey*

(continued)

Puzo, Mario, *The Last Don*
Rampersad, Arnold, *Jackie Robinson*
Rendell, Ruth, *The Keys to the Street*
Rice, Anne, *Servant of the Bones*
Riva, Maria, *Marlene Dietrich* (2 volumes)
Salamon, Julie and Jill Weber, *The Christmas Tree*
Shaara, Jeff, *Gods and Generals*
Snead, Sam with Fran Pirozzolo, *The Game I Love*
Truman, Margaret, *Murder at the National Gallery*
Truman, Margaret, *Murder on the Potomac*
Truman, Margaret, *Murder in the House*
Tyler, Anne, *Ladder of Years*
Tyler, Anne, *Saint Maybe*
Updike, John, *Rabbit at Rest*
Updike, John, *Golf Dreams*
Whitney, Phyllis A., *Amethyst Dreams*